The *Duty* trilogy

Book one: The Derelict *Duty*

By: James A. Haddock III

Websites
Jameshaddock.us
Haddockpublishing.com

Copyright © 2019 all rights reserved

D1733384

PROLOGUE:

The Blaring klaxon jolted me out of a sound sleep. I threw my covers off and was halfway to my Vac-suit locker before I was fully awake. It felt like I had just fallen to sleep, having just finished a long EVA shift. It would be just like Dad to have an emergency drill after an EVA shift to see if I had recharged my suit. I had, I always did. Both Mom and Dad were hard task-masters when it came to ship, and personal safety. Vac-suit recharging was top of the personal safety list. If you can't breathe, you die. Easy to remember.

Donning a Vac-suit was second nature for me, after 16 years of drills and practice exercises. I had been doing this, literally been doing this all my life. I loved life on our Rock-Tug. I was reaching for the comms when I felt the ship shudder. *"That can't be good."*

Mom's voice came over ship-wide, "This is not a drill, this is not a drill, meteor strike, hull breach in Engineering." Mom's voice was just as calm as if she was asking what's for lunch. This was a way of life for us, we trained and practiced so that when the reality of working in "The Belt" happened you didn't panic, you did your job. You didn't have to think, you knew what you needed to do, and you did it.

I keyed my comms, "Roger, hull breach in Engineering, where do you need me Mom?"

"Get to Engineering and help your Father, I'm on the Bridge trying to get us in the shadow of a bigger rock for some protection," Mom answered. My adrenalin was spiking, but Mom's calm voice helped to keep me calm.

I sealed my helmet and left my cabin, heading for Engineering. The klaxon had faded into the background. My breathing was louder than the alarm.

I kept telling myself, "stay calm, just do your job, stay calm."

I had just reached Engineering, when the Tug was rocked by a succession of impacts, each one harder that the last. The hatch to Engineering was closed, and the indicator light was flashing red. That told me there was hard vacuum on the other side.

I switched my comms to voice activated, "Dad? I'm at the hatch to Engineering it's in lockdown. I can't override it from here. Dad? Dad? Dad respond! Mom, Dad is not answering, and Engineering is sealed, you will have to evac the air from the rest of the ship, so I can open the hatch."

Mom's steady voice replied, "Understood emergency air evac in 10 seconds."

Those were the longest 10 seconds of my short life. The hatch indicator light finally turned green and the hatch door opened. The Engineering compartment was clear. No smoke, no fire, some sparks, but lots of blinking red lights. I looked over to the Engineering station console, there sat Dad. He had not had his Vac-suit on when the ship's hull was breached.

Hard Vacuum does terrible things to the human body. I suddenly realized that I had not heard Dad on comms the whole time, just Mom. She probably knew what had happened, but was sending help hoping Dad was all right and that maybe the comms were down.

I heard Mom in the background declaring an emergency and calling on the radio for help.

Her voice still calm somehow, "Mayday, mayday, this is the Rock Tug *Taurus*, mayday. We have taken multiple meteor strikes. We have multiple hull breaches, please respond."

"Come on Nic, think! What do I need to do?" I asked myself. I closed the hatch to Engineering, to seal the vacuum from the rest of the ship. I turned and started back toward the bridge. There was an impact, a light flared, and sparks; time seemed to slow, there was no sound, we were still in a vacuum. I felt shuttering vibrations and saw sparks. Holes seemed to appear in the overhead and then the deck. It was so surreal.

The meteors were punching holes through our ship like a machine punching holes through metal on an assembly line.

"Meteor storm" I thought. I lay there looking at the overhead, thinking it would take a lot of work to fix all these holes. I then realized I was lying on the deck, I tried to sit up. Something was wrong. My left arm was not working.

I looked to my left and saw why, *"No wonder it's not working, it's over by the wall."* Sweat was stinging my eyes, I looked down at my body and saw my right leg was missing too. "Mom!" I shouted, something crashed into the left side of my helmet!

I sat bolt upright in my seat, straining my seatbelts.

"Whoa, easy there Belter, that was just the station clamping on to the ship. Sometimes they are a bit rough," the man next to me said.

"Yeah, thanks." I said, trying to play off the nightmare I was waking up from. You would think after 10 years the nightmares would ease up, but every so often I would be back on the *Taurus,* torn apart and helpless.

CHAPTER 1

Everyone seemed to be trying to get off the ship at the same time. The aisles were full of standing people bustling like they needed to get to the bathroom right now. I turned to look out the window, I couldn't see much, just the side of the station. They all look the same, some patched more than others. Some painted, some not, no rust in space, so why waste the money. Nobody looked at the outside, anyway.

I "blinked" up my comm screen, I figured I might as well run my diagnostics while I waited for the rush to clear. I read through the list, vision setting normal spectrum 20/20. Hearing normal. Noise canceling ON, Comms inactive. Right leg reaction 50%, tactile sensitivity 50%. Left arm reaction 50%, tactile sensitivity 50%. All systems normal operation, all systems nominal.

I reset my arm and leg to 100%; I had dialed them back to 50% because of the sleeping tab I had taken. Good thing too. Being jolted out of sleep by the nightmare might have caused me to break something or someone. That was one thing you learned to live with when you had cybernetic limbs.

Vision settings were ok, I turned my internal comms on and noise canceling off. I had my P-comm, but it was easier to just "blink" comms up through my cyber-optic implants. The vision and hearing upgrade had cost a lot of creds, but they were worth it.

I turned my P-comm on; it was a redundancy, but I kept it to keep people from asking about my eye. I don't know why. I'm not vain, I guess. I don't advertise how cybernetically enhanced I am. I didn't want people to call me "Cy". Being called "Nac" is all the nickname I need.

I had gotten the nickname because everyone said I had "the knack" to fix anything, well almost anything. So "Nac" had stuck, even though my name is "Nic".

The crowd had thinned out, so I grabbed my bag from the overhead and moved toward the exit. Moving down the gangway, I enjoyed the cold fresh air. It felt good on my face after 36 hours stuffed in that tin can of a passenger ship. It felt good to have a fresh lung full.

I followed the crowd and the signs to Security and Operations. The line at security move fairly fast, shortly I was standing in front of a bored looking security man. He took my ID card and scanned me into the system.

He pointed at the floor, "Stand on the yellow line, and look into the camera". I moved to the line and looked into the camera. He handed my card back, "Welcome to Conclave Station. Next".

I shouldered my bag and followed the signs toward Operations. I moved to the next available service window and handed the attendant my card. A nice-looking lady with short red hair scanned my card.

"How can I help you, Mr. Haydock?"

She handed my card back, "I'm just arriving, and I wanted to check to ensure that the systems in my Hab-hanger had been initialized. And everything was in order for me to take up residence," I said, returning her smile.

"Let's see." her fingers clicked over the keyboard. "HH-AA12, Wow that's one of the original hanger-habs."

Nodding my head, "Yeah, my family has been out here from the beginning. They helped open the belt and mine this asteroid out and later put in habs."

I was proud of my family heritage; we had a proud history of opening the belt and helping other belters.

Out here that was a given, as my Granddad used to say, "When a belter sent out 'the call' everyone came running throttles to the firewall." I don't remember it, but they told me that's the way it was the day Mom had set out "the call". Every Rock Jockey in the sector dropped their loads and did a "Turn and Burn". 26 minutes later I was in a stasis pod on the way to Conclave Station's Trauma Center.

The attendant snapping fingers in front of my face brought me back to the here and now. I focused on her smiling face.

"Oh, there you are. There is someone home after all," she said.

I could feel my face turning red, "I am so sorry, I don't think the sleeping tab has completely worn off."

"I know what you mean," she chuckled. "I hate those things, but how else could you stand being strapped in one place for all those hours."

"Exactly," I replied.

She looked back at her screen, "Now as I was saying," she cut her eyes at me and smiled. "We got your e-forms and deposits. We have initialized the systems. Air, water and power are on, you can move in right away. I'll make a note in the file you checked in with Ops and you are moving in. You are moving in, correct?"

"Yes ma'am, as soon as I leave here, I'm going there. I also had containers shipped, have they arrived?"

"Hmm, yep, they are ready for delivery, would 1300 tomorrow be all right?"

"That would be fine." I answered.

"Is there anything else I can do for you? Set-up comms? Notifications? Cup of coffee?" It took a couple seconds for the "cup of coffee" to register. I'm sure I had a confused look on my face. She patted my hand chuckling, "That's ok, you go get some sleep, when it finally registers, you comm me."

I laughed, "deal, I promise I'm not usually this thick headed, or at least no one has said anything if I am."

"We'll see Nicholas Haydock."

"Just Nic," I said as I turned toward the doors marked Main Habitat/Promenade.

***

I followed the signs toward the S-Tube. Things had changed in the 10 years I had been gone. I didn't come over to the Port of Entry much even back then. We own a hanger-hab and were residents. I had to admit things had grown. There seemed to be more people here now. Going in and out of the shops, buying and selling, doing what people do.

I kept following the signs down two levels to the S-Tube terminal and found the tube I needed to get out to the Alpha spoke of Alpha Ring, or AA. Looking at the map I realized how much Conclave Station had grown. The original miners had built their habs in circles like a ring with spokes and a center hub. They isolated each ring from the others for safety. No one failure could cause a catastrophic failure to all.

They were all inter-connected by S-tubes, but these had redundant safety systems in them. As far as I remember, there were only 12 rings on the hab when I left. Now there were 15 and 3 more were under construction. I guess business is good with all this growth. I noticed that 2 of the main lines went out to the Industrial Zone. One was to the refinery smelter factory. The other went over to the shipyard. Both had grown according to the map.

My P-Comm was getting pinged with all kinds of ads. I had about an hour of travel before I got to Alpha ring so; I brought up some to the local news feeds. It was mostly stuff about the refinery and shipyard expansions and how much it would help the local economy.

There was opposition to the expansion saying it would open the door for more immigrants taking jobs away from the locals and forcing out smaller locally owned companies. A lot of those small companies were family owned and operated and had been for generations.

For all the growing business expansions and prosperity, I noticed crime was up. Some feared with these new expansions, organized crime would expand as well.

The sports page was kind of sparse, mostly fights of one kind or another. Boxing, wrestling, all kinds of mixed martial arts and MMA. Good, I can keep up with my training, I had an MMA Instructor's Comm contact. I had started MMA 5 or 6 years ago, the therapist said it would help with the coordination and balance of my cyber-limbs.

I had trouble at first ever finding an instructor to work with me because of the cyber-limbs. We finally found an MMA gym run by a former Space Legion Marine who himself had a cyber-arm. The therapist was right, it really helped me with my coordination and balance, but also my self-esteem. I'd never be an MMA champ, but I can take care of myself.

There were help wanted ads, owner operator ads for rock tug drivers. For cargo ship jobs you had to belong to "The Union" to get those jobs. That looked kinda suspicious, I guess the organized crime worry might have some basis in fact.

It looked like lots of "Big" money was moving into the Conclave and bringing both good and bad with it. The Van Dam shipyard was still in business. Mom and Dad did a lot of business with them, they had a few job openings too. I would check on that once I get settled.

"Next stop, Alpha hub," the overhead speaker said. I glanced over to the blinking light on the S-tube map. The car wasn't crowded, but I let everyone move to the exit before I got up. I threw my bag over my shoulder and stepped off the car. I was almost overwhelmed with the feeling of nostalgia.

A lot had changed, new paint, new kiosks and booths, but the underlying sights, sounds, and smells were still there. It said "Home". I moved up the wide staircase to the main floor, taking it all in.

Looking at the storefronts that were new, and the old ones I recognized. That place where we used to eat, and that place where we used to shop. I'm sure I looked like an "Outbacker" that was on his first visit to the Hab. There was the fresh smell of "green" in the air. The Hab used wall ivy as part of the air cleaning system, and the sound of water splashing was soothing.

A disturbance from a sidewalk café shattered the peace. It looked like a big fight had broken out. People, tables, and chairs were being thrown around. I moved over to the wall to stay out of the way. But I must admit I was curious about what was going on. There was a large man in a nice suit on his back, both his legs were out stiff and kicking everything he got close to. My first thought was convulsions, but no, he was yelling and cursing a blue streak.

I leaped over the café railing and yelled, "does he have cyber-limbs?" As I broke through the crowd.

"Yes," one man who was trying to hold him yelled. I grabbed and turned over a trash can, grabbing all the foil I could reach, I then grabbed a metal plate off the table scattering food all over the place.

They were all looking at me like I had lost it. "Flip him on his stomach!" they stared at me while the man kept kicking. "Flip him now, I need to get to the control module on his back!"

Flipping the big man over was no easy task. It looked like the main event at a Wrestling Royale. We finally got him over enough I could slap the foil and metal plate over the cyber control module. As soon as I did, he stopped kicking and lay still.

I looked around and pointed to a maintenance cart by the wall.

"See if there's any rigger's tape in that maintenance box over there." There was, and they threw it to me. I was holding the plate and foil firmly in place.

"Okay sir, I need you to get up onto your hands and knees but move slowly so I can keep the CCU covered."

The big man nodded, gritting his teeth as he slowly raised to his hands and knees. "Here, wrap this tape around him so it will keep the plate in place." Nodding, a man took it and we wrapped the tape around the big man several times.

I sat back, "ok sir, let's get you into the chair, but no sudden moves." He nodded, and they got him up into the chair.

The big man shook his head, "Son, that was worse than riding in a rock tug with a flaring thruster, with a max load in front of ya."

Everyone was smiling, and a few chuckled.

"This happens sometimes, but this was by far the worst it has ever been. How'd you know what it was?" He asked.

I smiled and rapped on my left arm, "Had something similar happen once, but nowhere near this bad. Your RF shielding must be weak or there's a crack in the CCU casing. It caused an overload, and off you went. That foil and plate will hold until you can get to the Med-Center and get it fixed." His men were clearing the way for the EMTs to get to him.

"I'll not forget this; I remember those who do right by me. If you need anything, come see me. Ask for 'Jocko', everyone knows me."

"No worries sir, glad I could help."

"Nac?" I turned to see who had called out.

"Jazz?" She came over and hugged me, "You can't help yourself, can you? You just got here, and you are already fixing things," she laughed.

Jocko watched the exchange as the EMTs moved him toward medical. He leaned over to one of his men.

"I want to know everything about him."

His man looked back at Nic and nodded, "yes, sir."

"Coffee?" Nic asked Jazz, motioning toward the café that was about ready to reopen after the excitement.

"Sure." She stepped toward a table in the back. As we took our seats, a waiter appeared to take our order.

"2 coffees please," I said. The waiter nodded and headed into the café.

"So, you're just getting here?" Jazz asked.

"How can you tell?" Jazz pointed to my bag with her chin.

"Oh, yeah," I laughed.

The waiter returned with our coffee and a plate of pastries. I looked quizzically at the pastries.

The waiter smiled, "compliments of the owner, for helping one of our guests."

"Thank you, that is most kind of him."

"Our pleasure sir, enjoy."

I turned back to Jazz. Taking a sip of the coffee, "mmm, good coffee."

"So, how was the trip?" She asked, reaching for a pastry. I put down my cup and reached for a pastry too.

"Long, that last leg was 36 hours, I had to take a sleep tab to relax and get some sleep. I hate those things."

"I know what you mean, it will take you a few days to get over it and get back in the swing of things," Jazz said.

"Yep, I can hardly wait to get in a bed and stretch out."

The pastries were "melt in your mouth" good and the coffee was the best I have had in a long while. I watched Jazz out of the corner of my eye; she had changed from the pretty girl I had a crush on, into a beautiful woman.

"Judging by your flight suit, I guess you are still a rock-jockey."

"Yep, I work on shares for the Mercer family. I'm flying one of their old 50 KLT tugs. It needs some TLC, but we're doing okay. They give me my own place so that cuts down on my expenses."

I knew the 50 KLTs were real work horses and had served for years. They were only about a quarter of the size of our family tug ship that was rated at 200 KTLs. The "Our family tug" thought kinda stopped my wondering mind.

The conversation dragged into the ordinary. Who was still around, who had moved on, who had married, who had kids. I smiled and let Jazz talk, enjoying the company and the sound of her voice.

The waiter came around and refilled our cups.

"Seen Mal recently?" I asked.

"Yeah, when he comes out of his cave," she laughed. "You remember how he was; he gets so engrossed with his computers and programming he'd forget to eat. And if anything, he's worse. He forgets to take a bath," she laughed.

"There's no one better with computers, computer hardware, and programming. You know he was going to take a computer college course. But he was so far ahead of the instructors they couldn't understand half the stuff he was doing; he hasn't been back." Jazz said.

I raise my hand for the waiter to get our check.

He approached our table smiling, "sir, your check has been taken care of by Pierre, the owner, we hope you'll come again."

"We certainly will," I said, "the coffee and pastries were exquisite." I left a nice tip, and we eased out into traffic and headed toward HH–AA12.

As we walked, Jazz tried to catch me up on all the happenings of the last 10 years. Most of it whizzed right past me. I caught that she now had her multi-engine pilot's license and dreamed of someday owning her own tug, maybe a 100 KLT model. She'd had that dream forever.

"I saw an ad they were looking for owner/operators. You thought about maybe doing it that way?" I asked. That brought her up short.

"Not likely, that's that new refinery group, they want to lock you into an exclusive contract with them for everything. Sell to them, buy from them, even maintenance on your tug by them. All at their rates. No, thank you." She turned and continued walking.

"Well, I'm glad we got that cleared up," I said, chuckling.

As we neared the end of Alpha Spoke, I saw two locks with "A12" on them. One was a small personnel lock, the other a cargo lock. We stopped at the personnel lock, I inserted my new key card into the terminal, entered the keycode and placed my hand on the scanner pad. Everything was now updated and reset for me.

"You never said where Mal's cave was," I said, as the personnel lock swung open.

"Funny you should ask that," Jazz said.

I had forgotten how big our hanger was, I mean I knew it was big, but... There she sat, my throat closed a little, and the tears made it hard to make out the name that was scrolled across her side. I didn't need to see it to know that *"Taurus"* was what it read.

I blinked away the tears and had to smile, looking at the "nose art" of a bull snorting steam with a rock held between its horns. This was the first time I had seen her since "that" day. I close my eyes, took a few deep breaths and got my emotions under control. I heard my Mom's gentle voice saying, "Big boys don't cry," that made me smile.

"Need a minute Nac?" I open my eyes, looked at Jazz and smiled.

"No, I'm good," looking back at the tug. "Ya know from here she doesn't look too bad."

"Yeah, well, wait to see the other side and top. She took some hard hits. It's a wonder she held together. Oddly, the strikes missed any main structures, they blew through her." She stopped talking, looking away from me. "Well, you'll see." Her voice seemed a little strained, I knew how she felt. I let my eyes wander around the huge hanger, there was plenty of room to park another *"Taurus"* in here with room left over.

My eyes drifted over the parts and equipment storage area, remembering the times Jazz, Mal, and I had spent climbing and playing. Later it was "our" place to plan our futures.

Jazz would be the best rock jockey in space, I would own a shipyard and build the best ships ever launched, and Mal would build all the computers for the new ships.

CHAPTER 2

"Nac!" Mal came bounding down the ship's ramp.

"Mal!" I laughed as he bear-hugged me. Jazz joined in the hug.

"It's great to have you back," Mal said.

"Well, the gangs all here," I said, we all laughed.

Mal looked at Jazz, "have you told him?"

"Oh no," she chuckled, "I told you that was your job, it was your idea, you explain it."

"What idea is that, my scheming friend?" I asked.

"Well, what had happened was," Mal looked around the hanger. "I kinda told my parents I needed my own place; I was too old to live at home."

"And?" I nodded, encouraging him to continue.

"And so Jazz mentioned," He started.

"Oh, no you don't, this was all your idea. You get all the credit for this one," she laughed, enjoying Mal's discomfort.

Mal raised his hands in surrender.

"Ok, ok, I told my parents you had rented your hanger to me if I would rebuild and upgrade *Taurus'* electronics and computer systems and pay utilities."

"I see, and your parents believed you?" I asked.

"Of course, I had emails."

"What emails?" I asked.

"Oops," Jazz said, laughing.

I looked between them.

"I had to show them something to prove you agreed to have me living and working here," Mal said. I stared at him, slack-jawed. Jazz was laughing so hard she was crying.

Mal just shrugged his shoulders.

"I had to give them something, you know how they are."

"Yeah, I know how they are. You know they will ask me about you living here now that I'm back, right?" I asked.

"To be honest, I really didn't think that far ahead," He said.

Jazz was getting her second wind. "This is priceless," she wailed. Jazz was now hanging onto me unable to make a sound just shaking her head doing the silent laugh thing.

"Ask him," she gasped out. "Ask him how long?"

"How long what?" I asked. She couldn't take it any longer and just fell on the floor kicking her feet in the air.

Mal was looking at her with disgust, "it's not that funny Jazz."

"How long what?" I asked.

Mal rubbed his hand over his face and mouth, "five years," he mumbled.

"I'm sorry! Did you say five years? You've been living here for five years?"

"I'm sorry, okay! My parents were driving me crazy! Mom wanted me to get out and meet a 'nice girl'. Dad wanted me to go to college or get a job fixing computers."

Jazz finally got her breath back. "You guys are killing me, I haven't laughed this hard in like...forever."

I couldn't help myself; I shook my head. "Well, we always said I'd fix and build ships and you'd put the electronics and computers in them. I guess we got started a little sooner than I expected."

"But wait!" Jazz said using her best announcer salesman voice. "There's more!" Mal looked as if he was hoping the deck would open and swallow him.

"Jazz you are enjoying this entirely too much," Mal said.

"Oh no, I have been waiting for this moment for literally years, why don't we go in, you can meet your cook."

"Cook? You have a cook?" I asked.

"Well, technically 'we' have a cook," He said.

"And who, pray tell, is this 'we' of whom you speak?" I

asked.

"Well technically, in this case, the 'we' is 'our' company," He said.

"What 'our' company?"

Jazz shook her head, "As much as I enjoy watching you two playing 20 questions, this is just too painful. Let's go inside, we'll explain later."

"Inside" was the hanger's living quarters, at one time our family was large. So were the living quarters 4 floors in fact. The sub levels housed storage. First level, company offices and re-pair shops. Second-level, common area, galley and crew quarters. Third level was family quarters. Most of the areas had been closed, to save on expenses.

Mom, Dad, and I didn't need the room. We mostly just use the second and third levels, and not all of that. Looking over my shoulder at the hanger, I remember the reason it was so big. At the height of our operations, the family owned four tugs.

Over the years we sold them to make upgrades to other areas and tugs. Then the fleet was downsized to match the size of our aging family. In the end, it was just Mom, Dad, and I.

They finally sold the last two 100 KLTS and bought *Taurus*. She was a 200 KLT tug that was designed for longer runs and had a crew and family quarters.

She had become our home for a few years before...well, before... As we approach, the hatch slid open to allow us in. These were newer than the big main hatches that swung open. I steeled myself for what I knew would be another emotional roller coaster.

We moved through the reception area and down the hall-way toward the back stairs. All the offices were dark, I didn't stop to look in Mom's or Dad's offices. I didn't trust myself to be ready for that yet. As we reached the bottom of the stairs, I smelled coffee and cinnamon.

We moved through the second-level den and living room it was one large open area Mom called it an "open floor plan". I could see someone in the galley. They were leaning down looking at one of the ovens. The cinnamon smell was getting stronger. Mal headed straight for the coffee urns at the side-board.

Without turning, a gray-haired lady said, "dinner will be at 1800 as usual, don't be late."

Jazz and Mal both smiled and answered, "yes ma'am."

The cook turned toward us, "Aunt J? You're our cook?" I asked.

"Well, I am unless the boss replaces me."

I looked over at Mal, he shook his head, "nope not me, that would be you, boss."

I look back at Aunt J; she wasn't really our Aunt, but we had known her all our lives. Her name was Julie Moore, and she ran a small breakfast bar called the "Breakfast Plus". All the kids just called her Aunt J.

I looked at her for a moment, turned and got myself a mug of coffee. I looked at my "partners" who were just standing there smiling waiting to see what I say.

"The Breakfast Plus?" I asked.

"Sold it."

"Uncle J?"

Her eyes saddened, "heart attack, three years past."

"I'm so sorry, I hadn't heard."

She smiled, "he had a good life, went fast, didn't suffer. He always worried he would linger in his old age, becoming a bur-den on his family. That's something, I guess."

"Did it happen on his tug?" I asked.

"No, he was at home when it happened. We parked his tug outside your hanger. "

I glanced at Mal, "why didn't you bring it in, there's plenty of room?"

"I didn't want to presume too much." I just looked at him, I heard Jazz behind me chuckling.

"Uh-huh," I said.

I turned back to Aunt J, "we'll get her inside, that will save you docking fees at least." I cocked my head, thinking. "Are you interested in selling her?"

"Are you interested in buying her?" she asked.

"Might be," I said.

"Do you know someone you can get to fly her?" She asked, smiling.

"I might know a hotshot rock jockey, but I'll have to check with him." I said.

"Him!?" Jazz screamed. "I will punch you in the throat!"

"You have a job," I said.

"You didn't have a tug."

"I still don't, I'm just thinking out loud."

"Well, when you get one, I'll be the one flying it!"

Aunt J laughed, "yep, just like old times."

She turned and open the oven, pulling out a pan of cinnamon sugar cookies. She sat the cookies out on the cooling rack. I couldn't help myself and reached for one.

A "you'd better not," froze my hand in place. "those are for AFTER dinner."

Withdrawing my hand, "yes ma'am," I said. Everyone laughed.

Aunt J set out dinner buffet style, we served ourselves and moved over to the table. I was hungrier than I thought, the sleep tab had lost some of its edge. The food was great, and the conversation with old friends was better. After the meal, we all cleared our places and racked our dishes in the big industrial dishwasher.

Aunt J finished wiping down the cabinets and grabbed a cuppa. She joined us at the table, bringing the cinnamon sugar cookies with her. I grabbed one and dunked it in my coffee. Aunt J sure could cook.

"So, tell me Aunt J, how did Mal convince you to be 'our'," I did the quotation fingers in the air, "cook?"

"Well, after Jazz told me about Mal, 'renting'. " She did the finger quotes in the air.

Everyone looked at Mal, "I will never hear the end of this, will I?"

"As I was saying, after Jazz told me, I knew he would turn into a hermit if someone didn't check on him. Jazz and I convinced him that if he was going to have a repair company, he needed a cook. Rather than eating out all the time, and it would be cheaper in the long run. I threw in housekeeping and cooking."

I nodded, sipping my coffee, "and what princely salary is the company paying you for your services?"

"Well, as I said, I sold 'The Plus' and Uncle J is gone. The kids have moved to Titan. It was just me in that apartment. I told him I'd work for room and board, and a share in the profits once the company was up and running."

I glanced over at the clock, 2200 hrs.

"Okay that's a starting place. You've given me a lot to think about, and it's only my first day back. It has been a long one. If you'll excuse me, I will find a bunk and crash."

"The master suite is ready, but so is your old room, whichever you prefer," Aunt J said.

"I think I'll just take my old room for now, thanks."

We all rose, I racked my coffee mug, "good night all."

"Good night," they replied.

Jazz surprised me with a tight embrace, "it's good to have you home Nic." As we held our embrace, I realize that the girl I had had a crush on was no longer just a girl, but a full-grown woman and she smelled wonderful. She smelled like her namesake, Jasmine. As I released her, she kissed me on the cheek, "good night."

"Good night." I replied.

I grabbed my bag and headed up to my room on the third floor. My room was the first one at the top of the stairs. I open the door to my room; I looked down the hall toward the master suite at the far end. No, definitely not ready for that yet. I stepped into my room and closed the door behind me.

***

I woke up and looked at the clock, 0300. The clock was in the wrong place.

Momentarily confused, *"oh yeah, home."* I got up and went to the bathroom, took care of the needful.

I started to go back to bed. Stopped and headed back to the bathroom and took a long hot shower. I was reaching for the soap and froze.

"She called me Nic, not Nac, but Nic." I stood there under the hot shower with a goofy grin on my face. It was good to be home.

It was too early to start anything, so I laid in the bed staring at the ceiling. I can't stand doing nothing. I sat up on the side of the bed, looking around the room, pictures, posters and drawings on the wall.

I smiled, I had covered one whole wall with ship drawings and building notes. The room seemed smaller than I remembered. I looked over at my bag, wondering when the rest of my luggage would be delivered, and if they had delivered my shipment. I sat there, deep in thought. I could see no reason to unpack and put away my things, only to move them into the master suite later.

Leaving my room, I walked down the hall to Mom and Dad's room. I stood there looking at the door. My mind drifted through the past.

"Suck it up, Buttercup," I said, and palmed the entry pad.

The door slid open; I stepped in and turn the lights on. At some point in the past, someone had packed all Mom and Dad's things. I walked to the foot of their bed. When I was little, I thought it was the biggest bed in the world. It seemed smaller now, even though it was a king-size.

The family pictures were still on the wall, I moved through the suite. Wet bar, or rather coffee bar. Mom loved her coffee. Sitting and desk area, Mom's mostly. Dad usually worked from the downstairs office.

"What? you couldn't find a bigger vid-screen?" I said.

Man, that thing is huge. Bathroom, double everything, a huge shower. While shipboard everything was compact and utilitarian, but when we were home, we like to spread out. No time like the present, I went back to my room, gathered my stuff and moved into the master suite.

*****

At 0600 I could wait no longer; I went down to the galley. I needed coffee. Aunt J was already in the galley starting breakfast. I grabbed a mug and filled it with the fresh hot nectar. I held it under my nose and breathed deeply.

"Omelet?" Came from behind me.

"Please," I said turning, "You always up this early?"

"After all those years of running the Plus, you know habits and breaking them. What would you like in it?" pouring eggs in the pan.

"Ham and cheese, if you have it," I said, taking a seat at the bar.

"Coming right up," she said.

"What time does Mal usually come through?"

"Well," she said, laughing. "That depends on what project he's working on."

"What project is he working on?" She slid my omelet in front of me.

"Nothing major, that I know of, just the regular electronic and computer repair stuff he takes in. He works out of the repair shop downstairs, when he's not working in the *Taurus*. He's also been doing work for the Van Dam's when they get something they can't handle, that man is a genius with computers." She slid into the seat next to me with her own omelet.

"Yeah, tell me about it, we used to tell everyone he was a computer robot," I laughed. I dug into my omelet and finished before I knew it. I racked my plate and got another cup of coffee. "So, Aunt J, how long have you been working for us?"

"A little over four years. Mal was a mess, eating junk food, sitting in front of the computer for days at a time. We were really getting worried about him. So here I am."

"Whose idea was it for opening the repair shop?"

She smiled, "he was already helping the Van Dams, I mentioned that there was a repair shop downstairs that was not being used, and that I bet there were others who had electronics and computers that needed fixing. He needed encouragement, I pointed him in the right direction."

I nodded, "he seems to be doing good."

"Jazz helped with that," she said smiling. "She may have hinted, that if he wanted to be part of your business, showing you, he could run a repair business would be a good place to start. He took off with it."

"What about Uncle J's tug?"

"Oh, that's only been parked out there about a week. I have been leasing it since Uncle J died, but they had not been keeping up on the maintenance on her. I finally had to take them to arbitration. The tug failed the maintenance inspection, turns out they had not pass one in three years.

The arbiters found them in breach of contract, awarded me all the escrow funds, and canceled the rest of the contract. We moved her over here to save the docking fees. We knew you'd be home soon. So there she sits. I was sure you would bring her in once you got here."

"How bad does the maintenance report say she is?"

She pulled out her P-comm, "I'll send you the report, see what you think." My P-comm chimed, and I pulled up the report and scanned it.

"You're right looks like they did just a minimum to keep her working. Drives are mis-aligned and out of calibration. Gravitonics overloaded, 25% of the force emitters burned out. Yeah, they definitely rode her hard."

"Are you thinking of buying her?"

"Let's get her in the hanger and see what we got, then we'll talk. I'll have to check that the enviro-fields are fully operational before we try to open the hanger doors. We can use the hanger's main grav-slings to lift her and bring her in."

Mal came in and headed for the coffee.

"Omelets?" Aunt J asked.

"Yes please, just cheese." He looked at me, "plans?" We caught him up on our conversation about Uncle J's tug. "Well, don't buy any parts until we talk, part of my deal with the Van Dams is I get to salvage the old parts yard, so we may find some things we need for repairs."

"I bet you already got a room full of computer stuff, don't you?" I said, Mal just grinned.

"I reprogrammed the security system when I first came in yesterday, I guess we need to get everyone reentered into the system under my new credentials."

Mal gave me 'The look'. "Really," he said.

"Oh yeah, sorry, forgot who I was talking to." I racked my cup, "I'll be out in the hanger."

Mal nodded, "I'll be out shortly, need more coffee."

I found my shipping crates by the front lock. They all look like they made the trip okay. I opened the first one and got my tools out. Strapped on my tool belt, grabbed my tool bag. I headed for the enviro-field control panel and ran the diagnostic routines.

The board was green except for one amber on an emitter feed. I checked the feed, cleaned the connections, and reran the diagnostics. That cleared the amber. It was all green now, just to be sure I checked the field generator itself.

The diagnostics checked okay, and the visual inspection was good. Returning to the control board, I brought the field generator online. I watched the gauges, they all held good at 100%. I called over the comm to the galley.

"Aunt J here."

"Aunt J I've checked out the enviro-field and I'm about to open the hanger doors, is Mal still in there?"

"No, he's probably in the shop."

"Thanks." I re-keyed comms to the shop, "Mal, you in the shop?" I saw Mal walking toward me.

"Everything check out okay?" He asked.

"Yep, we are ready to open the hanger door. I've had the field generator running, and it's held at 100% and the backups are online. We'll open the hanger doors just a little to start with to make sure everything holds." Mal nodded.

I opened the doors just a bit and waited. Everything held at 100%. "Okay, bringing the grav-slings online," diagnostics were all green. "If you'll stand by the board here, I'll go operate the grav-sling and get Uncle J's tug inside."

I ran the local checks and got an all green board. I signaled Mal to open the hanger doors. We watch the doors open without a hitch, I traversed the grav-sling toward the door and locked onto the tug and lifted it with no strain on the system.

The auto-adjust grav-deck plating worked perfectly, lowering the gravity as the grav-sling move the tug into the hanger. I got her positioned and lowered her into place. Mal closed the hanger doors as the tug cleared the entrance. I powered down the grav-slings and secured boards from ship movement ops. Mal had done the same to the doors. We did a walk around inspection of the tug; she was an older 50 KLT model, not in real bad shape for her age. She just needed some TLC.

Mal was looking at the keypad at the tug entry lock, "We will need the key cards from Aunt J to get inside."

I nodded, "figured, we'll get them later, I wanted to get her inside for the time being." We turned and looked at the *Taurus*. Mal just stood there waiting for me to decide.

CHAPTER 3

"Been working on her, huh?" I said.

"Yep, made a few improvements to the control systems and control runs, replaced the computer systems and programming, I think you'll like the improvements."

"I'm sure I will."

"Come on, I'll show you some of the new systems." Mal said, starting up the ramp. I nodded and followed him up, Mal stopped at the entry hatch. I looked at him expectantly.

"Place your hand on the palm pad, I've got her locked down." I place my hand on the palm pad, it's scanned my palm, turned green, and the hatch slid open.

A smooth, mellow female voice said, "access granted, welcome aboard Captain," I looked at Mal he was grinning from ear to ear.

We stepped inside, "ship status?" Mal asked.

The response came back immediately. "Main engines off-line, auxiliary power units off-line, gravitonics off-line, currently operating on shore hookups for power and water, 'ACE' systems operating at 89%, current mission state, in drydock for repairs and upgrades. Further diagnostics currently unavailable."

My grin matched Mal's, "yeah, but can she cook?" I asked.

"Main galley off-line," the ship answered. We both laughed.

"Mal, that is awesome."

"You haven't seen the best yet, let's go to the bridge."

I stepped inside and glanced down the hallway toward engineering. Someone had cleaned up everything.

"Nac, if you need more time, I understand. Hey, I'll go get us

a couple cups of coffee. You take your time, I'll be back in a few."
I nodded, and he left me standing there.

I stopped at the hatch to engineering, looking at the deck. They had cleaned everything. Most of the holes in the deck and overhead were still there. Mal was a computer geek, not a welder.

I turned back and hit the touch pad and the engineering hatch opened. I could tell things had been repaired but there were still a lot of work to be done. I moved over to the engineering console, the last place I had seen Dad. The console was dark, no power. I patted Dad's chair and left engineering.

I headed toward the bridge, noticing the damage; it was bad. I stuck my head in my old room, it looked like nothing had changed. My bed was still unmade. Climbing the stairs to the command deck, it shocked me to see the condition of the galley.

"Galley off-line, was an understatement" That whole area of the ship was crushed in. The bridge itself look pretty much untouched the report and said Mom had probably been killed from the major impact, I'm guessing from the galley hit.

I stood behind the command chairs looking out the main armor glass, not really seeing anything. In my mind I was looking back to all the happy times I had had.

I heard someone coming up the stairs, "Nac, I got your coffee."

"I could use it," I called back.

Mal handed me a cuppa, "so what do you think," pointed to the bridge with his chin.

"I noticed a few changes," I said turning to look where he was pointing.

Smiling, "yeah, a few," he replied. "Misty, bring command deck online." All the consoles came to life.

"Command deck online, all diagnostics are green," Misty replied.

"You named the ship, Misty?"

"No, I named the A.C.E. System 'Miss. T', it sounds like 'Misty', the 'T' stands for *Taurus*."

"What's an A.C.E. System?"

"Automated Control Engine, it's a new program I've developed. It's like, one step below an AI. Misty, what level of integration have you completed?"

"Present level of integration stands at 47%."

"Misty, estimated level of integration upon completion?"

"Estimated max level of integration will be approximately 87%."

"Only 87% huh, no wonder she can't cook," I said.

"Main galley off-line" Misty answered. We both laughed.

"Okay, so here's what I've done so far."

Mal and I spent the next few hours going over all that he had been able to do within his bartering and credit budget, and his expertise.

"Mal, this is amazing, I'm blown away."

"It's the least I could do, since you were letting me live here and all."

I gave him 'The Look'. "Don't mention it, and I really don't want you mentioning it around your parents. That's not a conversation I'm looking forward to. Let's break for lunch," I said. "I'm starved, and Misty better not say it." We both looked up, but no response was forthcoming.

Aunt J had sandwich fixings laid out on the counter for lunch and hot soup in the cooker. We built our sandwiches and grabbed a bowl of soup.

"I was wondering where you guys had gotten off to, it was too quiet, so I knew you were into something."

I swallowed and wiped my mouth, "we got your tug inside and Mal was giving me a tour of all the work he has done on the *Taurus*."

"What did you think of Miss. T, or Misty as Mal calls her."

"She is amazing, I don't know of anyone except maybe the Navy that has anything like her."

"What did you think of Uncle J's tug?"

"We are planning on checking her after lunch, we'll need your keycard." She handed it to me. "We should know more by dinner time. Anyone know if Jazz is coming over for dinner?"

Aunt J chuckled, "you know for someone as bright as you are, sometimes that bulb is a little dim." I looked at Mal, he shrugged his shoulders. Aunt J shook her head, "Men."

We racked our dishes and went to check out *Uncle J's* tug. Mal read off the inspection checklist and we cross-referenced it to the mediation inspection report.

We're almost done when I heard Jazz, "Hey guys, Aunt J says it's dinnertime."

I backed out of the engine crawl space, "sounds good, I'm ready for it." We all headed for the galley.

The galley smelled wonderful. Aunt J had the table already set, and we moved over to it. Jazz took me to the head of the table, and I guess technically it was "my" table, it felt kind of odd. We were all enjoying our food, and our conversation.

"There's apple pie and coffee for dessert, but you have to rack your dishes first," Aunt J said as she rose, racking her dishes.

We all followed suit. We all pitched in, clearing the table. Aunt J brought out the hot apple pie. Sliced and plated it. We all filled our coffee cups and returned to our seats.

"So, what did you think of Uncle J's tug?" I swallowed my bite of pie and took a sip of coffee, considering my answer.

"Does the tug have a name; I mean, calling her Uncle J's tug is a bit of a mouthful."

Aunt J shook her head, "nothing official. Some names he called her aren't worth repeating. Just the registration number, which is also mouthful." She thought a moment, "why don't we call her the *Uncle J* instead of Uncle J's tug." Everyone nodded.

"So back to my question, what did you think of her?" Aunt J asked.

"How bad is she Nac?" Jazz asked looking at me.

"The worst of it is her pulse interrupters, and balance coil emitters."

"Stop," Jazz said, putting her hand on my arm. "Nac, I'm a pilot, put it in pilot terms."

I looked at her for a few heartbeats, "stuffs broke, I will fix it." I said, smiling.

"That's my man." Jazz said, then slapped her hand over her mouth, eyes big, and face red. Jazz looked at Aunt J.

Mal chuckled, "it ain't like it's a secret." I sat there smiling.

Aunt J just shook her head, "you two have been head over heels for each other since... Well, since I've known you. Everyone in Alpha Ring knows it, so you two might as well get on board. It's obvious to anyone with eyes."

Jazz cleared her throat, "I'm sure Nac had a girl or two back on Titan."

I cleared my throat, "and I'm sure Jazz has guys here."

Mal barked a laugh, "not since she clocked that last guy for talking smack about you." I looked back at Jazz, she was looking daggers at Mal. She started to say something, but I interrupted her.

"Actually, there were no girls on Titan." I shrugged my shoulders, "never had time between surgeries, hospital stays, school, and work. Besides, I always knew I'd be coming back home." I looked up from the table into mesmerizing blue eyes that always took my breath away.

"Yep," Mal said. "They've got it bad. Sitting there staring at each other like two idiots."

Jazz's eyes never left mine, "don't make me hurt you, computer boy."

Mal just leaned back in his chair with his hands up, "just making an observation."

Aunt J was grinning, "back on the topic, what do you think of my tug?"

"We can do all the repairs in-house including recertifications. We need a few parts, Mal can probably barter for some of those." I answered.

"So, now that you've crawled into the belly of the beast, you interested in buying her?" She was grinning at me. I picked up my fork to take another bite of pie, giving myself a moment to think. Mal and Jazz were looking back and forth between myself and Aunt J. Deciding, I took my fork and tapped it on the side of my cup.

"I call this meeting of the Haydock Mining and Shipping company to order." They were really staring at me now. "Present at this meeting are Ms. Jasmine Duvall, Chief Pilot and Chief of Flight Operations, Mr. Malcolm Calhoun, Chief Information Officer, me Nicholas Haydock, Chairman of the Board. Before the board this evening is a proposal to buy the 50 KLT tug *Uncle J.* We'll now open the floor for discussion."

Mal and Jazz were staring at me slack jawed. Aunt J was sitting there with her hands folded in front of her, watching the show.

"Chief Information Officer?" asked Mal.

"Yep CIO." I answered.

"Chief of Flight Operations?" asked Jazz.

"Uh-huh" I answered. I let that hang a minute, watching everyone.

"Thoughts anyone?" I asked. Jazz and Mal looked at each other, then at Aunt J.

Mal looked back at me, "are you hiring us?"

"Nope, making you partners."

"Partners?" Jazz said.

"Yep, partners, just like we've planned since we were kids." Jazz put her hand on my arm.

"Nic, that was just kids dreaming, you can't just split up your family's business like this."

I covered her hand with mine, "Jazz all the family I have left is sitting at this table. All my trusted friends are sitting at this table. I'm not 'giving' anything away. You have already earned it and will continue to earn it. Getting this business back off the ground won't be easy."

"So, we'll start with the *Uncle J.* In its present condition is worth far less than if it was fully functional and had up-to-date certifications." I looked at Aunt J, she was nodding. "Aunt J could spend the money on parts and labor and then offer it for sale," again she nodded. "Or there may be another option."

"I'm listening," Aunt J said.

"You use the *Uncle J* to buy a percentage of the company." I said. "What percentage would that be?"

"The Tug as is, 10%".

Aunt J just stared at me, "20%".

I stared back, "15% and the escrow money goes for tug parts and repairs."

She considered it for a bit, "If I may ask, what is their percentage in the company?"

"15%." I answered.

They looked at me; I kept watching Aunt J.

"And in what position do you see me serving?" she asked.

My coffee cup was empty, I got up and walked over to the coffee urns. "You don't strike me as someone who is looking for retirement. If you were, you'd have moved in with your kids and grands. I think you're looking for a new opportunity." I returned to my seat, "Let me ask you, where do you see yourself serving, doing the most good, and doing what you enjoy?" I said, sipping my coffee.

She got up and refilled her cup and stared into the galley for a moment, sipping her coffee. She nodded her head, coming to some conclusion, returned to her seat.

"Supplies and Acquisitions, that's where I think I can do the most good. My tug, plus the escrow money for 15% of the company."

"If you decide to sell out, the company gets first right of refusal."

"Nic dear, with you three working together," she said, shaking her head. "There's been nothing built that you can't fix. Mal is so far ahead of everyone with computers, the only thing the rest of us understands is where the 'On' button is. Jazz can out fly anyone with anything that has an engine strapped to it. Sell out? Not likely, if nothing else, this will be one heck of a ride."

"Then we have a deal?" I asked.

"We do" she replied.

I looked at Mal and Jazz, "all in favor of taking on Aunt J as a partner at 15% for her tug in escrow signify by and say 'aye'." Jazz and Mal both said aye. "There is no opposition, Mrs. J. Moore, Chief of Supply and Acquisitions, welcome to the Haydock Mining and Shipping company. I looked at Jazz, "Well, Chief of Flight Ops, we have a second ship."

"Yes, but when will it be ready to fly?" Jazz asked.

"Barring anything too crazy, she should be ready in about a week I'd guess."

"Two," Mal put in, "I have upgrades in mind."

Jazz nodded, "all right, once you have her repaired and re-certified, I'll give notice to the Mercer's. They can replace me easily enough. I'll fly for HMS."

Aunt J raised her cup, "to HMS".

"To HMS", we replied raising our cups.

***

The next two weeks went by in a blur. Get up early, work on the *Uncle J*. Jazz would help when she wasn't wrangling rocks for the Mercer's. We enjoyed dinner together, and after, I'd walk her home. Wash, rinse, repeat as Mom used to say.

We took 17 days to finish, mostly because of Mal's upgrades. The escrow creds more than cover the repair costs and filled all *Uncle J's* tankage. We moved *Uncle J* out on the run-up pad and locked her in place with a grav-field. Jazz and Mal were on board doing a system check and engine run-up.

I stayed in the hanger in my Vac-suit, on emergency standby.

"*Uncle J* to HMS hanger, we've got greens across the board. Release grav-field, we've got clearance from Conclave traffic control for local maintenance test flight."

"Roger, *Uncle J*, releasing-field. Take it easy on her Jazz, don't scratch the paint." They took a long flight, but I monitor them closely. After the first 30 minutes, everything was still green. Jazz put *Uncle J* through her paces.

"*Uncle J* to HMS hanger, still all green, and she can really dance, you guys work wonders. We'll grab a rock as a final test, might as well make the test flight profitable."

"Roger *Uncle J* make sure you clear it with Conclave traffic, HMS hanger out."

"Yes, mother. *Uncle J* out." I switched the monitoring channel to hab wide and went to the galley for some coffee.

"How's the test flight going?" Aunt J, asked.

"All green, they're doing a final test, grabbing a rock to pay for the test flight. Jazz seemed happy with the ship's performance so far." Aunt J nodded.

They were back by 1700; I stood by the hanger controls but had them do a remote hanger entry. Everything worked perfectly. Jazz landed *Uncle J* and the hanger door closed smoothly.

I waited for them to complete their shutdown procedures and post flight checks. Jazz came down the ramp with a big grin on her face.

"That ship is awesome! All the repairs and upgrades meshed great, but with Mal's control systems it made the operations as smooth as silk. I love being able to talk to the ship, how cool is that?"

"Cool," I replied. Mal was standing behind Jazz, smiling at her enthusiasm.

"How'd the systems check go?" I asked Mal.

"About like Jazz said, a few things needed to be tweaked, but I did it on the fly, nothing Major."

"In that case I'd say *Uncle J* is ready to go to work." Both Mal and Jazz nodded.

"I'll give the Mercer's my notice in the morning and start wrangling rocks for HMS."

Jazz was back early the next morning, bags and baggage in tow. She left her luggage at the cargo hatch.

"Jazz is everything okay? I didn't expect you until later."

"Yeah, I'm good, just finished up with the Mercer's quicker than I thought I would. I gave them my notice, told them I was going to work for HMS."

"They thought it was great; they know how close we all

are. They released me right away, said I didn't have to work a notice, they had a pilot that could start right away. So, I packed my things and here I am. That's okay, right? I know we didn't talk about me moving in, I kind of assume since everyone else lives here..."

"Of course, it's okay, I assumed you move in here too."

"Great, which room do I get?"

"Take your pick, any one you want."

She got a funny little smile on her face, "we'll see." she started toward the hab door, she sure looked good walking away. The "we'll see" finally clicked. I knew I was in trouble. I hope it was the good kind of trouble. I headed for what was now my office on level 1.

CHAPTER 4

If Jazz was going to wrangle rocks, I needed to make sure all of HMS' accounts were up-to-date and active, so the rock creds had a place to go. I messaged my lawyers, Harper and Harper. The family had used the same ones for years. Their reply came back almost immediately. They would come to my office at 1400 if that was suitable.

I confirmed the appointment and made notes on things I should ask. I noticed the computer in here was far newer and nicer than the one in the master suite. I commed Mal and ask him to come to my office. He walked in less than a minute later.

"I noticed the computer in here is, well if not new, newer and upgraded."

"Yeah, I upgraded the whole hab."

"Sounds good, what program have you got running it, I mean I know you have ACE running the ship's systems, I assume you will do the same in here."

"Yes, but more interactive and user-friendly, designed to help us with everything. Answering the door, delivering messages, trading, ordering supplies, doing research, whatever anyone needs, just ask."

"How long before you'll be ready to bring it online?"

Mal pulled his P-comm out, tapped a few icons and said, "Initialize Major-domo program."

A few seconds later a baritone male voice said, "Major-domo initializing please stand by..., Major-domo online."

I shook my head, "I don't know what I was thinking, please continue." I sat down at my desk.

"Major." Mal said.

"Yes Mal, what can I do for you?"

"We are no longer in developmental test mode, we are moving into full implementation mode, you have permission for full integration into all HMS systems, hanger and hab, including all security protocols." Raising my eyebrows, I kept watching and listening.

"Understood, starting full integration into all HMS systems, hanger and hab, including all security protocols. Please stand by."

"Interesting name you picked." I said.

"I didn't want to call him 'House' or 'Butler', then I remembered reading the meaning of Major-domo, so Major seemed to fit."

"I like it. You're right, it fits."

The main wall monitor came on showing percentages to all systems Major-domo was integrating himself into. In a few moments everything was showing 100% integration.

"Mal, clarification required," Major said. "Are all HMS systems outside of this hanger hab designated HH-AA-12 to be included in the Major-domo integration?" Mal and I looked at each other, I shrug my shoulders.

"State location of HMS systems outside location HH-AA-12." Mal said.

"According to system archives and public records, HMS holding includes two other locations. Designations are HH-AA-11, and HH-AA-14. There are also several HMS accounts listed." Major answered.

"Display all the HMS holdings and accounts." A list appeared on the wall monitor. The list included the company bank accounts and accounts with some other businesses, some names I recognized, some I did not; some showed a balance some did not. There at the bottom of the list was A11 and A14.

"Major, are A11 and A14 occupied?"

"A11 is being used as a storage facility and is leased to the law firm of Harper and Harper and subleased to Van Dam Shipyards. A14 is unoccupied." Something didn't sound right.

"Major, what rent is Harper and Harper paying for the use of A11?" "1000 credits per month, deposited into HMS account at the Conclave Bank."

"Is there a record of what Harper and Harper rents A11 to Van Dam Shipping for?"

"According to public records Van Dam Shipping pays 4000 creds per month for the lease on A11."

"Something's not adding up here. Major, can you send a message to Harper and Harper?"

"I can, what is your message?"

"I need to cancel the 1400 meeting today due to a scheduling conflict; I'll reschedule later."

"Message ready, shall I send it?"

"Send it."

I looked at Mal, "Do you think you can get us in to see Mr. Van Dam?"

"Yeah, I'm sure I can."

"Today?" I asked.

"Let me make a call. "

"Major show me the blueprints for A14." The A14 blueprints appeared on the wall, I got up and walked over to the monitor taking a closer look at the drawings.

Mal joined me, "Mr. Van Dam will meet with us at 1400 today."

"Good," I said.

"I'm guessing these are the blueprints for A14?"

"Yes," I nodded, "Major is there an A13?"

"There is no A13 listed," Major answered.

"Major, status of A14 hanger, hab and systems." Mal asked.

"Minimum O2 present, pressure integrity reading 93%. They shut all systems down, or on safety standby. Showing zero occupants."

"In round numbers A14 appear to be twice the size of A12", I said.

Mal nodded, "if not a bit more," he said.

I turned to Mal, "ok, let's get A14 integrated back into the

HMS family, do a full diagnostic and we'll take a tour later."

Mal nodded, "Major, start full integration and safety protocols into A14 hanger, hab, and system. Bring it under the HMS company umbrella."

"Starting integration and safety protocols of A14 hanger, Hab, and systems."

"Once integration is complete raise hanger and hab temperature to hab standard, there is no hurry, but have it completed by 1200 tomorrow." Mal added.

"Understood, completed by 1200 tomorrow," Major answered.

"Let's go grab lunch and have a word with Aunt J." I said, leading Mal upstairs to the galley.

"You guys ready for lunch?"

"Yes ma'am, any pie left?" I asked.

"Ha! Not likely when Mal is around."

"You'll give me a complex," Mal said.

We fixed our sandwiches and moved to the table.

"Anybody seen Jazz lately?"

"She said she had to go check on some stuff," Mal answered around his sandwich.

"Aunt J, with all your business dealings I'm guessing you have a lawyer?" I said.

"I do. In fact, and a fantastic one, she works at one of the top firms on Conclave. Randall Jones and Associates, she's one of the Associates, Janet Jennings, she's also my niece. Don't you already have a lawyer?"

"Yep, but I'm considering a change."

"Anything wrong?"

"I'm not sure, but something doesn't seem right. Let's just say I may need to talk to your niece."

***

We arrived at the Van Dam shipyards just before 1400. I followed Mal into their offices.

"Hi Julie."

"Hi Mal."

"This is my friend Nac, we have a 1400 meeting with Mr. Van Dam."

"Pleasure to meet you Nac, I'll check and see if Mr. Van Dam is ready to see to see you." She went to the door of an inner office. She was only gone for a few seconds. "Mr. Van Dam will see you now." She ushered us in.

Mr. Van Dam was rounding his desk as we entered.

He shook our hands, "come in and have a seat. Nic, it's good to see you after all these years. You look great." He turned somber, "I'm sorry about your folks, they were good people, good friends."

"Thank you, sir, I appreciate you saying so."

"What can I do for you, gentlemen?"

"A few things, actually," I answered. "I know Mal catches some of your overflow work and I'd like to offer you the same service on the engineering side of the house."

"Nic we'd love to have you and I know you hold a bag full of degrees. Even before your degrees, you could fix anything man-made. The truth is, I couldn't pay you half of what that new shipyard can pay you. It pains me to say that, but you'd be better served signing on with them." I looked at him for a few moments.

"You know, as part of my rehab in dealing with the loss of my parents, and loss of my arm and leg. I read through all the reports of that day," I said. He quietly listened to me. "The hardest were the medical reports. I recall a report that said I was the only one still alive when the first help arrived, and just barely at that.

They did the best they could with what they had. They put me in a stasis pod; they didn't really expect me to live. Even with me in a stasis pod, we were a long way from Conclave Medical.

The tugs that had been first on the scene were powerful, but they were built to haul mass, not for speed. They said a call came in from a ship that was coming in at max burning, said to have my stasis pod ready to load soonest.

One of the old-timers said he'd never seen the like. Said that ship was at max burn one moment, then went zero burn; flipped ends and went full afterburners. Said it looked like a solar flare, but the ship came to a dead stop 100 meters from the rescuers and my stasis pod. The old-timer said as soon as my pod was on that ship that pilot went to full afterburners before the hatch was even closed."

Mr. Van Dam was staring at the floor. "The story picks up from the report from Conclave traffic control. The report said they gave repeated warnings about excess speed entering Conclave control space. They said the pilot showed 'total disregard for authority'.

His response to warnings was 'shut up, clear a lane to medical, you can write my tickets when I get there'. The Conclave medical report states, that the 'rescue ship' came in at full burn, flip went to full afterburners and full control jets coming to a stop 60 meters off Conclave Medical's apron. That pilot and ship got me there in time to save my life.

I got the maintenance inspection report filed by the insurance claim. The long and short of it was, the afterburners were totally melted. Injector nozzles melted. Gravity emitters, 98% of them burned out. The engine got so hot it melted 80% of the engine mounts. The only reason the whole back of the ship didn't fall off was the pilot had opened engineering to space to keep it cool for as long as he could." Mr. Van Dam was still looking at the floor.

"Whose ship was it, and who was the pilot?" Mal asked.

I got up and moved over to the sideboard that displayed a model of a Corporate Yacht. "The ship's name was 'June's Bride', and the pilot's name was Travis Van Dam." Above the display was a shadow box with several fight violation tickets. "I'm guessing these are the tickets Conclave control brought you when they arrested you at the medical center."

"Well, in my defense, I told them to meet me there." Travis

said, smiling.

"You?" Mal asked. "You were the pilot?" Mr. Van Dam shrugged his shoulders. I returned to my seat.

"I was in the neighborhood. I was on a shakedown run, I did what anyone else would have," He said.

"Be that as it may. You, a Van Dam, flying a Van Dam ship, is why I'm still breathing. The point being, it will be a cold day in hell, when I work for a competitor of the Van Dam shipyards."

"Don't feel too bad for me, we got so much business from that high-speed run we had to double our workforce."

"I'm glad you were at least paid for my rescue run, but we didn't come here too asked to be hired. Although we'll be glad to help with your overflow or when you get in a bind." I said.

"Okay, what you need?" Travis asked.

"We were going through some paperwork getting ready to get HMS back up and running. We came upon something that made little sense to us." Travis nodded for me to continue. "My paperwork says you are renting HH-AA-11 from us for 4000 credits a month."

"Yeah, that sounds right," Travis said. Mal and I looked at each other. "And?" Travis asked.

"And, according to my paperwork, Harper and Harper leased A11 from me at 1000 creds a month and subleased it to you for 4000 credits a month."

Travis sat there a moment, frowning. He got up and moved around his desk; he sat down and pulled up files on his computer. He stopped and leaned back in his chair, steepled his fingers.

"Nic, it looks like what you suspect is true. Before I call my lawyers, what do you intend to do?"

"I will hire another lawyer see what his advice will be. Then meet with Harper and Harper for an explanation."

Travis nodded, "Do you have a lawyer in mind, if not, may I suggest one?"

"I would appreciate the suggestion." I said. Travis picked up his P-comm and placed a call.

"Aaron Stein, please. Yes, I'll hold... Aaron, are you busy? Now if you can... Yes, it's important... Good, they'll be expecting you, and they'll bring you straight in." Travis hung up. "Aaron Stein will be here in a few minutes, he's one of the best lawyers I know. And for this particular problem, I think he's the guy you need."

Aaron Stein arrived, and Travis introduced us. We went through our story again, Travis verifying his part of the lease agreement. Aaron took notes and then consider for a moment.

"What do you want to do about this," he asked me.

"I think this is fraud, they were supposed to be handling my family's business. They or someone, has for lack of a better analogy, been skimming 3000 credits a month from me for the last 10 or so years. I'm not looking to see anyone go to prison, per se, but I want what's owed."

Aaron nodded, and turned to Travis, "And you Travis, what do you want done about this?"

"Nothing, we're just the company renting storage space. Although I'm rather ticked that they made me part of this, I want to see that Nic is fairly compensated."

Aaron nodded his head, "I don't see where Van Dam shipping will be involved, unless they push us to trial. Other than that, you are only the renter." He turned back to me. "They will more than likely settle; they will want to keep this whole matter quiet. Give me a few days to prepare, then we'll meet with them."

"Aaron are you an independent law office, or part of the firm?" I asked.

"Part of the firm, Randall Jones and Associates."

I glanced at Mal, "have you ever worked with Janet Jennings?"

"Yes, many times." he answered, "you know JJ?"

"Only by reputation, she is a niece of one of my partners. Will she be working with you on this case?"

He smiled, "she is now and no, it will not be a problem, no conflict of interest."

"Sounds good, call me when you're ready to proceed."

We all stood, shook hands, and departed. On the way back to A12 I sent Jazz and Aunt J a message that there would be a board meeting tonight after dinner. When we got home, we went up to the galley, I could tell by the look on Jazz and Aunt J faces the meeting would not wait for later. Before they could ask, I held up my hands.

"Let me get coffee and I'll tell you what's going on." We all filled our cups and took our seats. Mal and I explained what we found, what we had learned, and that we were going to sue Harper and Harper.

"Those thieving, backstabbing, lowlifes." Jazz started.

"Hold on Jazz, we don't know what how deep this goes." Aunt J said, patting the table.

"True," I said. "That's part of the reason I'm suing them, I want to know how deep this goes. And if HMS has been hurt anywhere else. Of course, I want my creds too."

"Who's representing you?" Aunt J asked.

"Randall Jones and Associates," I answered. "Specifically, Aaron Stein and Janet Jennings."

Aunt J chuckled, "Harper will have a fit when he sees them, Aaron Stein has quite the reputation."

"How did you find out about this in the first place, you didn't know HMS owned A-11?" Jazz asked.

I shook my head, "I didn't have a clue, Major was the one who found it."

Jazz frowned, "Major who?" I took a sip of my coffee, Mal was hiding a smile behind his cup. The ladies were looking at us expectantly.

"Mal, would you introduce the Major?"

"Why certainly," Mal said, smiling. "Major, please introduce yourself to the ladies." A figure of a man dressed in a tux appeared on the full wall monitor facing us.

Bowing at the waist, "good evening ladies I am the ACE Major-domo program for HMS, designation, Major." Both ladies just stared.

Aunt J looked at Mal, "I see you've been busy." Mal shrugged his shoulders and smiled. I looked at Jazz, she was still staring at Major.

"What do you think, Jazz?" I asked.

Her eyes never left Major, "We have a Butler?"

"Does he cook?" Aunt J asked.

"Main galley off-line," Mal and I said at the same time and laughed. I held up my hand, "sorry ladies, an inside joke."

Mal explained the capabilities of Major and how he could help streamline HMS operations. Everyone was suitably impressed.

***

A few days later Mal and I were working in the infamous "Main galley" on the *Taurus*, trying to remove the crushed cabinetry and hardware from the bulkhead.

"Is there a way to push the bulkhead back out? That would make it easier to remove everything," Mal said. I froze, looking at the tangled mess of the galley. "What?" Mal asked. I held up one finger, going deeper into my engineering mind. An idea took shape.

"It wouldn't be that simple. Could it be that simple?" I said.

"What?" Mal asked again.

I explained my epiphany with grand hand motions. Mal followed me, then he froze.

"What?" I asked. He held up one finger, I waited. His face broke into a grin and explained his epiphany we both just sat there staring at the galley engrossed in our thoughts and plans.

"Captain?" Misty said. Mal and I both almost jumped out of our skins, both of us laughed.

"Yes Misty." I answered.

"Major says there is a message from a Mr. Aaron Stein requesting a meeting at 1400 at Hab A12."

"Please have Major Send a confirmation for the meeting at 1400 and ask Aunt J to fix coffee and snacks for the meeting, please."

"Yes, Captain."

"Misty?"

"Yes, Captain."

"Send Jazz a message about the 1400 meeting, she'll want to be there."

"Yes, Captain."

We were all in the galley at 1345, Major announced that a Mr. Aaron Stein was at the A12 personnel hatch.

"Tell them I'll be there shortly, Major."

"Yes, sir."

CHAPTER 5

Mal and I met them at the lock and were ushering them toward the main hab conference room when Major announced over my internal comms.

"Security scans complete, security board is green." I glanced at Mal, he mouthed "later", and we continued to the first-level conference room.

As we entered the conference room Aunt J said, "Please help yourself to the coffee and snacks." She went to the table where Janet Jennings was standing, "it is so good to see you dear."

"You too Aunt J." We all got coffee and snacks and took our seats. After we exchanged pleasantries and introductions made, Aaron cleared his throat.

"If you'll allow Nic?"

"Of course, let's get to it." I replied.

He and Janet laid out what they had found and their suggested strategy. We all listened, asking a few questions here and there.

"Basically, if I'm understanding correctly, we will lie out what we found, and sue them. The negotiations will start at five million creds. Half going to Randall Jones and Associates and half to HMS?" I said.

"In a nutshell that is correct," replied Aaron.

"You think they'll pay that without going to court?"

"Probably not the 5 million, we'll probably end up at around 2 million. Their reputation is worth, well literally, their fortune."

I nodded, looking around, "You guys have any questions?" They shook their heads. "Will I, or we, have to be present when you present the suit?" I asked.

"Not if you don't want to be, and it may run smoother if you weren't, emotion sometimes flair."

"All right, I don't want to be there. When will you serve them?"

"Probably next Tuesday, if anyone contacts you from their office, just refer them to us, we're handling all this now."

I signed the paperwork, the meeting ended, and they departed. I pulled another cup of coffee and sat back down.

"I guess we'll see where the chips fall." I said.

Aunt J filled her cup, "Nic, don't feel bad, you aren't the bad guy in this. Harper and Harper or someone in their employ is responsible for this."

"I know, that's why I didn't want to be there, I'll let the lawyers fight it out."

Mal and I went back to the workshop, "Ok, what was the deal with Major informing us about security scans? I didn't even know we had security scans."

"I added them a few years ago, it's part of Major's security protocols."

"What do these scans detect?"

"Weapons, explosives, facial recognition checked against who they say they are, and against the criminal database."

"Cool, I like it."

We continued to the shop to work on our new idea. After a week of long hours, we were almost there. Jazz came into the shop to let us know dinner was ready.

"What are you guys working on?"

"Nothing." Mal answered.

"I'm not your Mom, give it a rest," she said. I chuckled. She looked at me "You're in it too Buddy, you guys are cooking up something, so what's up?"

"You're right we are cooking up something, we had an idea and we're working on. A prototype but we're not ready to share yet." I said.

"When do you think you'll be ready?"

I shrugged, "a week maybe."

"Ok, dinner is ready, and Aunt J is waiting."

We got to the galley, and Aunt J looked at Jazz. "What were they up to?"

"Won't tell, being all hush-hush about it. Claims they're working on a prototype but wouldn't tell what kind." Jazz answered.

"Torture them, you think?" Jazz narrowed her eyes, thinking.

"No, let's give them a week, if they don't produce something after a week, well..." They both laughed.

Mal and I looked at each other and then back at them, "you guys are just mean," I said.

***

I was lying on my bed relaxing after a nice hot shower just letting my mind wonder, drifting towards sleep. My P-comm pinged, I blinked my internal comms; it was Jazz.

"You okay, Jazz?"

"Yeah, I just can't sleep, can I come up and talk?"

"Sure, come on up."

"Ok, I'll be right up," she clicked off. I got up and opened the door. I blinked to night vision and watched her as she came toward me. I love the way she moved, so smooth, no wasted motions. I reached out my hand and she took it. Closing the door, I led her up to the observatory dome.

"I had forgotten about this place. I loved it when we were kids. I see they added carpet and throw pillows. Nice touch."

"Yeah, this was one of my favorite places too. I love sleeping under the stars." We arrange the pillows and just lay there enjoying the starry heavens. After a bit Jazz looked over at me, then moved over and put her head on my chest. We kept watching the stars.

"I can hear your heart beating," she said.

"Yeah, I thought it was kinda loud." I said, she chuckled. "I have always loved the smell of your hair," I said, and felt her smile.

"I know, why do you think I've always used that shampoo."

"Am I really that transparent?"

"To me, yes." The quiet stretched for a bit. "You know how in all our emails over the years you sign off with 'love you'?" She asked.

"Yeah." She turned toward me, raising up, putting her hand on my chest. "I realized we've never said it face-to-face." I nodded. "I love you Nic"

"I love you too, Jazz."

"Say my name," she whispered.

I pulled her tighter and to me. "I love you Jasmine, I have since we were 10 years old, and more so now." She melted into my arms.

One thing about living on a hab, there's not really a sunrise to wake up to. My P-comm pinged. I blinked it up; it was Mal. Jazz was still in the same place I remember from last night, wrapped around me, head on my chest.

"Yeah, Mal?"

"Hey, you guys will have to come down for breakfast, because we don't have room service."

"If that's Mal, I'm gonna kill him," Jazz said. Mal hung up.

"Want breakfast?" I asked.

"We need a shower," she answered.

"Yep, as it happens, I've got one down in my room." We made it into the showers, I noticed Jazz staring at my arm and leg, and how they attached to me. "This is who I am, Jazz. Are you okay with this?"

"Of course, I am my love, I was just admiring the view," She said smiling.

"I know exactly what you mean, I'm enjoying the view myself." We made it to the galley... In time for lunch.

Aunt J came to us smiling, gathered us into a hug. As she

turned, walking back to the galley, "about time," she said. Mal shot coffee out of his nose.

"In my defense," Jazz said, "He told me I could have any room I wanted." Everyone laughed.

"Nic, there is a message from Aaron Stein." Major announced.

"What's the message, Major?"

"He is requesting a meeting with you and the partners at 1500 in the offices of Randall Jones and Associates."

"Confirm the appointment, Major."

"Appointment confirmed."

We all got cleaned up, changed and headed to our meeting. We arrived at 1445 and were shown into their conference room.

"Please help yourselves to the coffee, tea, and snacks. Someone will be with you shortly." Before we finished getting our cuppa, Aaron, Janet and Randall Jones he joined us.

"Thank you for meeting with us on such short notice." Mr. Jones said.

"No problem sir, I'm guessing you have something to share with us of some urgency." I replied.

"Quite right young man, quite right. Shall we get to it then?" Mr. Jones said, waving us to our chairs. "Would you start us off, Aaron?"

"Of course, sir." Aaron looked at us, "per our agreement, we sued Harper and Harper in a civil court for five M-creds. The judge gave us a week to see if we could settle it out of court. If not, he would set a court date for trial.

They threaten countersuits, there was some back and forth. Long story short, they offered to settle, but have a list of requirements. What you need to decide now is, do you accept their offer, counter the offer, or go to trial."

"Ok, why the urgency?" I asked.

"We need to tell the judge our decision by 1000 in the morning."

"I see what's their offer." Aaron looked at Mr. Jones.

"3.4 to 3.7 M-creds depending on appraisals." Mr. Jones

said.

"Appraisals? I take it this is not an all creds offer." I said.

"Only about 1 million in creds, the rest is in hard assets." They handed each of us a hard copy list of assets. "Their holding company owns a small shipping company, a couple of ore haulers, a cargo ship, four tugs, two of which are nonfunctioning. All the parts are there, just nonfunctional. Miscellaneous parts, tools and equipment."

I scanned the asset list, "This looks like a fire sale and they are just getting rid of all their junk, so they can write the whole venture off their taxes and clear their books."

Mr. Jones nodded, "That is exactly what they're doing. They got caught with their hand in the cookie jar. They are trying to get out of this as cheaply as possible, trying to gain some good out of it."

"You said they had demands?" I asked.

"You will all have to sign nondisclosure agreements concerning the whole civil action. You must take possession of assets and move them from their yards and hangers within two weeks or pay for storage thereafter."

"Anything else?" I asked.

"No, that sums it up."

"Can you give us a moment to talk this over?" I asked.

"Before you do, let me sweeten the deal a little." Mr. Jones said. I nodded for him to continue. "We think you'll be in the market for a new law firm to represent HMS. We would like to be that firm. If you agree to make us your law firm, we be willing to waive our normal fee of 50% on the civil suit, taking a flat 250K creds in fees. We would start immediately by doing a 100% audit of all your assets including the ones you will gain from Harper and Harper and get everything as tax-sheltered and protected as possible."

"And the cost of this audit and tax sheltering?" I asked.

"Covered in the 250K cred fee."

I nodded, "if you would give us a few moments to discuss our options please."

"Of course, just open the door when you're ready."

They left the room, closing the door. I got up and filled my coffee cup and returned to my seat.

"Thoughts?" I asked.

Jazz looked at me and smiled, "wherever thou goest."

I smiled, "I appreciated that, but I also needed your thoughts and advice."

She nodded, "we need to see firsthand what condition all these assets are in, I'm not trusting the appraisal of someone who has already shown they are dishonest."

"I agree," Aunt J added.

Mal was nodding, "me three."

"What about taking Randall Jones and Associates on as our law firm? Aunt J you've dealt with them, what say you?"

"The best I can say is, I'm still with them. They handle all my legal affairs." Mal and Jazz were both nodding.

"I liked the settlement flat rate, they quoted. 250K creds is better than 1.5 million creds. We're all in agreement then?"

"Ask for a month to move assets." Jazz said.

"A month after the independent appraisals are complete," Aunt J added.

"Good points," I nodded. "Anything else?" I asked. "All in favor say aye." "The ayes have it."

I open the door, and our new lawyer came back in, and we all took our seats.

"We accept the terms with Harper and Harper with two changes." They were taking notes. "One, we want an independent audit survey, an appraisal done on all the assets they are offering in the settlement with HMS reps present. Two, we want one month to move all the assets to an alternate location, time to start once we accept the independent audit, survey, and appraisal." They made the changes; I signed the papers including making them HMS' law firm.

We waited while Aaron contacted Harper and Harper with our counteroffer. They accepted it within the hour. The topic over dinner that night was the surveys and appraisals of the settlement assets.

"Is there enough room to park the ships outside the hanger?" Aunt J asked.

"Yeah, HMS owns a few sections of land, it's part of the original state claim. You'd have to check with the Chief of Supply Acquisition to see what her plans are." Aunt J gave me "The look".

"How are we going to move all the ships, parts, and equipment?" Jazz asked.

I frowned, looking at her, "I don't know, you'll have to check with Chief of Flight Ops and see what the plans are." Mal chuckled.

Jazz turned to Aunt J, "airlock?" Aunt J close one eye, thinking over her options.

"Possibly, but there's all that paperwork to fill out afterwards, but we have lawyers now." I held up my hands in surrender.

"I have an idea, let's put everything over in A14." Mal said. Jazz and Aunt J looked at each other, then at me.

Mal stood up, "I got to go check on..."

"Hold it right there, computer boy," Jazz said. Mal froze.

"Take a seat", Aunt J said. Mal sat. Jazz lean forward with her elbows on the table chin in her palms.

"Nic honey, who owns A14?"

"HMS," I answered, looking over at Mal. He shrugged his shoulders.

"Hmm, and how long have you known about A14?" She asked sweetly. I wasn't fooled. She was thinking about throwing us out the airlock again. I looked over at Mal he was looking everywhere but at me.

"We found out about A11 and A14 at the same time. It kind of got pushed to the side."

Jazz set back, "ok, fair point. Have you been over to see it?"

"Not yet. Major, status of A14?" I asked.

Major appeared on the wall screen, "atmospherics pressure holding, ambient temperature at Station norm. Safety systems are all green, all other systems are off-line or in safety standby. A14 is fully integrated under Major-domo protocols."

Jazz looked at Aunt J, "you know, as Chief of Acquisitions, you need to see the new hanger."

Aunt J nodded, "true," she said. "And as Chief of Flight Ops you need to see it to know where to land, and how much maneuvering room you have," Looking at Jazz.

"Shall we?" Aunt J asked.

"I think we should" Jazz answered. They both rose and started down the hall.

"You boys coming?" Aunt J yelled as they headed down the stairs. We both jumped up and ran to catch up.

***

We gathered at the personnel hatch at A14. Jazz reached to palm the hatch security pad. Before she touched it, she looked at Mal, then palmed it. The pad read her print, turned green.

"Access granted."

Jazz was still looking at Mal, "you dodged a rock, computer boy." Aunt J chuckled. we moved inside. "This place is huge" Jazz said.

"According to the blueprints, it's more than twice as big as A12. The hab is six levels instead of three. More storage, bigger shops. Well, like I said, bigger everything." I said.

As we walked across the hanger, lights came on. A side door read, "auxiliary power," I stuck my head in, generators looked in decent shape, I'd have to run diagnostics to be sure.

Everything probably needed maintenance and updating. We passed by the hanger door control board it was showing all green. There were twice as many grav-slings and a huge test pad outside.

Mal was looking up, "there are overhead gantries. They set this place up like a small shipyard.

"Makes sense, when they first settled here, they had to be

self-reliant." I said.

The hab had the same basic layout, just more of it. More and bigger offices, more crew quarters, the main galley was huge, two elevators, one service, one personal. The master suite was larger and had its own small galley, dining area, a den and a balcony. Jazz and Aunt J were on the balcony looking across the hanger.

They turned back to us, "Sold!" Jazz yelled.

"We'll take it," Aunt J added. We all laughed.

"As it happens ladies, I know the owners. I think we can get a good deal on the place. I looked at Jazz, "sorry there's no observation dome."

"The observation dome is on the opposite side of the quarters," Major said. We all turned, and a wall panel parted. The hatch behind slid open. Mal was the first to arrive.

He stopped in the hatch, "oh, my." We all stuck our heads in.

"Amazing" Jazz said.

We took three steps down into a sunken area about 8 meters across. It was like looking through a glass ball, out onto the plains and the cliffs in the distance.

"Millions of stars" Aunt J said. Everyone had stepped down into the sunken area and sat down and stared at the heavens.

"God's handiwork, that's what Mom used to call a view like this, I have to agree."

***

It was another week before the new asset survey started. We all went over to get a firsthand look at the ships and equipment. It was about what we expected. Harper and Harper were having a fire sale and made the best out of a tough situation. The ships and tugs were used but not total wrecks. The cargo ship looked to be the best of the bunch.

There was a lot of containerized equipment, but all part of the package. We spent half the day there. No one wanted to do an extended stay in a Vac suit, walking the yard. We'd wait for the reports.

10 days later we had the reports. We read through them, the appraisals came in at 2.5 M-creds, plus 1.25 M-creds cash, not as much as we'd hoped, not as bad as we feared.

We accepted the settlement and signed the paperwork; we paid Randall Jones and Associate 250 K-creds making them HMS's lawyers. We got them started on sheltering our new assets.

They figured taxes would get about 20% but we would have a lot of business expenses. None of the ships had been flown for at least six months, no one knew why. We needed to move our new ships over into HMS area yards and hangers. We were sitting around the galley table having coffee, talking over how to handle the movement of assets.

"I have a question," Jazz said. We all looked at her expectantly. "Is there any reason we can't move over to A14? I mean our business is growing we will use it for storage and maintenance of the new assets. We'll need soon employees to handle the workload and operate equipment, and they will need quarters. I think we should move HMS operations to A14, and lease A12."

I had already been leaning in that direction but had said nothing. I looked at Mal, "any reason from an infrastructure standpoint, that we should hold off moving?"

Mal took a swallow of coffee thinking. "All the electronics and computers need to be upgraded but we'll just be trading equipment between A12 and A14. No need to buy new, whoever leases A12 can buy their own computers. The only thing that will cost us is time and manpower."

"Aunt J?" I asked.

She pursed her lips and rocked her head from side to side, thinking. "The galleys are the same, equipment wise. A14 just has more of it. It's fully stocked with pots, pans, dishes and things. We'd need to move our stores from here to there. No, I can't think of any reason not to move. I think Jazz is on target with her reasoning."

I nodded my head, "I think so too; all right let's talk logistics. We'll need to hire people, at least temporarily. Jazz, do you know a good pilot that needs a job?"

She nodded, "I think I know someone who does, but I need to check."

"Okay hire us a pilot. You take *Uncle J* and move one of the new tugs over here. We'll do a full diagnostic on her and get her flying. Then we'll have two tugs moving equipment. Mal, do you know a couple of techs who you'll let touch your stuff, and help you move all the computers and electronics?"

Mal laughed, "Yeah I know a few guys, but I want to keep Major and Misty undercover. I'm not ready for the public to know about them yet."

I nodded, "ok by me, that's your area. Aunt J would you get the crew roster for the cargo ships and ore Haulers, let's check them and see how many we want to hire to re-crew the ships. Let's use this opportunity to get rid of any rotten eggs, and deadweight. We need to get those ships working ASAP, if they aren't hauling freight, they aren't making us money.

CHAPTER 6

We were up and at it early the next morning. Jazz had *Uncle J*'s preflight completed. She had coordinated with the H&H yard to pick up the best of the tugs to bring in for me to inspect.

She kissed me, "be back in an hour." She fired up *Uncle J* and was gone. I went over to the EL shop, Mal was there packing up the items he wanted moved.

Jazz was back in less than an hour and set the new tug down on the test pad and parked *Uncle J*. I opened the hanger doors and powered up the grav-slings. Jazz came walking over.

"Any problems?" I asked.

"None, smooth as glass." I grav-slung the new tug and moved her into the hangar.

"Did you check on that pilot you were talking about?"

"Yeah, she wants to come and talk to us about the job and look at the tug she'll be flying."

"Then I guess I'd better get busy and have her something to check out." I called Mal and ask him to help me with the new tug.

"If you'll start on the electronics, I'll start on the mechanicals". Mal nodded, and we got started. She wasn't in too bad a shape. She needed fine tuning, a few parts, and Mal replaced a few control boards. We got all green boards and were satisfied to put her to work. We were standing at the foot of the ramp comparing notes when Jazz called out.

"Hey guys," we turned toward her. "This is Jade, a friend of mine. She's the pilot I was telling you about." Jade was not as good-looking as Jazz, but she didn't miss by much. She had spiked blonde hair in the typical pilot cut, and she worked that flight suit. "Jade, this is Nac."

"So, you're Nac. Jazz has been talking about you forever. She was right, you are good-looking."

"Down girl, he's mine, hands off. This is Mal, our in-house electronics genius." Mal was staring at Jade with his jaw hanging. Jade was smiling at him.

"Close your mouth dear, you'll swallow a fly." Mal's mouth clopped closed. "Smart, cute, and follows instructions. Where have you been all of my life?" Jade chuckled.

"Prison," Mal deadpanned. Jade's smile faded, and her eyes got big. "Gotcha," Mal said. We all busted out laughing.

Jade laughed the hardest, "we'll get along just fine, smart guy."

"Why don't you ladies do a preflight on her," I said pointing at the tug. "See what you think. Then we can move you out on to the test pad for a power test." We watched them go up the ramp into the tug. "Mal," I said. He looked at me. "You're drooling."

"Well, yeah, duh," he answered.

Their preflight went perfect. We grav-slung them out onto the test pad and locked them in place with the grav-field.

I keyed the comms, "HMS hanger to HMS tug one, you're clear for a full power test."

After 15 minutes Jazz called in, "HMS *Tug One* to HMS hanger, full power test all green. We have received local space test run clearance from Conclave Control, requesting grav-field release."

"Roger *Tug One*, grav-field release. Don't scratch the paint."

"Roger, *Tug One* out."

"Major, continue monitoring HMS *Tug One*, until their return let me know if they call."

"Yes sir," Major answered.

Mal's help arrived, and he put them to work. I packed up my office, which was only one box of stuff. I set it to the side.

"Major, status of *Tug One*?" I asked.

"All boards are green heading out on final tests to capture a rock," He answered.

"Continue to monitor."

"Yes, sir."

I told Aunt J that we would probably have a guest for dinner. A few hours later Major said, "*Tug One* on final approach all boards are green."

"Good, open hanger doors."

"Remote landing operations already in progress," he answered.

I headed for the hangar and watched *Tug One* enter the hangar, settle down on her landing gear and power down. Mal joined me as we waited for the ladies to exit the tug. They came down the ramp and did a walk around inspection of the tug. When they finished, they came over to us.

"How'd she handle?" I asked.

"Not as good as *Uncle J,* but she'll do," Jazz answered.

I looked at Jade, "do you think you'd like to fly it for us?"

"What are you paying?"

"You have to talk to the Chief of Flight Operations about the pay scale, but I must warn you she's tough."

"Ok, when do I meet her?"

Jazz stuck her hand out, "standard class III tug pilot pay, plus room and board."

"Food any good?" Jade asked.

"Aunt J is our cook."

"No way!" She looked at us. "Seriously, Aunt J's cooking for you guys?" We all nodded.

"Ok, but one more thing," Jade said.

"What?" Jazz asked.

"Can I have the smart one?" she chin pointed at Mal.

"He's not housebroken," Jazz said.

"Oh good, a challenge." Jade smiled at Mal. The ladies joined arms laughing headed for the hab.

I looked at Mal, he was watching Jade walk away. "You know you're in trouble, right?"

"God, I hope so." We laughed and went to catch up with the ladies.

We were enjoying our after-dinner coffee.

"When can I move in?" Jade asked.

Jazz looked at me and I nodded. Jazz looked back at Jade, "will tomorrow be soon enough? We're all moving over to A14."

"What time?" Jade asked.

"About 0800."

"In that case I'd better go get packed."

"Can I walk you home?" Mal ask.

"That would be nice, thank you Mal." Mal was smiling from ear to ear when they left. Jazz and Aunt J looked at each other and chuckled.

"What?" I asked.

"Nothing dear," Jazz answered. I look at them through squinted eyes for a moment.

"Why do I get the feeling Mal just got worked?"

"All right, Jade has had her eye on Mal for a good while, she was just waiting for the right moment."

I looked back and forth between Jazz and Aunt J. "We never stood a chance, did we?"

Jazz smiled getting out of her chair came over and kiss me on the head. "No, dear, you didn't." Taking my hand, she led me out of the galley.

I heard Aunt J chuckling, "nope, never stood a chance," she said.

In the end we hired a moving company to move us from A12 to A14 it was all done in a day. We ordered takeout that night, so Aunt J wouldn't have to dodge movers while she tried to cook. Everyone went their separate ways, unpacking and setting up their rooms.

Jazz and I had unpacked, put away our things, taken our showers, getting ready for bed. I took her hand, "open observation room." The wall and the hatch slid open. We lay on the floor looking at the stars.

"Nic?"

"Yeah, babe?"

"You don't feel bad about moving from A12 and your parents' room, do you?"

"No baby, I don't feel bad, that was Mom and Dad's room, this will be ours. She raised up looking at me."

"I love you, Nic."

"And I love you, Jasmine." We sank into our love and passion for each other.

***

With Jazz and Jade flying all day every day, it still took us two weeks to move everything from H&H's yard to HMS A14. We parked the ships on the yard in a grav-field lockdown. No one could get in to the grav-field. We were still inventorying, and storing parts, opening containers, inventorying and storing more parts and equipment.

One container we opened had six automated mining machines, those would come in handy. There were a lot of mining tools and portable grav-generators. We would sell anything us couldn't use, but I had a few ideas working. I wanted to explore them before we sold anything.

"Sir," Major's avatar appeared in my HUD.

"Yes, Major?"

"There is a Mr. Jocko at the hatch asking for you, security protocols have flagged him as Amber. He is under investigation by the authorities."

"Understood, ask him to come in, let Mal and Aunt J know we have company."

"Yes, sir."

Jocko was coming through the hatch, and Mal and Aunt J joined me in greeting him. Red pips appeared on my HUD, showing where Jocko was carrying weapons.

"No explosive devices detected," Major said in my ear. "There are also two armed men waiting outside in a grav-car." I nodded my head.

I extended my hand, "good morning Mr. Jocko, you seem to be walking better than the last time we met."

He shook my hand, smiling, "I am. Malcolm," he shook Mal's hand. Turning to Aunt J, "Julie, how have you been?" Aunt J hugged him. Apparently, they knew each other.

"Fine, and yourself?" She said, stepping back.

"Been doing better since Nicholas fixed my cyber controller."

"Oh?" Aunt J looked at me.

"He didn't tell you?" Jocko looked at me.

"No, he didn't."

I shrug my shoulders. "I was in the neighborhood," I said, stealing Travis' line.

Jocko laughed, "so were a lot of other people, but you were the one that helped me."

"Do tell" said Aunt J.

"It'll cost you a cup of coffee." Jocko smiled.

"Come on up, I got a fresh pot on." We all moved up to the galley, got our coffee, and moved to the table.

"So, there I was. That's how all good stories start," Jocko said, chuckling. "Flopping around like a fish out of water. My boys were trying to hold me down. Seems my CCU picked that moment to go crazy. Nicholas here jumps over the divider, and dumps over trash cans, grabbing dishes, throwing food all over us." Jocko was laughing, really get into the story.

"Nic is yelling 'flip them over", 'flip them over'!" People are running over each other trying to get away from this 300-pound flopping fish and flying food." We were all laughing now. "My boys managed to get me part of the way over, Nicholas comes sailing in to join the dog pile. He slams a metal dinner plate to my back, covering my CCU.

It was like he hit the off switch for my legs. I was never so relieved in my life. Long story short, Nicholas taped the plate in place, and they got me over to medical. Although I'm not sure which was more embarrassing, flopping around like a trout, or being wheeled face down on a gurney through the Promenade with a big silver plate taped to my butt."

That did it. Everyone was laughing so hard tears were flowing.

"To add insult to injury someone took a picture of my gurney ride and posted it to the web!"

Aunt J had stood up and was bent at the waist waving her hands, "no more, I can't take anymore." We all finally settled down, sipping our coffee. Aunt J smiled, "Lou would have loved to have seen that."

Jocko nodded, "he'd still be laughing."

"Who's Lou?" Mal asked.

Aunt J patted Mal's arm, "that was Uncle J's real name." Mal and I looked at each other.

"I always thought his name was Joe or Jim, something that started with the J," I said.

Aunt J chuckled, "you kids just called him Uncle J, you figured if I was Aunt J that made him Uncle J. He always got a kick out of all the kids calling him Uncle J."

"Yes, he did." Jocko whispered, looking down. Aunt J refilled everyone's coffee from the carafe on the sidebar then sat back down.

She took a sip of her coffee, looking at Jocko. "As much as we enjoyed your story, you're not widely known for social visits, though you're welcome here anytime." She patted his arm, "what can we do for you?" Jocko looked around the table at the four of us.

"I appreciate the invitation, this is both social and business. I wanted to thank Nicholas in person for what he did for me. I didn't know who he was, so I had him checked out." He said looking at me. "I knew your folks, they were good people, sorry for your loss, truly I am."

I nodded my head, "Thanks."

"As I was saying, I had you checked out. I know pretty much all there is to know about you." I didn't know how I felt about that, but what was done was done. "I know what you're thinking Nicholas, but in my line of work I have to know who I'm dealing with, not doing so could be bad for my health. You're an interesting young man. The universe took a hammer to your life. You got your body put back together, got multiple engineering degrees etc. etc. etc. The one thing that stuck out is out of all your accomplishments, you are the same 'Nac' that left here 10 years ago.

Most people after helping me would have asked for some boon or would have been bragging about it from here to Titan. You didn't even tell your closest friends. Neither did Jazz who witnessed your actions. You've asked for no favors. Made no brags. In my experience that is uncommon, even unheard of.

So, thank you, I hope you will count me as one of your friends, and judging from who I see here and others I know of, that's an elite group of people." I rose from my seat; he did as well. I offered him my hand, and he took it.

"I would like that sir, truly."

"Call me Jocko."

"Call me Nic."

"And the business?" Aunt J said from across the table.

Jocko shook his head, looking disgusted. "The Doctors at the med center can't do any more for me. I'd have to go to Titan to have my CCU looked at. I hate to make that trip. I was hoping Nic could look at it and see if he could do anything."

I nodded, "sure, grab your coffee, let's go down to the shop. This will probably be Mal's area of expertise."

"You guys go, I need to get dinner started, will you stay Jocko?"

"Can't tonight Julie, I have a prior engagement, maybe another time?"

"Sure, drop by anytime." We went downstairs to the EL shop. Mal led us over to a workstation.

"Have a seat Mr. Jocko, and I'll get you hooked up."

"Just Jocko, Malcolm."

"Ok Jocko, just Mal."

We got Jocko hooked up and ran diagnostics. We all watched the screens, Mal narrowed his eyes. "That's not supposed to do that, and that's wrong, and why did they do that?"

Jocko looked at me smiling, "he always talked himself?"

"We both do occasionally, it's how we process problems," I chuckled.

"Whatever works. I knew a guy once, who sang the whole time he was working on things." Mal was typing away, fixing and patching lines of code.

I suddenly remembered something, "you know my Dad used to sing while..." I looked at Jocko he was smiling at me, nodding his head.

"Yep, your Dad. A heck of an engineer worked on my tug several times. He could make those engines sing. That was back before me and my tug got caught between two rocks. Not the career change I was looking for, but life happens."

"Yes, it does," I answered.

"Jocko, I need to shut down your CCU to make the program changes," Mal said. "Just lean on the workbench for support and balance on the stool." Jocko did as he was asked. "Nac, come over here so I can plug in to your CCU, something is way off with his programming."

I moved around, and he plugged me in. Mal was studying the screen, comparing the lines of code. "That part is right, but this part is... Oh, I see what the problem is. It's an easy fix, shouldn't take long. Just need to clone some code, then copy it to the CCU."

"He's talking to himself again." Jocko said.

"That's a good thing. When he stops talking, I worry," I replied.

"Y'all know I'm sitting right here, right? Ok, that's got it." Mal unplugged me and brought Jocko's CCU back online. Diagnostics were all green. He reengaged the control program for Jocko's legs. Everything stayed green. "Ok, Jocko try that." Jocko slowly stood up, turned, bent, twisted, kneeled, his smile growing bigger by the Moment.

"Nic loan me a shoulder, just in case." I moved over to support him. He ran in place, slowly at first and faster. He was grinning from ear to ear. "Guys, I have not been able to do that in years and you fix it in less than an hour. What was the problem?"

"Where did you get your CCU?" Mal asked.

"Why?" Said Jocko, suddenly becoming serious.

"It was a bootleg copy, probably a copy of a copy. Jocko nodded his head, "well, buyer beware, I suppose. What do I owe you?"

"Nothing," Mal and I said at the same time.

"Jocko we don't charge for helping friends, especially on body parts, I'm kind of funny that way." I said.

"Well in that case, as my gramps used to say, 'thank you until you are better paid'. I better get going, my boys will wonder where I got off to." We moved toward the door.

"No, they're still waiting for you in your car." He turned and looked at me, tilting here his head a little. "Security monitoring systems" I answered the unasked question.

He nodded, "wise my young friend, wise. Nic, in the brief time you've been back you've made friends; you've also made enemies. The biggest enemy is Harper and Harper. Well, the son anyway. He's mad he got caught, and madder still you got all his toys. He had plans for those toys, and you threw a monkey wrench into those plans."

"In what way?" I ask.

"He bought that shipping company, made it look like he would do some big-time mining and shipping. He was making a show, so that the new shipyard and refinery would buy him out. He was positioning himself to double his money."

"That explains a lot." I said.

"Rumor is, he is also getting in tight with the new union leaders they're bringing in. You watch your dealings extra careful and added security is a good idea."

He left, lifting his hand in goodbye as he went through the hatch.

"Security board is green," Major said in my ear. We went back up to the galley Aunt J was fixing dinner.

CHAPTER 7

"Were you able to help Jocko?" Aunt J asked. We filled our coffee cups and went over to the counter.

"Yeah, Mal fixed his CCU completely, I think someone may be in trouble." I said, Mal nodded.

"What makes you say that?"

"It turns out someone sold him a bootleg copy of a program running his CCU." Mal answered.

Aunt J looked serious, "oh my, yes, I would say someone may be in trouble. Jocko is not someone you cheat or cross without repercussions. That's one reason the three rings run so smoothly."

"Three rings?" I ask. Aunt J was looking at something in the oven.

"Yep, A, B, C."

"A, B, C?" She closed the oven door, turned to look at me.

"Three rings, Alpha ring, Bravo ring, and Charlie ring." She came around out of the galley, filling her coffee cup. "Come sit down" we did.

"Jocko has a gangster or Mafia reputation. He even instigates it sometimes, but what he really does is watch over the three rings. He controls what happens in the three rings. Crime is low, unemployment is low, when compared to other rings. He watches the union to make sure they are on the up and up. He backs the Workers Association but pushes no agenda.

He lets the free market work; he watches the market to make sure it stays free. Just make sure when you see and interact with him in public, be very respectful. Its kabuki theater for public consumption."

Mal and I nodded, "sure, no problem."

"Good, now dinner is almost ready, and the girls should be here soon."

***

It took another two weeks to get everything inventoried and stored. Some things stayed in the containers out on the yard. Most everything fit in the hanger with room left over to work on our tugs. The girls were still wrangling rocks generating income, but we needed to get the haulers and the cargo ships working.

"Major, cross-reference parts and equipment inventory with what ship they fit." The list appeared on my screen; each page was the ship the parts on that page fit that ship.

"Compare list to ship's maintenance inspections and repair list." I studied the list, "remove parts from lists that are excess to bring that ship to full mission capable status." The list shifted, but not by much.

"Add parts to the list we need to bring the ships to FMC status, but are not in HMS stock, and highlight." The list shifted. "Cost of parts needed but not in stock." The list shifted.

"Display the list of ships that have all the parts on hand for to bring that ship to FMC status." The correlated list showed we had the parts to bring two of the three tugs and the cargo ship to FMC. "Thank you, Major."

"You are welcome, sir."

I went up to the galley, Aunt J was puttering around making cookies.

I got a cup of coffee, "got a minute Aunt J?"

"Sure Nic, what do you need?"

"Do you know another cook we can hire?"

She cut her eyes around me, "Planning on getting rid of me?"

"That depends, do you want to stay in the galley, or take on the supply and acquisitions and operations role?" She thought about it, continued to make her cookies.

"I've been thinking about that; I think we need to hire more staff."

"How many are you thinking?"

She smiled, "Operations Manager, Cook and two mess attendants. HR generalist, Security Manager, four security men, and a medic or EMT with security training."

I laughed, "is that all?"

She thought a moment, "for now, but I think we need to talk to Travis Van Dam."

"I'll bite, why Travis?"

"He may have someone he can recommend for Operations Manager, and the Van Dam yard is slow on work. We might can get some of his people to install all those parts we have sitting on shelves. You said you wanted to get those ships out working and generating income. He may also have advice on the captains and crews for those ships sitting in our yard."

"Anything else?" I asked.

"Nope, that covers it."

"Ok, I'll get right on that."

"Oh, and Nic, Travis will join us for lunch." She said smiling.

I shook my head, turned and walked away. "I should've put her in the front office," I mumbled.

"What was that Dear?"

"I said, I love you Aunt J."

"I love you too dear," she said, laughing.

Travis joined us for lunch. Jazz and Jade were there too, which I'm sure was how Aunt J had planned it.

Aunt J ushered Travis to the table, "thank you so much for joining us."

Travis took his seat, "are you kidding, and miss out on some of Miss. Julie's cooking? You know the Breakfast Plus just ain't the same without you, they have started calling it 'The Minus'."

We all dug in, enjoying the food and the company. There

was the usual good-natured bantering and the playful slaps on shoulders.

After we finished lunch Aunt J announced, "there is pie and coffee for dessert, but it will cost you." We all grabbed our dishes and racked them in the washer. Travis, being no slouch, picked up on the action and followed suit. Coffee cups filled, and pie dished, we settled in.

Travis cleared his throat, "Now that I have been sufficiently plied, what's it really going to cost me?" He said, laughing.

"We need advice," I started. Travis watched me, sipping his coffee. "We have grown so fast that there aren't enough of us to get the things done that we want done, or there aren't enough hours in the day."

Travis nodded. "I know what you mean. That is the nature of the beast, feast or famine. Either too much business or not enough. How can I help?"

"We'd like to hire an Operations Manager, and we thought you may have suggestions. We also need engineers to install parts and make minor repairs, so we can put our ships to work. We also need a HR person who understands the shipping business."

"Anything else?" Travis asked, smiling.

"We also have the crew manifest for all the ships sitting in our yard, we want to see if you could give us any insight into the crews, and captains."

"Ok, the easy stuff first. I have a couple of names in mind. The guy at the top of the list works for us as an Assistant Operations Manager. I'll lose him eventually, anyway. There is nowhere in the yards to move him up.

I'd rather lose him to you than someone else. If you're interested, I'll talk to him, and if he's interested, we'll set up an appointment. His name is Robert "Bob" Johnson. I'd love to keep him, but like I said..." He shrugged his shoulders.

I have the same issue in HR. Pam Whitman, Assistant HR Manager. She has trouble fitting in. Before you ask, prosthetic legs. Birth defect, teen years were a little rough.

Engineers to install parts and minor repairs. We are kind of slow at the moment. I would have to cut back hours to keep them all. I can have 20 engineers over here in the morning, there will be lead men in the group."

I slid the parts list over to him, "got any of these parts in stock?"

He looked the list over, "probably most of them."

"Prices look okay?"

"Yeah, I can do these prices, give or take."

"Wow, that solved, or partially solved most of our problems."

"Let me see your crew list," he said. I slid our hauler crew list over to him. He read down the list, "no, no, no, oh my God, no." He scanned the rest of the list. "No one at all on that list. I wouldn't hire them to sweep my shop floors."

I slid him the other hauler list. He scanned down the list, "half of these guys are passable, barely." I slid over the cargo ship list. He looked at the list, "Captain Reginald Smyth, formally of the Earth Space Foreign Legion Navy." He slid the list back, "if they are on Reggie's ship, they are top-notch, he accepts nothing less.

If he hasn't been scarfed up already, get him if you can. Him and his crew. As far as the other ships' crews, how about I send you over the names of a couple of captains I know who are looking to get off the beach. Good men just caught in fleets mergers."

"We appreciate this, Travis." Aunt J said.

"No problem, it's a win for both of us. So how about a tour of your hanger before I have to go." We toured the hanger, winding back up at the *Taurus*. "Making progress on her I see." Travis said patting the side of the ship.

"Yes, she's a work in progress but we're making progress. Come on inside and look around." We headed inside he looked here and there. We made it up to the galley.

"Lots of work left here, but I see you tore out the bulkhead cabinets." He looked closer, "no cut or burn marks, how'd you get them down?"

"We use our grav-bar." I said.

"A what?" He asked

"Grav-bar."

"Never heard of it."

"it's like a crowbar or a prybar but uses force emitters."

"I've never seen one"

I reached over and picked up the grav-bar, walked over to the bulkhead and stuck the end of the bar behind the cabinets I push the activation ring, and slowly raised the power level. The cabinet popped and dropped off the bulkhead.

"Where did you get that?" He asked wide-eyed.

"Mal and I made it."

He looked back and forth between us, "you made it?"

We nodded, "want to try it?"

"Do fat kids love cake, yeah!" I showed him how to use it and he positioned it behind the cabinets, raised the power level and the rest of the cabinets dropped to the deck.

"This thing is amazing." Turning toward me, I grabbed it and pointed it up.

"Make sure it's turned off. It does funny things when you pointed at people," I said.

"I didn't think it was so funny," Mal mumbled, rubbing his chest.

"Let me make sure I understand you correctly, you guys invented this, this grav-bar."

We both nodded, "yeah."

"Have you applied for a patent yet?"

"Yeah, last week."

"Don't show this to anyone else until you get your patent registered and confirm it." We both nodded.

"That thing is awesome." He said.

"If you think that is awesome you will love this." Mal said patting the test box beside him.

"What does it do?"

"It's the grav-bars big brother. We were waiting until we

got the cabinets off the bulkhead to test it. Want to give it a test?"

"Sure." We open the box, so all the force emitters were in the open, and plugged in the power cord.

"First you power up the mag locks to lock it in place." Mal was giving a play-by-play. "You enter all your ship's specs, so you know where the frame superstructures are. You turn on the scanner's, so the computer gets a reading on where it is sitting in relation to the superstructures and the damage, in this case a bend in the ship's hull." Mal said

"Once that is done, you tell the machine what you want it to do. In our case, push the bend back to the location listed in the ship's specs and our own entered information. Once all that is programmed into the machine, you tell it to execute the program." We look to Travis, Travis was looking at the box, then the bulkhead, then us, then the box.

"What's to keep it from just being crushed into, or through the deck, when power applies to push the bulkhead?" "Reverse force emitters pushing against the superstructure, but the 'secret sauce' keeps that from happening."

"Secret sauce?"

"What really happens is a program starts slowly pushing out, in concentric circles rather than trying to push the whole section out at the same time."

"Ok, I follow you, make sense."

Mal looked at me, "ready to test it?"

"If your program is loaded, I'm ready."

I looked at Travis, "want to watch?"

He nodded, "fat kids and cake."

We all stepped back, Mal took out his P-comm and linked it to the box controls. He looked at me and I nodded. Mal sent the execute command, and we watched as the bulkhead and hull was pushed out. The only sound was a low hum of a vibration, and two welds popping loose. Five minutes later the bulkhead and the hull were back within specs.

The machine beeped, "program complete." We all walked

over to the bulkhead, and examining it, it was warm to the touch.

"Let's check the outside and all the superstructures." Travis said. For the next hour we crawled all over the *Taurus*, ending up back in the galley. "What do you call this one? Grav-box?"

"No, we call this one a Grav-Ox."

"Applied for a patent?"

"Yep, same time as the grav-bar."

"Don't show this to anyone else until they confirm your patent. You may not realize it, but these will make you rich." Travis was staring at the Grav-Ox. I looked at Mal getting his attention, I looked up at the speaker in the overhead then pointed my chin at Travis raising my eyebrows. Mal looked at Travis, considering for a moment, then he looked back at me and nodded yes. I nodded okay.

"Things been slow at your yard, have they?" I asked Travis.

"Yeah, everyone who can wait is waiting for the new ship-yard to come on-line. That way they can start a bidding war between the Van Dam yards and the new guys. It was bound to happen, a good strategy on the shipowners' part."

"What if you could offer them something, they couldn't get anywhere else?" Mal ask.

"That's the holy grail of business, isn't it? What did you have in mind?"

Mal looked at me, "Captain, it's your ship."

I nodded, "Misty?"

"Yes, Captain?"

"Were you monitoring the last test and repair to the bulk-head and hull?"

"I was Captain."

"Status report on those repairs and any damage caused while making those repairs."

"Galley bulkhead in alignment or within 97% of factory specs. It broke three welds along the joining face of bulkhead hull. No other damage noted during that repair operation, Captain."

"Status of the ship?"

"All systems are off-line pending final inspection and repair, tankage unchanged, operating on shore power and connections. Main galley off-line." Mal snickered. "Present ACE integration 92%. All other systems on safety standby, Captain."

Travis was looking at us, "who or what was that?"

"That is what no one else can offer. That is our holy grail. That was Mal's invention"

"Ours" Mal said.

"Patented?" Travis asked.

"Intellectual property." Mal said.

"AI?"

"No, I call it an Automated Control Engine program, or ACE program. People get a little antsy when you say AI. It's a situational learning program."

"Can it control the whole ship?"

"It can control as much or as little as you wanted it to, within reason."

"It can't cook," I interjected. Mal and I looked up. Then both laughed. "Sorry, inside joke."

"So, it's not an AI?" Travis asked again.

"No, it's not an AI. It's a situational learning program, it can't think for itself, it has no independent thoughts." Mal said.

"How many ships have you installed this on?"

"Just this one, we also have a version running in the hanger and hab."

"If this program can do what you claim, the earning potential is unlimited. We need a full test, you need to get the ship fully operational, so we can get a full capabilities test. If it tests to the level we hope, what split of profits do you want?" Travis asked.

"What do you think would be fair?" I asked.

Travis thought a moment, "you lease us the rights to install the program. You train my guys to install, test and troubleshoot the problems of installation. All the work to be done at the Van Dam yards for a 75%–25% split. 75% going to you."

Mal shook his head, "no, 65%–35% we'll take the 65%. This agreement only covers ACE programs to be installed on ships nowhere else. Hab models are a different item with no connection."

"Agreed. The Van Dam marketing and research will come up with the sales prices."

"NDA?" I ask.

"Until all is decided no one outside our group needs to know all the details and capabilities."

"Agreed."

"Misty?"

"Yes, Captain?"

"Did you witness and log the NDA just agreed upon?"

"Witnessed and logged, Captain."

Travis looked up at the speaker, "the universe just changed."

***

It had been a long day and late night. As soon as Travis left, I called a board meeting and included Jade. The first item on the agenda was everyone's signing NDA's, that covered the legal stuff. Mal and I spent the next two hours explaining every-thing we had shown Travis and the tentative agreement we had reached, pending board approval. Everyone wanted to see the prototype. Aunt J said we needed to call Aaron Stein and JJ and get them in to cover the legal side of things.

The next morning Aaron, and JJ joined us, and we started the briefing including showing them the prototypes and the ACE programs we told him about the proposed deal with the Van Dam shipyards and what we wanted but asking if that was all we needed. Aaron and JJ asked a lot of questions and so did we. They left at 10 o'clock, saying they would get back with us soonest. The family, that was how we had started referring to ourselves, continued talking and planning until after midnight.

We were all gathered around the breakfast table, with a large dose of coffee and light conversation. Right at 0800, Major's avatar appeared on the galley's wall screen.

"Sir, Mr. Van Dam and company are at the hatch requesting entry."

"Allow them entry, we'll meet them in the hanger."

"Yes, sir."

We all went down to meet Travis in the hanger. The workmen stayed by the hatch, while Travis and another man approached us.

"Security board is green." Major said in my ear.

"Good morning, Travis." I said, shaking his hand.

"You're here earlier than I expected."

"Yeah, after our talk yesterday, I thought we'd get the show on the road.

Let me introduce Bob Johnson." We all shook Bob's hand. "He'll be overseeing the crews working with you."

"With your permission sir, if you'll give me your inspections, reports, and parts list I'll get the men started."

"Sounds good." I took out my P-comm and flipped him the paperwork he needed.

He quickly looked over the list, "thank you sir, we'll get right to it. Ladies, gentlemen, a pleasure meeting you." With that, he turned to get the teams started.

"Did you talk to him about possibly coming to work for us?" I asked Travis.

"I did, he's interested. We thought this would be a good opportunity for you to see him working and managing, and he'd see what your place and people were like."

"I like it." I nodded.

"Did you discuss the proposal with your board?" He asked.

"Yes, we were up late, no offense meant, but those Documents also included our lawyers."

"None taken, I did the same thing. I hope I did not overstep, but I set up appointments for you."

"Oh?" I raise my eyebrows.

"Pam from HR will be here at 0900 for an interview, Captain Smythe will be here at 1000, and 2 hauler captains will be here at 1100 and 1200."

I laughed, "anything else?" Which is becoming a popular question around here. He reached into his pocket and took out a "coin" drive.

"A mutual friend asked me to deliver this, and to expect someone at 1500." I took the coin-drive and handed it to Mal.

Aunt J leaned in and look at Travis, "Jocko?"

Travis nodded, "We, how should I say this, don't always walk the same path, but we are usually headed in the same direction."

"How Zen of you." Aunt J said, smiling.

Mal held his P-comm out, "it's an encryption key code, no message."

Travis nodded, "you can never be too careful, business is war."

"So, I've heard," I said.

"I'd better get back to the yard." Waving, he took his leave.

"Looks like we will have a busy day. If you ladies will interview Pam Whitman, Mal and I will drift around the hanger looking in on the crews and Bob. We'll all gather back at 1000 to meet the captains. Does that suit everyone?" Everyone nodded.

"Oh, and we have a new cook and mess attendants who will audition during the lunch meal," Aunt J said.

"Good, anyone else? Ok, let's get to it."

Everything was going well in the hanger and the yard. Bob said he would have a repair schedule for us by the end of the shift. Aunt J was in the galley with the new cook, going through cold storage and ordering more food. Feeding an additional 25 people had not been in the plan, but Aunt J said it would be a great test.

CHAPTER 8

At 0900, Miss Whitman arrived, and the ladies took her into the company conference room. Captain Smythe arrived at 1000, the ladies were still in their interview so Mal and I showed him into my office. We had him sign the NDA.

He noticed me looking at his cyber hand, he held it up "space is a dangerous place."

I held up mine, "indeed it is."

"Glad to be left out of the club." Mal said, holding up his hand. We all chuckled.

I looked at him for a moment; he appeared to be in his 50s, fit, with intelligent eyes.

"Let's walk while we talk, shall we?" We all rose, "let's get coffee first." We headed up to the galley. It was a beehive of activity; more tables and chairs were being set out. Orders were being called back and forth, but it was all well managed.

We grabbed our coffees and toured the hanger, watching work in progress. We talked of his career in the ESFL Navy, and his cargo ship experience. He asked of ours and the direction we headed with HMS. We wound back up at the coffee urns for a refill and headed back down to my office.

We took our seats, "are you familiar with the term, 'Ride for the brand'?"

He thought for a moment, "I can't say I am." I nodded.

"It was a term coined in the American West. The ranchers branded their horses and cattle to identify who the animals belong to. The cowboys who worked the ranch and were loyal to the rancher were said to 'ride for the brand'. In exchange for their loyalty the ranchers were in return loyal to them." He was nodding. "I guess what I'm saying is, we're looking for a Captain that will be loyal to HMS, and we in return we'll be loyal to him.

You've been highly recommended by someone we trust; we will need to trust you and lean heavily on your experience and advice. We don't know the cargo business; we are miners and ore haulers; you have probably forgotten more than we know about cargo shipping.

We'd like you to come to work for us and Captain our cargo ship. We understand if you'd rather go with a more established company." He nodded, looking down into his coffee cup.

"I don't haul contraband, I don't smuggle."

"Not on our ships you don't, not if you want to keep your job."

"My crew?"

"We're told that if you have them as crew members, they are top-notch. We'll let you run your ship, hire and fire at your discretion."

"How long before your ship will be ready to sail?"

"Maintenance should be done by weeks end." He nodded again, looking at Mal then back at me.

"In that case Mr. Haydock, I believe I can 'ride for your brand'. Salary?" He asked.

"What do you think would be fair?" I asked.

"Standard contract rate for that size cargo ship, plus 10% of profits, crew shares based on positions and ratings." He said.

"Standard contract plus 12% for you, you'll most likely be picking most of your cargo. You decide what rate to pay the crew."

"Any special orders?"

"Don't lose money and don't scratch the paint." I said, smiling.

"I'll do my best... Not to lose money, anyway." He chuckled. Reaching across my desk we shook hands.

"Welcome to HMS, Captain."

Captain Smythe departed to gather his crew, he said he would contact us tomorrow to check the status of the ship. The next captain's interview went to smooth as the first and we had our second Captain. The third Captain canceled, saying we were too young of a company, too young to be owners for him to work for. On a whim, I sent Captain Smythe a message, asking if he knew another Captain who was looking for a home.

He sent back, his first officer who had his Captain's ticket was interested in the position, he wholeheartedly endorsed him. I showed Mal the message.

"Do it." He said. I messaged Captain Smythe back and told him to tell the new Captain to gather his crew, and for both to let me know when they were ready to go to work.

Since we had no 1200 interview, we were through until our mysterious appointment at 1500. Jazz stuck her head in the office and asked us to come to the conference room. We followed Jazz.

"Pam, this is Nic and Mal."

We shook hands, "pleased to meet you."

"We offered her the HR manager job. We were explaining to her, as part of the in-processing Mal, to run diagnostics on her CCU. For safety, because of all the RF in the hanger area." Jazz was looking pointedly at Mal and I.

"Great, we can get that out of the way, we don't want any accidents." We started for the door.

Aunt J said, "I need to check the galley, lunch is at 1200, and we have 25 guests."

We went down to the EL shop, Jazz and Jade came with us with Pam in tow. Pam seemed a little apprehensive.

"Nic was having problems with his cyber limbs, and Mal fixed him right up." I look back smiling and nodded my head. Jazz and Jade set up a work screen and acted as chaperones. Mal passed the diagnostic cable to Jade to plug into Pam's CCU. That done, he ran his diagnostics. The girls talk about girl stuff while Mal was working. Mal stopped, look closely at the lines of code, and shook his head.

"Pam, how long have you had your cyber legs?"

"This set? About five years." This set? Mal and I both

mouthed.

"Pam, can I open the access panel on the calf of your right leg?" Mal ask.

"Sure." The girls moved screen a bit, and Mal knelt and open the panel to another test port. He made the connections and look back at the screen. He glanced around to make sure the girls wouldn't see him and mouthed the word "junk". I nodded.

"Pam, did they discuss the compensations package with you?"

"Yes sir, they did." Came from the other side of the screen. Jazz raised up and looked at me, lifting an eyebrow. We unplugged the cables and let Pam get her clothes rearranged. Once done the ladies moved screen out of the way.

I sat looking at her, "Pam, we'd like you to come to work for us." Jazz and Jade were both nodding behind her.

"I will add a caveat to the job offer. When I moved back here and into our habs, I had to have upgrades done to my CCU. You may have heard about a recent incident at a café on the Promenade when a man's CCU malfunctioned."

"I read about that." Pam said. I was trying hard not to smile.

"So, the thing is, we will include in our offer to you, that we pay for the upgrade of your cyber limbs or replacement whichever is the most cost-effective." Jazz and Jade were grinning from ear to ear.

"HMS will pay for my legs?"

"We're looking at it as an investment, and part of your medical package, we are kind of sticklers for safety around here." Pam looked around at Jazz and Jade.

"Really?"

"Safety first." Jade said, both girls nodding. Pam looked back around at me, considering the offer.

"Ok, if it's part of the medical package, and for safety, I accept." She said smiling. She suddenly lost her smile and looked at me.

"There may be a problem, the last time I had work done and checked on replacement legs, it was a 3 to 6 months wait."

She looked crestfallen.

"Let me make a few calls, I may know someone who can help. Let's head up to lunch and see how the new cook is doing. I'll meet you up there."

They headed for the galley and I stopped in my office, using my new encryption key I sent Jocko a message. Told him what I wanted and why. We want the best model they had available to fit her without surgery. Money was not an issue. That sent, I joined everyone in the galley.

The main table was set. Food covered the table, "family-style" as Dad used to say. I walked the serving line, looking at the offerings. Seeing it was the same food as was on the main table, I nodded to the chef and returned to take my place at the head of the table. Everyone was looking at me and waiting, "let's not let it get cold, dig in." Everyone laughed.

The food was amazing, nobody was talking, everyone was eating. The only sound was the "mmmms" from around the table. The galley seemed kind of quiet I looked across the galley all the workers were eating not talking, just shoveling food and in and nodding their heads.

Dessert and coffee served to the main table. The same was being plated on the main line. The only difference I could see was the main table had an attendant refilling drinks and removing empties. I noticed not a few workers glance at the main table to see what we were being served and nodded when they saw we were all eating the same foods.

As the meal wound down, I stood and tapped my water glass with my knife, getting the galley's attention. The chef was looking over the galley, making sure all was well.

I raise my voice, "my compliments to the chef and his staff!" The galley broke out into applause and "here-here" were heard from all over. The chef waved his staff out, and they all were bowing and mouthing thank you. When all was quiet again. I shouted, "engineers!"

The whole Van Dam crew shouted back, "engineers!"

"And now, you lot get back to work," I said, laughing. "And

rack your dishes, your mother doesn't work here!"

I sat down, housekeeping rule set in place. I noticed everyone at our table was staring at me.

"What?"

Aunt J raised her glass, "to HMS!"

We all followed suit, "to HMS!"

Aunt J was smiling looking at me, "you sure know how to make an impression."

I shrug my shoulders, "Mal told me what to do."

Jade grabbed Mal and said, "that's my man!" Then slapped her hand over her mouth, turning red and looking around at Jazz. We all laughed so hard we cried.

"Incoming message." Major said in my ear. I took out my P-comm and read the message and smiled.

"Pam, you have an appointment at the Med Center's Cybernetic Department at 1000 tomorrow. If you like, Jazz and Jade may accompany you to make sure all paperwork is taken care of. I don't think there will be a problem, they are expecting you." Pam looked askance at Jazz and Jade, nodding her head smiling. They nodded back. "All right, that's taken care of."

Aunt J left the table and went in the back of the galley. Later she returned with the chef.

"Everyone, may I present Chef Jean-Claude." We all clapped out of appreciation for a wonderful meal. Aunt J looked at me and nodded.

"Chef would you consider coming to work for HMS?" He bowed his head then looked up at me.

"Sir, that depends, Ms. Julie said you were only looking for a chef's crew of three, we are six. We would accept the position but only as the complete crew of six." Everyone's head swung back to look at me.

"I'm afraid, sir," I paused, "that I must accept your offer. Otherwise I may have a mutiny on my hands," everyone was laughing. "Today's lunch of over 30 guests and crew has shown me I may have underestimated the need in our galley. We would love to have you and your crew join HMS." Everyone applauded.

The next appointment arrived at 1445 I met him at the hatch. Major showed him as green, no weapons. From his build, and the way he moved, I didn't think he'd need one. We went to the conference room; the usual suspects were there.

He introduced himself, "Jim Jones and no Kool-Aid jokes please, I've heard them all." We all chuckled.

"Well, Mr. Jones we might be interested in some security or at least a security assessment." I said.

"Mr. Jocko said you might."

"How do you know Mr. Jocko?" Aunt J asked.

"We augment his security detail from time to time," He answered.

"We don't need a full-time security detail; we'd like a security assessment with recommendations. A threat assessment with recommendations. An on-call security detail if we are going somewhere and feel we need one. An emergency comm number in case the sock hits the fan."

He was nodding and taking notes, "timeframe?" I looked around the table.

"Did Mr. Jocko say why he thought we needed security?" Aunt J asked. He thought a moment.

"Not specifically, no ma'am, some businesses make enemies. Sometimes business gets rough, some more than others. I won't know which category you fall into until we do a threat assessment."

"What's your security background, Mr. Jones?" Jazz asked.

"My team are all former ESFL Marines, counterintelligence, security, cyber counter-cyber, and interdiction."

"How large is your team?"

"That would depend on the needs of the client and the threat level."

"Timeframe starts now, we'll want your call numbers before you leave, assessments as soon as possible." Mr. Jones took out his P comm and flipped us a contract, we read over it and signed it, and flipped it back to him.

"We'll get started on the threat assessment today, two

members of our team will be here in the morning to start the risk and security assessment. You may call those numbers 24/7 someone will always answer. Here is a list of codewords specific to HMS. If there is nothing else, we'll see you in the morning." We saw him to the hatch.

Bob Johnson was waiting for us when the meeting with Jim Jones was over.

"I've got the work scheduled for you to review," He said. I took the list and looked over it. The closest ship to being ready for space was one hauler and it would be ready in three days. Cargo hauler ready in six days. The other hauler in 10 days. As they finished each one of these, we would shift the work crews to the tugs.

"Do you have any problems with the crews moving into the ships as your work proceeds?" I ask.

"Not at all, might even make the work go faster if the crews help with the grunt work."

I nodded, "when can the crews move in?"

"Anytime, they are on shore power, aired up and heated."

"Good, I'll let you know when the crews are ready to occupy."

The family was enjoying our after-dinner coffee. Dinner had been great. Chef had cooked and set everything on the serving line. He and his crew had cleaned up, so we sent them home for the day. We did our usual cleanup after dinner, racking our own dishes. Chef and one of the attendants were married and didn't need a place to stay. The assistant chef and the other three attendants would move tomorrow.

"Today was a good day," I said. "I think we got some good people."

"I think so too," Aunt J said. "Chef and his team are top shelf."

I nodded, "the food was outstanding, but what cinched it for me was that he was feeding everyone the same food, no special food for the master's table."

"I agree," she said, "and don't think the crew didn't notice."

Jazz reached over and put her hand on my arm.

"You did a good thing for Pam; she is very insecure about her legs. She had had trouble throughout school with them. She and her family could never afford good ones. She always had to make do with the cheap ones, they were usually knockoff cheap ones."

"I was wondering what was taking you guys so long in the interview," I said.

"We took our time with her talking, it really seemed to help her when we told her you had cyber limbs and had had trouble as well. Thank you, and you too Mal, for going along with her diagnostics for safety."

Mal raised his cup, "safety first." Jade leaned over and kissed Mal on the cheek.

Jazz leaned over and kissed me on the cheek, whispering in my ear. "Tell them they need to move up to the family level." I nodded, sipping my coffee.

After a few Moments, "I've been thinking." They looked at me, "with more crew being hired on and moving in the HMS hab, I think Y'all need to move up to the family level. You're not the crew, your family." Jazz was nodding her head looking at them. Jade was looking at Mal.

"We accept your kind offer, and to cut down on over-crowding we should share rooms." He said, looking at Jade raising his hand toward her. Jade looked down at the floor, shaking her head.

"I'm sorry Mal, but Aunt J has already asked me to share a room with her." Mal just sat there looking crestfallen, blinking his eyes in confusion.

"Gotcha! Mr. I was in prison." Jade jumped onto his lap, hugging his neck. We all laughed.

"Yep, he is definitely better with computers than with girls." Aunt J said, shaking her head.

"What rooms can we have?" Jade asked.

"Any of them but mine." I answered.

CHAPTER 9

The next morning chef had the galley opened at 0600 with coffee, pastries, and omelets to order. At 0800 Major announced Bob Johnson and a crew of 50 had arrived. I told chef word got around about his cooking and to expect 60 for lunch. I met Bob at the hatch.

"Brought friends I see."

"Well, two things happen. Word got around about your new chef, the whole yard wanted to come. Second, Mr. Van Dam wanted to push up the timelines, so you could finish the *Taurus* project. He also sent over all the parts you ordered."

"I've already told chef you brought friends." I smiled.

"Let's get them to work then." Bob said.

At 0900, Jazz and Jade left to get Pam for her appointment at the Med Center. As they were leaving Jim Jones' men arrived. Major had them listed as Amber and had red pips on both, marking shoulder holsters. I called Mal to meet us to talk about security. Mal joined us.

"Who handles your cyber security?" One of them asked. I nodded toward Mal.

"Your system is good." Their cyber guy said. Mal chuckled, "Oh I'd say it was better than good, you guys have been trying to hack in as soon as we sign the contract with your boss. He left a bug with an encryption cracker in our conference room. It didn't survive.

We knew the moment you started, I wanted to see how good you were, so far you haven't even scratched the surface of our system. I had your server painted 10 seconds after you started. I could've smoked your servers, but I know you are just doing what we asked you."

The guy laughed at Mal, "ok, your system is good, but no way do you have us painted and even if you did, you could never smoke it." Mal took out his P comm and tagged his app. Five seconds later cyber guy got a comm call, then his P-comm smoked. The other guy got a comm call.

He answered it, "yeah?" He listened, "the entire system?" He listened more; he gave his P-comm to the other guy.

"Yeah?" He listened, "yeah, it got smoked." He listened, "Roger, out." He handed his partner his P-comm back.

"Mr. Jones asked, and I quote, have your system take its boot off our systems throat and don't smoke it, it's very expensive, end quote. Apparently, I let my crocodile mouth overload my Hummingbird butt."

His partner looked at him, and in an imitation Chinese voice said, "hmm, his Kung Fu is stronger than yours." We all laughed.

"Yeah, yeah, I'll take the hit, but I want a rematch."

Mal looked at his P-comm and said, "boot off, no smoke." I smiled and asked Mal if he would take them around on a security survey. Bob was waiting to talk.

"How do you want to handle the *Taurus*, Mr. Haydock?" I walked him back over to the *Taurus*, thinking.

"Patch the holes in the decking and overhead, replace the galley. We'll run a full system check after that and see what more they may need, which shouldn't be much. Whatever happened to the Van Dam's corporate ship, the one he almost melted the tail off?" I asked.

"As far as I know it still sitting over in the yard's corner where it's been since the day, he melted her." Bob said.

"Interesting. Ok, if you have any more questions about the *Taurus*, call me or Mal." He nodded and gave orders.

The girls weren't back by lunch. The security guys stayed to eat and after lunch said they must have missed areas and would be back tomorrow in time for lunch. We all laughed. The girls finally got back in 1700.

"Everything go okay?" I asked.

"Everything went fine, no problems at all. We had to go shopping. The new legs made her clothes fit wrong and her shoes did not fit. Since it was our replacement legs that caused the problems, HMS paid for those replacements." Pam was looking at me, almost biting her nails.

"Seems only fair." I said. Pam let go a breath she had been holding.

"They wanted Mal to run another diagnostic and sync everything to be sure." Pam said.

"That's exactly what we'll do, safety first." I said.

"Jade, if you will take Pam down to see Mal, I think he's in his EL shop." They headed down the hall, Pam walked like a new person. I turned to Jazz, "how did it go to the Med Center?"

She chuckled, "I don't know what Jocko told them, but they fell all over themselves serving Pam. They showed her three different models of legs. She would go for the cheaper set, but I reminded her that her package was paid for it. We told them we'd take the best they had; it was funny to watch them jumping through hoops."

We went up to the galley for coffee. Pam, Jade and Mal joined us a little while later.

"Everything check out?" I asked.

"Yep, just tweaked the CCU." He nodded. Pam raised the hem of her dress, showing her new legs, and her new shoes.

"Aren't they wonderful?" She had opted for the skin tone models.

"They are, indeed, Pam, they are indeed." It amazed me, the change that had come over her in such a brief period.

"I can't wait to show Mom. They said it would take a while before they fully integrated." I nodded.

"I have exercises that helped me, I bet they'd help you too."

"I've got to run," she laughed. "Mom will flip, see you tomorrow." She waved as she left.

"Do I want to see the bill for the clothes and shoes?" I asked.

"No," Jazz answered, smiling.

"I didn't think so," I said. "But seeing the new Pam, I'd say it was worth every cred."

"K-cred," Jazz and Jade said laughing. Mal and I shook our heads and were wise enough not to say a word.

We finally seem to get into a normal workday 0600 early breakfast, 0800 work crews arrived. This morning Aaron Stein showed up with the paperwork for us to sign. It was all straight-forward, no surprises; it protects everyone's interest. He assured us that the Van Dam shipyards was getting the same. Aaron left, and Pam stuck her head in the conference room.

"Do you have a minute?" She asked.

"Sure, come on in," I said.

She came in followed by an older couple, "my parents wanted to meet you. This is my Mom, Rebecca Whitman, and my father, Earl Whitman." We all rose to greet them.

"Please come in and have a seat." Aunt J messaged chef for coffee for the conference room.

"We want to thank you for all you've done for Pam, it's like she's a new person." Mrs. Whitman said.

"I think it's the new shoes." I said everyone looked, Pam was wearing her new pair of red high heels.

Grinning, she clicked her heels together, "there's no place like home." We all laughed. Her father pointed at her, "you see? Who is she, what have you done with our daughter?" He said, laughing.

Aunt J picked up the conversation, "where do you work, if I'm not being too nosy?"

"Earl is a retired engineer and with the slowdown I'm only working part-time with an accounting firm." Mrs. Whitman said.

"I'm too old to be climbing all of those ships anymore." Earl said.

"Accounting?" Aunt J asked.

"Yes, I handle several of the mid-size Mining and Shipping accounts." Rebecca said.

"She's great." Pam said. "She is amazing with numbers; I

don't know how she keeps track of all those accounts and creds."

"The same way you do with all those HR rules, and names." Rebecca said.

"Want a job?" Aunt J asked.

"I don't know," she said looking at Pam. "What'd you have in mind?"

"Come on into my office, lets girl talk." All the girls got up and left the room. We three men watched them leave. Earl turned back around, took a swallow of coffee, looking at Mal and I over his cup.

"You ever feel you are just along for the ride?"

Mal and I nodded "all the time," I said sipping my coffee, "engineer, huh?"

"How long have you been retired?" Mal asked.

"14 months."

"Bored yet?"

"God yes, I'm breaking things, so I have something to fix." He smiled. I had an idea where Mal was going with this, so I let him run with it.

"We are about to build a newly patented tool, and we need an engineer to oversee production." Mal said.

"What kind of tool?"

"Let's go down to the shop and we'll show you, I think you'll like it." He loved the Grav-bar and was speechless over the Grav-Ox.

"May I?" He asked. Mal nodded. He opened the Grav-Ox, grabbed the test probe and light, and talked to himself. We both smiled. We have found a kindred spirit. His probing and mumbling went on for 30 minutes. Finally, set back and looked at us.

"Amazing. Genius application. Tamper-proof?" He asked.

"Yep, if anyone tries to open the control module it will slag itself leaving nothing behind but carbon in silicon." Mal said. He nodded, pursing his lips.

"Interested in a job?"

"As Travis Van Dam would say, 'fat kids and cake'."

"You know, Travis?" I ask.

"Used to work for him, I helped refit what they called their 'Corporate yacht', the one he slagged getting you back here to medical. Never regretted it though and never bragged about it either. Didn't have to, really. They had the tugs place her over in the yard's corner where she could be seen from the observation deck. Everyone came to see the ship that Van Dam had slagged during a rescue.

I'll tell you though, if it were any other ships and probably any other pilot that came for you, you would not have made."

"Why is that?" Mal ask.

"There was not another ship this side of Mars that could hold a candle to her for speed and for handling. She was originally an ESFL gun and pursuit ship. They stripped the guns out of her and sold her, said she wasn't cost effective to operate. The girl was over-engineered, frame, shields, engines, thrusters, gravitonics, she was a beast, but beautiful."

"Interesting." I said.

The Whitman's joined us for lunch. Chef continued his winning streak. By the end of lunch, we had hired an accountant and an engineer. We gave them two living quarters, that and chef won them over. They would start work tomorrow and move in by the weekend.

Work was proceeding on schedule, even a little ahead of schedule. They sealed *Taurus'* hole and the decking, and the overhead repaired. They were starting on the galley; they should finish it in a few days.

"Captains Smythe and Williams are here to see you, sir." Major said in my ear.

"Let them in, I'll meet them at the hatch."

Captain Smythe introduced his former first officer, now Captain Williams.

"Good to meet you, sir." He said as we shook hands.

"You as well Captain, do you gentlemen have your crews ready?"

Both men nodded, "we do, sir."

"Good, let me get Bob over here and you can coordinate

moving aboard."

"Before you do that sir, we have information for you." Captain Smythe said.

"Ok, shoot."

"The other hauler captain will turn down the job."

"You know why?"

"He will cite health reasons, or family health reasons."

"They have threatened him, I'm guessing," I Said. They both nodded.

"Were you threatened?"

They both smiled, "Not so much. Most of our crews are former ESFL Navy, and Marines. We don't react well to threats."

I nodded, "neither do I. Know any other captains looking for a berth?"

"No one close, we can send messages."

I nodded, "I'll let you know. Thank you for the heads up, let's get you with Bob so you can get started." I introduced them to Bob and sent them on their way.

"Major, message Jim Jones and ask him to come for a meeting, please."

"Done, sir."

I headed for my office, "Mr. Jones asks if 1000 would work for you?" Major asked.

"Yes, that's fine."

"Meeting confirmed, Sir."

I found Aunt J with her head together with Pam and Rebecca.

"You got a minute, Aunt J?"

"Sure." She followed me the conference room, she watched me as I close the door. "What's wrong?" She asked immediately.

"We will be short one Captain and probably a crew." I said.

"Someone spooked them." She said. I nodded and told her what Captain Smythe had told me. She nodded, "let me make some calls."

"Jim Jones will be here at 1000, I want to tell him about this and see if he knows anything, and if he doesn't, I want him to find out about it."

Jim Jones and his two cyber guys arrived at 0945, Major showed them as green with red pips. They followed me to the conference room where Aunt J and Mal were waiting. We grab coffees and sat down.

"It would appear that our enemies are becoming more aggressive."

"What happened?" He asked. I relayed the information as it had been told. They were taking notes.

"Do you have any information about this?" I asked.

"We don't have a complete risk assessment done, however there are rumors that someone is putting pressure on those who do business with you."

"Any ideas whose driving that tug?" Aunt J asked.

"Nothing solid, maybe a little from union workers, but no solid ties to union management.

"Some independent muscle?"

"Maybe Harper is holding a grudge." He said.

"Jocko know about this?"

"It wouldn't surprise me, but he wouldn't find out from us. We are under contract to you and don't share client information." Aunt J nodded her head.

"Advice?"

He nodded his head, "situational awareness, no one goes out by themselves. We'll need more information and evidence before acting." He said.

"We have some new employees moving in from their apartments, I want security for them to get moved in without being threatened." I said.

"Names?"

"The Whitman family, Pam, Rebecca, and Earl."

"Done. Anything else?"

"Not from our side of the table." I said.

"We finished the initial security survey and cyber survey, which I must admit was a little embarrassing. We have a list of suggestions for upgrading your physical security, and a proposal for the cyber security." Jim flipped the list of proposals for the physical security upgrades, some we had they had not seen them.

"And your proposal?" I asked.

"As I said, cyber security assessment was a little embarrassing. If you'd be willing to show my team what you are doing in your cyber security, increase our cyber security abilities by say, 25%, we'll cut our fees by 50%." Jim said.

"25%?" Mal asked.

"Sir, your 25% will put us so far ahead of competition, we'll blow them out of the belt." Jim said. I looked at Mal, shrugged my shoulders.

Mal nodded, "25% for a 50% reduction in all fees."

"Done." Jim said, "when can you train them?"

"Now, if you leave them with me." Mal answered.

"Great." Cyber guy said, "we get lunch."

"If I'm not careful, the whole team will come to work for you, just to eat." Jim said smiling. "I'll leave the walking stomachs with you; I'll go get started on the other stuff. The Whitman's will have an escort when they leave this afternoon."

I nodded, "we'll let them know to expect you."

***

The next few days felt like I was juggling plasma cutters. The Whitman's got moved in with no issues. The cargo ship, the *Star Duster,* was complete and fully crewed. Captain Smythe was loading her with exports going to Mars and Earth and would return fully loaded with what Conclave Station needed. I scheduled them to depart tomorrow. *Humpty* and *Dumpty*, our two ore hauler's repairs were ahead of schedule. *Dumpty* and her crew on board, completing preparations. We still needed a Captain for *Humpty*. *Taurus* was finally complete, and Mal was doing final tweaks on Misty.

"There is an incoming call from Captain Smythe, sir." Major said in my ear.

"Put him through, Major."

"On-line, sir."

"What can I do for you, Captain?"

"We're good here sir, on scheduled for 1700 departure to-morrow. Are you still looking for a corpsman, nurse or Doctor?" He asked.

"A corpsman or a nurse, I think a Doctor is little more than we need." I answered.

"How about all three in one?" He asked.

"I'm guessing there is a story in there somewhere." I said.

"Not mine to tell, sir. I've worked with him before, ; I think he's worth talking to, at least. He's looking for a berth."

"All right, send me his contact information."

"Done, sir."

"Travel safe, Captain."

"You as well, sir."

I looked at the info Reggie had sent me, John La'Gree. It wouldn't hurt to talk to him.

"Major, message Mr. La'Gree, and set up a meeting at his earliest convenience."

"Yes, sir."

"Major, are Jazz and Jade in the area?"

"They are sir, they dropped a load of ore, and are heading back out."

"Put me through to Jazz."

"On-line, sir."

"Jazz?"

"Nic, I told you not to call me at the office." She laughed.

"Well, this is a special occasion."

"What's the occasion?"

"I need a pilot."

"For what?"

"Mal and I are taking the *Taurus* out on the test flight."

"Don't you two dare! Jade and I are on the way, ETA 17 minutes, Jazz out."

CHAPTER 10

They were back in 15. Mal and I were waiting in the *Taurus* when they came bounding in.

"I thought you said you were taking her out?" Jazz said.

"We were. I didn't mean right that second. I told you we needed a pilot; we wanted a good one but..." That's when I had to duck.

Jade pointed at Mal, "don't say a word, smart guy."

Mal shook his head, "I ain't saying nothing, I don't even know that guy."

"Yeah whatever, get out of our seats."

"Okay, but before you do anything, we want to check things." I said.

"Ok, shakedown run. What do you want us to do?" Jazz asked.

"You are here to take emergency manual control of the ship if needed." I said. They both turned and looked at us.

"You've met Major and heard us talk about Misty. Now you'll meet her. Misty, introduce yourself."

"Good morning ladies, it's a pleasure to meet you, I'm glad to be working with you." Both girls were smiling.

"We want Misty to follow commands, and we want you to watch and verify the actions. Be ready to take over, just as a precaution." I said. The girls nodding.

"Misty, start preflight check please."

"Starting preflight check, generators on-line and green, gravitonics on-line and green. Engines online, in safety standby and green, shields online and green." Misty went through the whole checklist smoothly, line by line. Jazz and Jade confirming each action. "Preflight checklist complete." Misty said. We had Bob standing by the hanger control panel for safety.

"Misty, open hanger door, confirmed green board with door controls."

"Green board on hanger door controls confirmed, hanger door opening."

"Misty, once doors are fully opened, take us out to the test pad dead slow."

"Aye sir, test pad, dead slow."

"Misty, once we are clear of the hanger, close the doors."

"Closing hanger doors."

The rest of the pad test went fine, all green boards. I went back to the engineering section and made visual checks. Everything is green.

"Misty, request clearance from Conclave Control for local space test flight."

"Requested and granted."

"Jazz, give Misty flight directions for our test flight."

Jazz nodded, "Misty, take us up 300 meters, come left 30°, increase speed to 100 KPH." Misty complied smoothly. Once Jazz was satisfied, she turned to me. "A rock?"

I nodded, "we are here to test, so let's test.

Got one in mind?" I asked.

"I do now that we have this big baby out here. Misty, take us up to section Bravo two-three." Misty turned smoothly, heading for B23.

"Misty, bring tri-dar online."

"Tri-dar online."

"What's tri-dar?" Jade asked.

"Tri-dar is a combination of radar, lidar, and a kind of space sonar. Combining all three sensing devices increases the accuracy of the readings exponentially." Misty answered.

"Something new?" I asked Mal.

"Only the combining of them, I wanted to see what would happen."

"Which rock you want Jazz?" I ask.

"That one over there." She highlighted it with the pip.

"Misty, scan the highlighted rock with tri-dar for mithrilium."

"Scanning... Mithrilium content 23%." We all looked at each other.

"Misty, verify scan." Mal said.

"Scanning... Content 23% verified."

"Wow, 12% would've been great, 23% is dancing in the aisles percentages." Jazz said.

"I have no dancing shoes." Jade said.

"I'll buy you some when we sell that." Mal said, laughing.

"Oh, you're so sweet."

"Misty, engage gravitonics and capture highlighted rock."

"Capture complete."

"Misty, take us back to Conclave Station." We got under way to Conclave Station.

"This will be a good payday." Mal said.

"Good thing too, we've been spending money lately, the chef is expensive." Everyone laughed.

"Captain, you have an incoming encrypted call."

"Put it through."

"Nic, I understand you've got *Taurus* out for a test run."

"We do, everything is checking out all green, so far."

"Great to hear she's back out working the belt. Going to grab a rock, I'm guessing?"

"Yep, already got one, and she's a shiny one too."

"Good for you, then this call is fortuitous, seems OEM refining and you share troubles." Jocko said.

"That so?"

"Yep, they would appreciate any business you can send." Everyone on the bridge was nodding their heads.

"As it would happen, we were on our way to OEM."

"Thanks, Nic, take care."

"You too, Jocko."

"Transmission ended." Misty said.

"Misty, take us to OEM refining."

"In route to OEM refining, ETA 43 minutes." I went over to the galley and looked in the cabinets to see if they'd stocked coffee and fixings. I looked at Mal, smiling.

"You didn't think I was flying out here without coffee, did you?" We started the coffee, drinking in the smell as it brewed. We fixed our cups and took cups up for the girls.

"They cook too?" Jade asked.

"Well, coffee anyway." Jazz answered.

Mal brought up the scan displays, reading it, frowning.

"Misty, scan captured rock with radar only for mithrilium percentage."

"Scanning... 3%."

"Scan capture a rock with lidar only for mithrilium percentage."

"Scanning.... 3%."

"Scan capture a rock with sonar only for mithrilium percentage."

"Scanning... 3%." We all just looked at each other.

"Incredible, 20% difference." I said.

"Misty, classify tri-dar as corporate secret and encrypt," Mal said.

"Classified corporate secret and encryption confirmed." Misty said.

"We need to start re-scanning places that have already been picked over, there may be some shiny ones at our doorstep rather than way out there." Jazz said.

"We need to be careful, other wranglers going to watch us if we catch shiny ones to consistently." Jade said.

"Approaching OEM refining." Misty announced.

"Open a channel to OEM, Misty."

"Channel open."

"OEM, this is the *Taurus*, where you want it?"

"Good to see you back online *Taurus*, drop it in the chute."

"In the chute, Roger."

"Handoff complete," Misty said.

"See you next time, OEM."

"Always welcome *Taurus* fly safe."

"Transmission complete," Misty announced.

"Take us home, Misty."

"In route home, ETA 15 minutes," Misty said. 15 minutes later Misty announced, "on final approach."

"Stand ready Jazz." I said, she nodded. "Take us in Misty, return us to the designated parking area."

"Taking us in," Misty said. "Door control board is green, hanger door opening... Entering hanger dead slow... Engines on safety standby, *Taurus* landing in designated parking," Misty said.

"Misty, initiate end of mission shutdown, and post flight checks," I said.

"Initiating," Misty said.

Everything went off without a hitch, green across the board.

"I'd say that was a successful test flight. Good job, Misty." Everyone applauded.

"Thank you, sir, it's a pleasure to serve."

It was almost dinnertime, and I was starving. I stop by my office to check messages. The first one was from OEM refining. Mr. Robert "BB" Browning needed to talk. I commed him.

"Nic Haydock returning Mr. Browning's call." They put me right through.

"Mr. Haydock thank you for returning my call."

"No problem, call me Nic."

"All right Nic, call me BB."

"What can I do for you BB?"

"This is kind of embarrassing, that rock you brought in was a real shiner, haven't seen one that good in months. The problem is, I don't have enough creds on hand to pay your account."

"I don't see a problem BB, unless the universes stopped buying mithrilium. You'll have it sold, and accounts cleared in what, 3 to 5 days? Just credit my account when you sell it." The comm was quiet for a moment. I suspected what was happening. I waited.

"I appreciate your understanding son; rumors have been spreading that I was going bankrupt and not paying accounts. Which is untrue, it's just dirty business, ain't how it's supposed to be.

I knew your folks did a lot of business with them over the years. When sales were slow, and creds were slow in coming, we all just rode the storm out together. It does me good to hear you do business the same way your folks did."

"Thank you for saying so BB. Don't worry about the cred I'm sure I'll get it when you get it. You've been in business a lot of years, you don't stay in business that long by cheating people and not settle accounts."

"You got that right, we all got bills to pay. If you find yourself over in my ring, drop in and see us, coffee is always on."

"You do the same, BB," I said. "travel safe."

"Travel safe." He said and clicked off.

I sat there a moment, thinking. Dirty business indeed. I went up to dinner, fixed my tray, and sat down to eat.

"Problems?" Jazz asked.

"Not really, we had a call from OEM refining."

Aunt J looked up, "what did BB need?"

"Nothing really, seems we may have some of the same problems. Speaking of problems, did you talk to the chef?" I ask Aunt J.

"I did, they are being taken care of."

"Good. Anyway, someone has been spreading rumors about BB and OEM going bankrupt, and not paying accounts. I suspect everyone wanted their creds at delivery. He was calling to tell us he could not cover our accounts."

"What'd you tell him?" Aunt J asked.

"I told him not to worry about it, credit our accounts when he made his sale."

Aunt J smiled and nodded, "that's the way we've done it for years."

I concentrate on my food for a bit catching up with everyone else.

"Mal, you never did say how the training was going with security."

"It's going, and they aren't totally lost. But is going to take a while."

I got more coffee, "we have an interview with a 'medic plus in the morning at 0900."

"Medic plus?" Jazz asked.

"Yeah, one of Reggie's contacts. He said it be worth it to talk to him."

We caught Aunt J up on the *Taurus* test flight. Dinner broke up, and we racked dishes.

***

Mr. John La'Gree arrived at 0845. Major had him marked as green with no red pips. He followed me to the conference room where I made introductions and we all got our coffees.

"How do you know Captain Smythe, Mr. La'Gree?" I asked.

"Just John, please. Reggie and I have worked together a few times in the past."

"ESFL?" I asked.

"He was when we first met, the ESFL subcontracted me, and that's as much as my NDA will allow me to say."

I frowned, "he said you were a Corpsman, Nurse, Doctor and that it was not his story to tell."

John took a swallow of his coffee, "I don't want to waste your time or your board's time sir. Reggie says you're an honorable man. So, as much of my NDA will allow, I'll tell you what happened.

I was working as a contractor for the ESFL. They sent in us to help people, families, caught between two opposing forces. There was a child that was hurt, and I could save her. Their beliefs did not allow me to help her. I helped the child anyway and saved her.

The father found out, he came and undid the work I had done. He was basically killing the child. I took exception to his actions and laid into him. The hypocritical thing was when his daughter needed help, he said no. When he needed medical aid, he wanted all we had to offer. I was the only Doctor there, and I was busy saving the little girl, I didn't have time for him.

So, NDA, NDA, NDA and so on. I was banned from working for the ESFL and lost my license. And NDA, NDA, and NDA. Now I work as a corpsman, nurse, O.R. Tech, whatever I can get. Thank you for seeing me. Tell Reggie thanks as well." He rose to leave.

When he reached the door, "tell me Mr. La'Gree." He turned and looked at Aunt J. "Would you do it again?"

"I've asked myself that many times, and the answer is always the same. Anyone who hurts a child forfeits the right to breathe the same air as I. I don't regret doing it. I regret doing in front of witnesses." He nodded and turned to leave again.

"John," I said. He stopped and looked over his shoulder. "Would you take a position as our CND specialist?"

He frowned, "CND specialist?"

"Yes, it appears we have an opening for a Corpsman/Nurse/Doctor specialist."

"What will my duties be as your CND specialist?" He asked, smiling.

"The first thing you would do would be to set up a med-bay for our hab. A fully functional med-bay, with auto-Docs. And anything else we might need in case of emergency if a Doctor should show up to help. Also, advise us on auto-Docs on our ships, and anything else you think you can help us with."

"A CND specialist, huh? Does that position come with room and board?"

"It does and a salary equal to a level III corpsman to start. We must keep our HR paperwork straight. We don't want the medical board claiming you are working as an unlicensed Doctor."

He chuckled, "nope we can't have that."

"Will you accept the position as our CND specialist, John?"

"I will, sir, and thank you."

"Thank you, John, and welcome aboard. Let's get you over

to Ms. Whitman in HR. She'll get you in processed, find you a room, and the galley. You can start on our med-bay in the morning."

The galley was in full swing at lunch. I found my seat; I spotted John La'Gree sitting at a table with Pam. Taking my seat, I ate.

"Mal, if you have a few minutes after lunch. I want to show you something."

"Sure, come down anytime you are ready." I nodded.

"Any luck on our hauler Captain, Aunt J?"

"Maybe. He said he may come by and see us today, or tomorrow. He's a character, I'll keep looking."

I went down to the EL shop after lunch and found Mal. We walked over to the engineering shop.

"You remember when the Grav-bar nailed you in the chest?"

"No, I remember when you nailed me in the chest with the Grav-bar."

"Whatever, the point being, that started me thinking." I took the baton out of the drawer. "I've been working on this, it's an FE baton. It's the same size as a security baton."

"I'm afraid to ask, but, what does it do?"

"It is three settings push, punch, kick. On the push setting when you trigger it, it will push someone back or down. On the punch setting, when you trigger it, it punches harder than you can punch. On the kick setting when you trigger it, it feels like you got kicked by mule."

"Have you tried it yet?"

"Nope, but I got a dummy set up over here." We tried it, and it worked great. It pushed him down, it punched, knocking him down, and it kicked, bouncing the dummy off the wall.

"That is so cool, let me see if I can tweak it with the program."

"I was hoping you would say that." I gave him the FE baton, and he went to work on it.

Travis Van Dam messaged me, checking on the *Taurus*. I replied that we had a green board, and we should meet. I told him we would come to him. He said he would rather come to HMS and bring his marketing department for a show and tell. He'd come tomorrow at 0900, and I confirmed.

I was looking around in the equipment area when I saw the mine drones again. I started past them but stopped and was staring at them. I open the access panel and looked inside to see how it worked. I got another epiphany and worked that idea in my mind.

"Nic," Bob said.

I looked up at him, "yeah Bob, what's up."

"You've been kneeling there for 30 minutes talking to yourself."

"Yeah, that's how I work through problems. What can I do for you?"

"That job offer still on the table?"

"It is."

"I'd like to take it."

"Good, when can you start?"

He chuckled, "I think I already have."

"I believe so, go to HR read your contract. If you accept, sign it."

"You have a contract ready?"

"We knew we wanted you, we were just waiting to see if you wanted us." I said.

"All right, I'll go check it out."

"Good, now quit slacking get back to work," I laughed.

"That was a short honeymoon," He said, walking away smiling.

I turned back to the mining drone, powered up, and ran its diagnostics. The only amber light I got was a low charge on his battery. I turned on its grav-pad and it raised up off the deck; I got it over to the service lift, and down to the engineering shop. I got up on my workbench and took it apart. I understood the theory, I wanted to see how they applied to it.

I must've been deep in the zone; someone was knocking on

my bench saying my name. I refocused; Earl was standing there with three other men. They were all smiling; I chuckled.

"Man, you were in deep, a good thing the place wasn't on fire." Earl said.

"You know how it is when you get into an engineering problem." I said. They all nodded, looking at the drone. "I see you brought company."

"I found these bums panhandling down on the docks, they followed me home." Earl said.

"Not true, he lured us here, said you are starting a retirement home for old engineers." One fired back.

"You saying I'm old?" Earl said.

"Nope, I'm saying you ain't an engineer." We all laughed.

Earl pointed and named them, "Fred, Warren, and RG." We all shook hands.

"Earl said he could use help here at 'the home'," Fred said smiling.

"Yep, we were trying to decide where to put shuffleboard." I said.

"To be honest Nic, we worked together at the yard. As my daughter would say, 'back in the day'. They know which end of a tester to hold. I thought we'd start small and get an assembly line set up, and as we got the flow figured out, we'd scale up using these guys as our lead-men." Earl said.

"Sounds like a plan, let's go look at the shop where I was thinking about putting you." We walked down to the shop. It had plenty of room for them to try different layouts. "Earl, this is your show, you figure out what you need. Anything you're missing, let Aunt J know, and she'll get it for you. Once you get set up, I want four Grav-bar's and two Grav-ox's." They went to work, and I started back to my shop, I stopped and went back and stuck my head in the shop. "And get these old folks up to see Pam and HR and get them on the payroll."

I was back deep into the mining drone, when someone put her arms around my waist.

"Hey baby, don't let Jazz catch us." I got smacked on the

butt.

"You wish," Jazz said, laughing. "What are you doing?"

"I had an idea, and I was just working out the details. While it's on my mind, Travis and company are coming over in the morning for a 'Dog and Pony' show. We will have a presentation of Misty's capabilities. I want you and Jade to do the same thing we did on the test run."

"Sure, who is Travis bringing?"

"He said he was bringing his marketing department. You can't market and sell what you don't know about. We will put on a show for them, the only difference will be we will not use the tri-dar." Jazz nodded her head.

"Sounds like fun. Let's go eat, we're late." I looked at the time, 1830.

"Time flies when you're having fun."

I was getting my first cup of coffee when John La'Gree stepped up to fill his cup.

"John, don't Marines call their corpsman 'Doc'?"

He smiled, "they do, at least the good ones who earn their respect by knowing their jobs."

I nodded, "morning Doc," I said picking up a pastry.

"Morning, Captain." He said grabbing a pastry.

"Let's take a walk, I'll show you where I'm thinking of putting the med-bay, you tell me if it will do what we want. More importantly, do what we need," I said. We went down and out into the hangar. We walked over to the parts and equipment storage area.

"This used to be the parts room." I open the door and entered. "It's about 15m x 15m, double doors for wider loads. It's on the hanger level for fast access and close to the main hatches. We can install anything you need for power, water, and O2, you tell me what you need, and we'll get it." He was looking around, measuring things with his eyes. He went back to the door, looking out, then looking in. I could tell he was in his own zone, running scenarios. I waited.

He walked around the room, nodding his head. He finally

ended back up beside me.

"What capabilities are you after?" I took a swallow of my coffee.

"Doc, I tried to error on the side of caution. If something goes sideways out in the hanger, or wherever for that matter-, and seconds means the difference between life and death. I'll do what I can to buy those seconds."

"Budget?" He asked.

"Open for discussion, I'm not saying 'no' to anything. I don't plan on buying 'top-of-the-line' new, but we aren't buying junk either," I said.

"I understand we have an in-house electronic and computer wizard?"

"That we do," I answered.

"In that case, I think I know where I can get what we need at a decent price. We'll just need our wizard to do his magic. I'll have your plan, and a list in a few days." He said.

"Glad to have you aboard Doc."

"Glad to be aboard Captain."

CHAPTER 11

Travis and company arrived at 0900. Major checked everyone in with a green board and no red pips. We went straight to the *Taurus*. Coffee and pastries were ready on board. Chef apparently had heard about the demonstration and had assigned a mess attendant.

We made introductions all around. Travis started the presentation to his marketing department. Mal and I finished it up, explaining how the ACE program came about.

"If there are no questions, we'll get the demonstration started." Jazz and Jade took the helm and navigation seats. "Misty?" I said.

"Yes, Captain?"

"Ship's status?" With that, the demonstration began. Everything was going as scripted. Misty took us out into the rock field.

"Captain, I'm picking up a distress call," Misty said.

"On speaker, Misty."

"On speaker, Captain."

"Rock tug *Jingles* requesting help, does anyone copy?"

"*Jingles*, this is the *Taurus*, what's your status and location?"

"Good to hear you *Taurus*, I've lost engines and gravitonics. I've picked up inertia heading toward the rock fields so you getting here sooner, would be better than later."

"I have him on radar Captain, we are the closest ship." Jazz moved for the controls, but I put my hand on her shoulder, she stopped.

"Misty, set a fastest time course for *Jingles*." Before I could say anymore the view out of the main armor glass skewed, and we felt and heard the main engines spinning up.

"Engines at 100%, request emergency override to take engines to 110%." Misty said.

"Emergency override granted." I said.

"ETA 2 minutes and 40 seconds."

"Roger *Taurus* copy 2 minutes 40 seconds." *Jingles* replied.

"Misty, gravitonics to 100%, standby for capture."

"Gravitonics to 100% standing by for capture, ETA 1 minute."

"Copy 1-minute *Taurus*, this will be close." *Jingles* said. Jazz was flexing her hands; it was making her crazy not having them on the yoke.

"Hang on to something *Jingles* this might get a little rough." I said.

"Roger, *Taurus*. Rough I can deal with, sudden stops on a rock I'd rather not try."

"10 seconds to capture… Five seconds, engaging gravs." *Jingles* was getting bigger and bigger through our front armor glass.

"Capture initiated, sweeping yaw 180 degrees, capture gravs at max and holding. Emergency override released engines back to 80% and in the green. Generators at 80% and in the green, gravitonics at 80%, and in the green, all other systems are green." Misty said.

"I don't want do that again anytime soon." Mal said.

"Me either, *Taurus*, me either." *Jingles* said. Everyone laughed, and that broke the tension.

"Status, *Jingles*?"

"I got knocked around, but I'm okay, I shut all systems down except life-support."

"Misty, take us home, best speed."

"Yes, Captain. Heading home, course to A14 laid in and started, ETA 47 minutes."

"Sit back and enjoy the ride *Jingles*."

"Roger, *Taurus*."

Jazz patted my hand that was still on her shoulder, "well

done, Captain." I leaned down and kissed her on the head.

"Captain?" I turned. "Were you worried about letting the ACE program control the rescue?"

"Not at all," I said.

"Have you practiced such a maneuver?"

"No."

"Then why weren't you worried?"

"Because I had the two best pilots in the galaxy at the helm, their hands were on the yokes. If at any time we felt Misty couldn't have completed the maneuver safely, we would have taken over manually."

"We don't need an ad campaign; this thing will sell itself." Travis said.

"I have an idea for some publicity." I said.

"You mean other than rescuing tugs in distress?" We chuckled.

"Sell me the ship you slagged rescuing me. Let your market guys hype it up."

"You going to fix her?"

"I will restore her; she's been sitting on the sidelines too long." He thought a minute.

"I'll trade you." I shook my head.

"Not the *Taurus*."

"I'd never asked that," Travis said. "You give me an ACE to run my hab and yard and I'll give you the yacht." I looked at Mal, he shrugged his shoulders and nodded yes. I look back at Travis, extended my hand, "deal." We shook.

***

"Captain, we're on final approach," Misty said.

"Execute standard hanger entry and landing, Misty. Set *Jingles* down easy."

"Aye Captain, a standard entry and landing." When we came down the ramp everyone was gathered and applauding, Aunt J was in front.

"What's this?" I ask.

"You guys are celebs."

"Why?"

"Someone recorded the whole rescue transmission with you and Misty riding to the rescue, it's gone viral."

Travis was ecstatic, "You can't buy publicity like this, we'll be rich!" He said, laughing.

We moved around to the front of *Taurus*, to see how *Jingles* had faired. The pilot was getting out of his tug. He was limping a little, but no other visible damage. As we approached, he offered his hand; I took it.

"Nic Haydock, of the *Taurus*."

"Lance White, Captain Haydock, thanks for the lift."

"We were in the neighborhood," I looked at Travis, smiling.

"Whatever the reason, I'm glad you were, I was about to become space-paste on the side of that rock."

I pointed with my chin, "how bad is she?"

"I'm afraid to look to be honest, I was trying to squeeze a few more runs out of her. She needed an overhaul; I just didn't have the creds to pay for it."

I nodded, "feast or famine, that's the way it always is. If you'd like, I'll have someone look at her and give you an idea of what you have to work with," I said.

"Bob!" I shouted and waved him over. "Look at *Jingles* and see what we have to work with."

"Yes sir, we'll get right on it."

"Lance?" We turned, Aunt J was approaching, reaching out to hug Lance.

"Julie?" They hugged.

"Are you all right?" She asked.

"Fine, fine, just a few bumps and bruises, nothing broken."

"How's May?"

"She's good. She will kill me when I get home, I think I may have toasted my tug," He said.

"She cares more about you than that tug." Aunt J said.

"Maybe, but once she sees I'm okay, then she'll want to

know about the tug, and that's when the beating will start," He said, laughing.

Bob came walking up, "how bad, Bob?" I asked.

"Not good, sir. She's slagged, she'll need a complete rebuild."

"Thanks, Bob." I said.

"That's about what I figured, I've been putting off the refurbish until I could have it done without taking a loan. I guess I pushed my luck a little too far on this one," He said.

"I thought you were a hauler Captain," Aunt J said.

"I got tired of driving for someone else, I bought a tug to strike it rich, not as easy as it sounds," He said.

"What will you do now, Lance, get a loan and rebuild?" I asked, looking over at Aunt J. She gave me the nod.

He shook his head, "No, I think I'm done. Today scared 10 years of life out of me. I think that was the universe's way of telling me it's time to move on."

"As it happens, HMS is in the market for a hauler Captain, you interested?"

Lance looked up, his eyes got big, "oh crap, here comes May." We all looked where he was looking. A little china doll came running through the crowd.

"Lance!" She ran up to him, jumping into his arms and hugged him tight. "I heard on the news you had to be rescued, and were almost killed."

"I'm okay baby, no harm done."

She looked at the tug, "how bad is the tug?" He gulped, swallowing.

"Slagged," He said. She smacked him in the chest, and then smacked him again.

"I told you we needed to fix it."

"It's okay baby, I took a job as a hauler Captain."

"For who?" May asked.

"Julie and HMS." He said, pointing at Aunt J. May looked around at Aunt J.

"That true, Julie? You going to hire this bum?"

"Sure, if we have any problems with him, I'll just call you."

May nodded, "you do that, can he start tomorrow?"

"Yep, 0800."

May nodded again, "good." May turned back to Lance, "what are you going to do with the tug?"

"I was just talking to Captain Nic about that. It will cost more to fix than I can sell it for." Lance said.

"Let me get it appraised and I'll buy it from you." I said. May looked at me.

"Ok, come on Lance, let's go home you have to go to work in the morning." May said, walking out, leading Lance like a lost puppy.

"Bob, get *Jingles* appraised, I think I bought another tug."

"Looks like, Captain."

***

The next week went by in a blur. I bought *Jingles* and got Bob started refurbishing her. We hired Lance as a hauler Captain, and he got his crew together.

Captain Williams and *Dumpty* made runs out to the miners hauling in raw ore. We kept BB busy. Travis' marketing team was running full speed, capitalizing on our celebrity status. They already had 10 orders placed for ACE ship programs, and Jazz and Jade were doing presentation runs.

Mal installed an ACE program in the Van Dam shipyard and hab and came back with a new corporate yacht. We hired a marketing firm to sell the Grav-bar's and Grav-Ox's.

We sent the first ones off the assembly line over to Van Dam shipyards to test and evaluate.

Doc came up with a list of equipment we needed, work request for fitting out the med-bay.

Doc introduced me to Gunny Smalls, formally of the ESFL. I pointed at Gunny, squinting my eyes at him.

"Scrounger," I said. Gunny smiled. I looked at Doc, "does he know what we want?"

"He does." Doc said.

"Let's get coffee and talk."

With coffee in hand we went to my office, I had Mal join us. We looked over the list. It was quite a list, but we had started from scratch. Gunny check the specs and ask about replacing things with other models.

I sat back in my chair, "Gunny, I've worked with a few scroungers. I found its best to give them your list, and free rein to work their magic. Let me add this caveat. I'm looking for solid hardened equipment equal to military grade, not bare-bones stuff. If you need clarification on capabilities, contact Doc, if it's equipment that may need to be upgraded, contact Mal."

"Do you need sales receipts?" He asked.

I smiled, "don't get me put in jail, and don't have to have me testify at any trials. I'll need receipts to show I bought it from you or your company, other than that, do your thing."

"Roger that, sir." With that he left, to what I can only assume, was to beg, borrow, or steal to get the equipment we needed.

"Have you got time to look at something?" Mal asked. I nodded and followed him to the EL shop. He opened a cabinet and held out what appeared to be an FE baton. It was a little bigger, and a little heavier than the prototype, but not by much.

"I take it you made upgrades?" I asked.

"Don't I always?"

"I'd be disappointed if you didn't." we laughed. "Give me the lowdown," I said.

Mal took the baton and started his hand model routine.

"Here, we have the new FE baton with three intensity settings and three ranges. It's powered by a removable battery. Each battery has enough charge to fire the baton 15 times on the low setting. 10 times on the middle setting and five times on the highest setting. Once the FE battery has been depleted, either change the battery thusly, or with a flick of the wrist it can be deployed and used as a standard baton. Some assembly required batteries, not included."

"Don't give up your day job," I said. "let's go down to the range and try it."

The settings were still push, punch, and kick. The range settings were near, middle, and far. Now with increased power output. The near kick drove the dummy into the wall so hard it broke all the dummy's ribs and one of its arms.

"Will it work with the baton extended?"

"Yes," Mal said

"Awesome! I will need to field test it before production."

"Whatever, come get the accessories in my shop." Accessories turned out to be a belt holster an extra battery pack. "Don't shoot yourself in the foot," Mal said.

"Yeah, yeah, yeah."

"What's up with your mining drone?" Mal asked.

"That's our next project, come check it out." I had the drone reconfigured for my purposes. "You know how drones are pointed at a rock, then follow a program to mine the rock to form tunnels? I've reconfigured it to do something like that on asteroids."

I had a rock sitting on the work stool in front of the drone. I powered the drone up, and flip the first switch, and the rock levitated. I flipped a second switch, and it drew the rock into the FE field. I flipped the third switch, and the rock crumbled into rice sized bits, forming a ball hovering in the center of the FE field.

Mal studied the ball of gravel for a Moment leaned his head to the side.

"You want to change the tugs to do this?"

I nodded, "then drop them into the ore hauler like this." I turned off the power and the ball of gravel dropped in his trash can.

"The FE field is pushing and pulling with alternating waves?" He asked. I nodded.

"We won't even need to change the configuration of the FE on the tugs, we need a program to handle the alternating fields."

Mal said.

"That's what I think to, want to try it on *Taurus*?"

"I'll just add the coding to Misty. They've moved the demo flights over to one of the Van Dam ship's, so testing will not be a problem," He said.

"I'll check the emitters to make sure they are aligned and can handle the load; you get our program ready."

Looking at *Taurus'* Capture Force Emitters, I could see some that needed to be tested and realigned. Some that needed to be replaced.

"Misty, run diagnostics on capture field FE's."

"Capture field FEs showing 93% green and we have one emitter showing red."

"Location?"

"Charlie 23." I moved over to the Charlie side, I looked at number 23. I could see that something cracked it, looking closer, it was cracked like an X from the top all the way to its base.

Mal was walking up, "what's taking so long?"

"You through already?" He laughed.

"No, I need to check some of Misty's lines of code. The interface controlling the capture field FEs."

"While you're standing there, toss me that emitter socket I need to change one out." Mal picked up the socket and tossed it. It suddenly stopped midair about a foot from me. It hung there not moving, I frowned looking at it.

"That's weird. Misty, is there any power applied to the capture field?"

"None showing on the diagnostics board."

I looked at Mal, "hand me a tester." He got it from the drawer and brought it to me. The emitter tested bad, and had a small current flow from somewhere, charging it.

"Something split this one into quarters; the test showed each quarter is charged with opposing polarities. It shouldn't be doing that, that should cause a complete burnout."

Mal moved back to the workbench, "Catch this." I nodded, and he tossed me a wrench. The same thing happened. It just stopped and hung there beside the socket.

"Hold on a second." I attached the test leads back to C23, "okay, toss me another one." The same thing happened. My test reading showed a slight uptick in power usage, then leveled off. I stood there deep in thought. "I wonder?" I moved over to the workbench and got a bigger wrench, and tossed it, same results. I picked up another wrench, this time I threw it hard, same results. I got the biggest wrench on the bench and threw it as hard as I could, same results.

We had several tools hanging in midair; we were sitting there staring at them.

Bob walked up laughing, "you've never seen one do that before?"

We shook our heads, "you have?"

"Yeah, it doesn't happen often, but I've seen it before. One of your emitters split, didn't?" Bob asked.

"They all catch and hold things?" I asked.

"Yep, well, the ones that split into an even number will. The one I had split in an odd number; it would stop whatever you threw at it and then drop it to the deck or would send it back toward you.

Once they split like that, you replace them. Anyway, the reason I was looking for you, was to find out when you want to get started on the yacht? We need something for the crews to do," Bob said.

"Go ahead and get started stripping out her engines, and let's see how bad she is," I said.

"Yes, sir." He walked away, calling his crews over. I went back over to C23, Mal followed me.

"There is something here everyone is missing. I don't know what but it's tickling my brain, I'm missing something."

Mal nodded, "I got that same tickle." I grounded out the emitter and tools hit the floor. Mal went to work on Misty's program, I replaced C23, and calibrated the rest of the emitters. I set the old C23 aside for further testing.

***

The hanger was a beehive of activity. Doc worked in the med-bay getting ready for equipment. The ACE program sold as fast as Van Dam yards could install them. Earl had added more workers to the Grav-bar line. Seems everybody wanted one. We made them standard equipment on all our ships.

We renamed our yacht *Beautiful Beast.* Bob had opened the engineering sections. She was a mess.

Captain White had his crews ready and occupied *Humpty.*

It took Mal and I a few days to work everything out with Misty's program and calibrate the emitters. We were now ready for a test run.

Jazz and Jade were at the helm prepping for our flight. I had Humpty stationed at the edge of the rock field. We were looking for shiners; we need a test subject. We rendezvoused with *Humpty* and moved to a likely place to test the new crusher program.

Humpty held station as we moved in to capture a rock.

"We'll start small to check everything before we put pressure on the system," Mal said.

Jazz grabbed a small one weighing about a metric kiloton (MKT). Mal ran through his readings and made tweaks.

"Ok, I think we're ready," He said, looking up from his screen. "Let's see what she does, run the crusher program." There was a vibration, but Mal was adjusting the program. The vibration stopped.

We're watched the power readings rise. Nothing seemed to happen. I looked at Mal, "wait for it," He said. The power readings on the FEs reached 50%, the rock crumbled, and formed the "Ball" of gravel.

"That is so cool," Jade said.

"Let's take this load to *Humpty* so I can adjust all the fields while making the transfer," Mal said. Jazz and Jade took us to meet *Humpty.*

We went through the process slowly so Mal could work through his program. We grav-pushed our load toward *Humpty*, she grav-pulled the load into her hold.

"Let's go get another one, a little bigger this time." We grabbed a 10 MKT rock, ran the crusher program. Mal watched his readings, it reaching 50% power before it made a ball of gravel. We returned to *Humpty* and made the transfer.

"Let's grab a big one and see what she can do," Mal said. Jazz swung us around and found our next victim. It looked to weigh around 100 MKTs.

"How about that one?" Jazz asked.

"Let's do it," Mal said. Jazz and Jade lined us up and captured it. Mal started the crusher program. Nothing seemed to happen for a Moment. The FEs power readings were rising. When they reached 80%, we got gravel.

"I think that will do it," Mal said. We loaded *Humpty* and went for another rock.

"Misty, bring tri-dar online." I said.

"Tri-dar online."

"Scan the area and find the rocks that have the highest concentrated mithrilium."

"Scanning..." We waited.

"There are several asteroids in the area that have a high mithrilium content, I've highlighted these on the screen."

"Good, capture, crush and deliver them to *Humpty*."

"Understood, executing."

Over the next four hours we filled *Humpty*'s holds, only needing to make a few adjustments along the way. While Misty made gravel, I made coffee. Misty ran the whole operation flawlessly. We signaled Humpty to take their load to OEM and return to HMS. We headed home, talking about how best to use the new crusher program.

CHAPTER 12

We got back to A14, Gunny Smalls was there making a delivery. Mal and I greeted him. Gunny and Doc were going over the delivery list.

"How's everything going Gunny?"

"Going well Captain, we got about a quarter of your requisitions filled. Doc was just confirming the shipment for payment." Doc handed me the shipping Documents.

"You satisfied, Doc?"

"Yes, Captain." I scanned down the list and the costs. I took out my P-comm and sent the invoice to accounting to be paid. Gunny's P-comm confirmed payment.

"Thank you, Captain, see you next trip."

"Doc, I'll get Bob to send you a crew over to help you with unpacking and placement."

"Thank you, Captain." Bob assigned a crew to help Doc in the med-bay.

"Bob, bring in two of the tugs, we're going to upgrade the FEs and add ACE programs to them."

"I'll get right on it, sir; we were running short on work. The men were ready to draw straws to see who would go back to the yard. No one wants to leave chef."

I chuckled, "we'll see what we can do to get more work for them."

Mal and I were walking toward the shops, "where'd the girls go?" I asked.

"Don't know."

"I think I will take Jazz for a walk on the Promenade and take her shopping. Y'all want to come?"

"Maybe later, I need to check in with the security guys."

"All right, later. Major, call Jazz."

"Yes, dear?"

"You want to take a walk on the Promenade?"

"Yes! But I need to change, meet me at the apartment." When I got there, she was getting out of the shower. "You. Shower. Now." I laughed and followed orders.

***

We strolled along the Promenade, looking in the shops. We got an ice cream, just enjoying the outing. We went into every shoe store and clothes store on the Promenade. She bought a dress I cannot complain about; she looked great in it. Of course, she had to have new shoes to go with a new dress. Apparently, that's a rule.

She had finished her shopping, "you want to get a cab or walk?" I asked.

"Let's walk, I'm enjoying stretching my legs."

We walked down Alpha spoke enjoying each other's company. We got to the 'T' where the spoke connected to the ring and turned right, heading for A14. Three guys fell in behind us as we made our turn. I glanced back at them; they were keeping their distance.

Jazz looked askance at me, "we're good, walk like nothing's happening. It's probably nothing."

"Hey belter!" Came a shout from behind.

"I guess I spoke too soon." We took a few more steps.

"I'm talking to you, belter!"

I let Jazz get a few steps in front of me and turned to face them. They stopped a few meters away from me. I looked at them, waiting.

"What you gonna do, Laddie?"

"I'm going to listen, you said you want to talk, so talk."

"You with the HMS group ain't-cha?"

"Yes."

"You sell your rocks to OEM?"

"Yes."

"Well OEM is going out of business, so you need to take your rocks over to the corporate smelter."

"I hadn't heard OEM was going under. Well, when they do, we'll do business with someone else."

"You ain't listening, Laddie. You don't sell to OEM no more."

"No, you aren't listening. I sell to who I want. And at the moment, I want to sell to OEM. If they go under, we'll sell to someone else."

"Did you no hear me, Laddie?"

"Ok, he's the stupid one which one of you two is the smart one?" I asked.

The stupid one pulled a pipe out from behind his back.

"When I'm finished with you, we're going to take our time with your girl."

My anger dropped into a cold rage, "until 5 seconds ago this was business, not good business, but business. Your boss hired you to scare off competitor's business. I get it, business. You threatened my family, that makes this personal."

"Well then, let's get to it, the girl's waiting." Stupid stepped toward me, swinging his pipe. He expected me to jump back, I stepped forward under his swing drawing my baton, flicked it open and broke his kneecap. I palm struck him in the side, breaking ribs.

I heard one of his partners coming in on my blindside. I ducked and spun under his reach and triggered a baton kick. We were at close range, so the kick lifted him off the ground and crashed him into the wall. He was out.

I felt a slash and burn across my back. I rolled away and triggered another baton kick. It caught a third guy in the shins, broke both his legs, and face planted him into the deck. He was out.

Stupid was trying to get up on his good leg. He swung his pipe at me again. I grabbed his arm twisted behind his back, dislocating his shoulder; he passed out.

Jazz was at my side, "Nic, your bleeding, he got a knife in you."

"I felt it, how bad is it?"

"Not good, we need to get you to Doc."

"Just a minute."

I pulled Stupid and his two friends over by the wall and slapped number two awake. He woke up blinking and confused.

"Tell your boss you delivered your message." He nodded. Stupid came around. I had to admit he was tough.

"I'm gonna kill," he started saying. I grabbed his hand in my cyber hand and broke a finger. He grunted and gritted his teeth.

"Now," I said.

"I'm gonna," he started again. I broke another finger, he grunted.

"It's not polite to interrupt people when they're speaking."

"I'm gonna kill." I broke two more fingers and dislocated his thumb. He almost passed out...almost. I grabbed his other hand and waited for his eyes to focus.

"Have I got your attention?" He nodded. "Good, I don't have a problem with your boss, he didn't threaten my family, as far as I know. You threatened my family, that makes this between you and me. Leave Conclave Station, if I see you again, I'll break every bone in your body. If you are unlucky enough, you may survive it. You understand?" He nodded. I punched him in the head hard enough to give him a concussion.

I looked at number two who witnessed my conversation with Stupid. Number two was having trouble breathing. I knew I had broken his ribs; he was probably bleeding internally. "Any questions?"

He quickly shook his head, "no sir, no questions."

"I have one, who sent you?" He shook his head no.

I took his hand in mine, "did you see what I did to Stupid's hand?" He looked at Stupid's hand. He looked back at me.

"I didn't say this, but Harper, the younger. Taking his P-comm, "I'm calling Med Services now, you may want to have your story straight by the time they get here."

"Yes, sir."

Jazz called A14 and told them we were coming in. When we got there, Doc was waiting, and took me straight to Med-bay. They got my jacket and shirt off and laid me face down on a med table.

Doc worked on me, "how bad Doc?"

"An inch lower and he would have punctured your kidney, you will need some internal stitching and a good bit of healing gel. Do you want to go to the Med Center?"

"No, I left a mess at the T-junction. Do you have what you need to do the job here?"

"We can do it here, just checking." Doc was about finished with me when Aunt J, Mal and Jade arrived.

"How bad, Doc?" Aunt J asked.

"He'll live, he will be sore for a few days. He'll have the full range of motion and three or four days."

"What happened?" Mal asked.

"I don't remember, I was looking at this pretty girl walking by and Jazz shanked me."

"I thought you said you didn't remember."

"It's all a bit fuzzy."

"What happened Jazz?" Aunt J asked.

"The condensed version is, don't threaten Nic's family, he'll go off the rails."

"We're gonna need a little more than that." Jade said. Jazz told her what happened, and what I told Stupid.

I shrugged, "you don't threaten my family, you guys are all I have." Aunt J shook her head.

"Harper. That boy, that jackass, is almost too stupid to breathe." She came over and kissed me on my head. "Rest dear, I need to make some calls." Doc wanted me to stay in med-bay for a while to make sure everything was holding.

"So, you used the baton? How did it perform?" Mal asked.

"That thing is awesome, I triggered two kicks, one bounced a guy off the wall and broke his ribs. The other face planted into the deck with what looked like two broken legs. I'd call that a successful test, we can start production."

"Wait!" Jazz said, "you guys made that baton?" Mal, and I nodded.

"What baton?" Jade asked.

"The baton Nic beat the crap out of those three guys with."

"You guys made something like that and didn't make us one?"

"Nic wanted to test it," Mal said.

"Thanks buddy, appreciate the help. The good news is," I said before the girls got on a roll." We have tested it and you'll get yours." I looked askance at Mal.

"Tomorrow, we'll start production tomorrow, and you girls get the first ones off the line."

"We better computer boy, or there will be trouble."

I spent the night in med-bay, Doc released me the next morning for breakfast.

"Thanks, Doc. Appreciate it."

"Just take it easy and don't mess up my work."

I smiled, "I'll do my best." I told everyone to keep our excitement quiet. I didn't want the rest of HMS knowing what happened. The topic of the morning was the terrible mugging that put three guys in med center. Supposedly six guys with pipes beat 3 miners bad. One was being shipped off station for further treatment.

I ate breakfast, taking the morning slow. Mal made four more batons and gave one to each of the girls, including Aunt J. We took them down to our test shop and trained them on how to use the batons. They were easy to use, and the girls loved them.

I was back in my office, taking it easy when Aunt J stuck her head in. "Meeting in the conference room."

"On the way." The board members were already there when I arrived, and Jim Jones. I grabbed a coffee and took a seat.

"Captain, you hired me and my team to see to your security. That outing yesterday was ill advised."

I held my hands up in surrender, "I agree wholeheartedly. In hindsight, I should've called you, won't happen again."

"I hope not, we don't enjoy losing clients."

Jim passed binder across the table.

"This is our threat assessment. The abridged version is, you've interrupted people's plans."

"Harper's," I said.

"For one, the local union for another. And the Corporation that owns the new refinery and shipyard. They've been quietly pushing out the competition. They had OEM on the ropes. Van Dam shipyards was right behind them until you showed up. Now they've set their sights on HMS."

"Anything station security can do about this?" Aunt J asked.

"No ma'am, not really, not enough evidence. Oh, they know what's going on, but they don't have enough to act on. These guys are smooth, this is not the first time they've done this type of thing.

You might even say it's their business model. They move in, buy out a big operation or build their own like they've done here and eliminate the competition. They always leave a few of the smaller operators so no one can sue under the monopoly laws."

"Recommendations?" I asked.

"I'd like to start tomorrow installing additional security monitoring equipment. Granted, you guys are already good in that area, but we can add some extra equipment. We'd also like to station men in the house, as a reaction force and escorts." Jim answered.

"How long will this last?" Jazz asked.

"I don't know, these guys don't quit. They have plenty of money, powerful owners, and time is on their side."

"Ok, coordinate with Mal on the additional equipment and integration. What kind of weapons will your team be carrying?" I asked.

"Standard pistols with non-breaching rounds, knives and

security batons."

I looked at Mal; he nodded, smiling.

"Mal, show him our new batons, if he likes him, issued them to his team."

"Come with me Jim, I think you'll like our batons better than your standard ones." A half-hour later Mal came into my office grinning with Jim right behind him.

"Jim, I take it you like our batons better than yours."

"Yeah, who I gotta kill to get the rest of my men equipped with them?"

"How many more do you need?"

"25."

"We got that many on hand, Mal?"

"Give me two days and we'll have them ready."

Jim nodded, "the guys will love these." He said as he left.

Mal had a baton in his hand, "replacement for your proto-type, I gave it a few upgrades and a new setting."

"What kind of new setting?" Mal shot me. It made me flinch; it was like a light slap. It didn't hurt, but you felt it.

"Training setting," Mal said, laughing. "I also ruggedized it."

We traded, "next time warn me jackass."

"Payback for shooting me with the Grav-bar."

"I will never hear the end of that, will I?"

"Nope," He said leaving my office.

The security detail moved in the next morning. It took two days to get all the new equipment installed and integrated into Major's security system. I was standing at the galley's armor glass looking out over the hanger enjoying a cup of coffee when Bob came up beside me.

"Morning, Captain."

"Morning Bob, how's everything going?" He took a swallow of his coffee, then pointed with his cup out the armor glass.

"Got two of the tugs upgraded and ready for testing."

"What took you so long, it's been almost 4 days?"

"I know sir, I'm sorry about that. But with the drinking and the bar crawling, the boys have been slow."

"Well, as long as you have a valid reason." We both laughed. "I'll get with Jazz and Jade about the test runs."

Jazz and Jade did their pre-flights on the two upgraded tugs, designated *Uno*, and *Dos*. We had *Humpty* standing by to take on gravel. Might as well make the test runs pay for themselves. They departed the hanger to rendezvous with *Humpty*.

I went over to *Beautiful Beast* and was looking at the aft section. She was in bad shape. Travis had literally melted the engines into the superstructure. It got so hot in the engine room the hull had buckled and warped. The hull was so warped they couldn't unbolt it. They had to use plasma torches to cut it open.

Bob came over, "lots of work to be done."

"Lots of work to get ready to do the work. We might as well just cut everything out. Save as much as the superstructure as we can and start with a blank canvas."

"I was thinking about making improvements. What's the inside look like?" I asked.

"Everything forward to the engineering section is undamaged. Van Dam had made that part look like an executive yacht. Leather seats, custom, well, custom everything and shiny accents. Flight deck was top-of-the-line 10 years ago, a good base to build on. She's missing a lot of her mil-spec equipment. Shield generators were standard industrial type." Bob said.

"I wonder if Gunny can help us with that?" I said.

The blaring klaxons made me jump.

"Emergency evac, all personnel evac the hanger deck! Emergency evac, all personnel evac the hanger deck! This is not a drill; this is not a drill."

"Major, report," I said, as I ran down the ship's ramp.

"Jazz has declared an in-flight emergency," Major replied. The hanger doors began to open. People were hurrying out of the hanger, and to the Hab per protocol.

"Open a channel to her."

"Open now, Captain."

"Jazz are you ok?"

"I'm okay, but Jade is not. The door side of her tug is crushed in, flight deck is badly damaged. I can't see how bad, and she's not responding."

"How far out are they Major?"

"They're on final approach, 60 seconds out."

"Inform Med-bay to expect casualties. Bring hanger emergency ship capture field online, prepare to receive runaway ship emergency override authorized if needed."

"Understood Captain. Med-bay standing by. The emergency capture field online at 100%, emergency override authorized. Ships are 30 seconds out."

The hanger was clear, everyone was watching through the armor glass in the galley. Through the enviro-field I can see the ships approaching. She was coming in hot.

"Major engaged test pad Grav-field and Grav-sling field to bleed off as much inertia as you can as she passes over the threshold."

"Roger, all Grav-fields are at 100%, the rescue crew is standing by. Five seconds to capture. All generators to 100% and standing by."

"My God, she's coming in fast." Jazz cut her engines and was just off the deck.

"Capture program initiated, test pad Grav-field redlined. Grav-sling redlined," Major said.

Time slowed; the emergency capture field engaged as the tugs slid through the environ-field. The test pad and Grav-sling had bled off some of her inertia, but I didn't know if it would be enough. There was a flash-boom and sparks from the right side of the hanger as one of the field generators gave way. The ships were sliding along the deck, slowing. I was running for the tugs before they stopped.

Using my cyber leg, I launched myself up on Jade's tug. It was bad; something crushed the hatch in. I increased power to my cyber arm and hand. I drove my hand down into the seam where the hatch met the frame and forced an opening.

Suddenly Mal was by my side with a Grav-bar. Mal drove

the Grav-bar into the gap I had created and applied power. We got the hatch open enough that I could leverage my cyber leg against it. I bent the hatch open enough that Mal could get through. I grabbed the Grav-bar and tore the side of the tug the rest of the way open.

Doc and his team were there with a rescue stretcher and took Jade as Mal passed her out. Her face was covered in blood. Her arm was bent at an odd angle, and she had a gray pallor. They had her on a stretcher and were rushing toward Med-bay. I jumped down, went over to Jazz. She was shaking and walking off the aftereffects of adrenaline overload.

"Jazz, you okay?" She flung herself into my arms, holding me. I held her, giving her the time she needed. She finally relaxed and let go of me, stepping back.

"This was no accident Nic, this was intentional. That other tug drove a rock right into Jade's tug."

"What? What tug? Did it have any markings, or a name?"

"No, all the I-dent's were blacked out. The tug was not broadcasting its safety warnings, markers, or warning lights. The only broadcast it made was to say, 'You scabs have been warned' then he drove the rock into Jade. I don't know what happened after that, I was concentrating on Jade."

"Major, comm the *Humpty*, encrypted."

"Encrypted Channel open, Captain."

"*Humpty*, this is HMS hanger."

"This is Lance, Captain. Did Jazz and Jade make it in? We are on our way in now."

"Yes, they made it. Jade is in med-bay, no word on her condition. Did you see what happened?"

"I didn't see it, but our cameras were on, so they might have captured something."

"Send us all that data and get here soonest."

"Yes Captain, transmitting data now."

"Major, analyze that data. See what we have on the incident. Log a complaint with Conclave Control about the accident, and the tug leaving the scene of an accident, not rendering help. Log a security report with Conclave Ops, looking for an unmarked tug."

"Complaints and reports log."

Jazz and I went to med-bay to see how Jade was doing. Aunt J was sitting in the waiting area, and Mal was pacing the floor.

"Any word," I asked. Mal shook his head.

"Doc will let us know something as soon as he can." Mal nodded his head.

"Nic, your hand." Jazz said. I held my hand up, looking at it. It was missing three fingers and was crushed.

"Mal and I did it getting the hatch open, my leg is gouged up some too. I can have it replaced, it's just a tool."

Mal seemed to come to himself, "Jazz, are you okay?"

"Yeah Mal, I'm okay."

He nodded, "thank you for bringing her back to me."

Jazz hugged him, "she's family Mal."

Doc came out, "she's gonna be okay. She's got a broken arm, four broken ribs. A sprained knee, a concussion and minor contusions. She's in the Auto-Doc, sedated. We'll see how she is in the morning." He looked at Mal, "you can go in and sit with her, but she's out."

"Go," Aunt J said. Mal nodded and went in.

"I assume you want her kept here rather than transferring her to the Med Center."

"Unless there is a medical reason for her to be transferred or something that will get you in trouble, I'd like to keep her here."

"No medical reason to transfer her, and all I did was clean her wounds, put air splints on her arm and knee, wrap her ribs and place her in the Auto-Doc. Just what any trained Corpsman would do." he smiled. "Now I have paperwork to do to cover our bases."

"If there's anything you need Doc, don't hesitate to ask."

CHAPTER 13

"Major, analysis of data?" I asked.

"We have a clear recording of the incident, Captain. However, Jazz was correct, they blacked all I-dents out. No warning beacons were broadcasting, no warning markers were operating."

"Did we pick up the audio transmission?"

"Yes Captain, audio captured."

"Send a copy of all that to Conclave Ops Security, and a copy to Aaron Stein with all logged complaints and reports. Send an encrypted copy to Jocko and Travis with an additional message of 'watch your six'."

"Done Captain."

Aunt J looked at me, "they messed with family," she said. I nodded once. She nodded and left.

I looked at Jazz, "let's go home, love."

Station's Security visited us bright and early the next morning, wanting to take statements. Aaron arrived minutes behind them and sat in on every interview. He had calls in to the station's chief and station prosecutor.

He held a press conference demanding answers, "How can a spacecraft fly around Conclave airspace, with no markings, no I-dents and no one had seen anything. Supposedly all tracking equipment was off line during the time of the incident. Was it poor maintenance or was someone paid off? The public needs answers."

Major had taken video feed from every source on the station and had traced the unmarked tug to its berth, with the pilot leaving the tug. The best part was a nice clear picture of the pilot. I called Jim Jones and gave him the data.

"I want to know all there is no about this guy. I want to know everything, if he has a cat I want to know how many times it goes to the litter box." Jim took the data nodding and left.

Jazz and I went to see Jade, she was out of the Auto-Doc but still in Med-bay on bed rest. Mal was at her bedside, holding her hand. When Jade saw Jazz, she reached out to her. They hugged and cried. Jade was whispering, "thank you" over and over.

Jade looked at me then my hand, "I hear I owe you a new hand."

"Nope, everything was going fine until 'tool boy' here decided to help me, he's the one who did this." I held up my ruined hand.

Jade looked at Mal, he shrugged, "he was going too slow."

Jade looked at Jazz, "have they always been like this?"

"For as long as I've known them, pretty much, yes." Mal turned serious, looking at me.

"You know who did it?" All emotion left my face. I nodded once. "You handling it?" I nodded once again.

I looked over at Jade, "they messed with family." Mal nodded.

***

Jade stayed in Med-bay two more days, then on bed rest for the rest of the week. Things were kind of back to normal. Station security still had no answers. Jocko and Travis had taken on added security. Aaron was still stirring the pot. Jim was still gathering info.

I needed a new hand; I had fixed mine to use in the short-term; I have ideas I wanted to try. I could get by with one and a half fingers and a thumb for a while.

"Captain, we have Gunny Smalls' cargo ship on final approach requesting clearance on encrypted Channel."

"Grant clearance. Inform Doc, Mal and the security team we have company."

We met Gunny at the space side cargo hatch.

"Good to see you again, Gunny."

He shook hands, "I brought more of the parts you requested, and some extras that might interest you." They unloaded crates.

"Captain," Major said in my ear, "facial recognition has identified that man as Admiral of the ESFL Coal." It highlighted the man on my HUD, I blinked acknowledgment. I glanced at Mal, he nodded slightly. We all went to the Med-bay. The Admiral was pushing a grav-cart of cases. We moved to the far side as they continue to bring cases and crates into Med-bay.

Gunny pointed to the grav-cart, "these are what I think you'll be especially interested in." He unlatched the cases and opened them. "Mark VI mil spec cyber limbs, four full sets, including exoskeletons for supports." We looked in the cases.

"Sweet." Doc said. I looked at Gunny for a moment, nodding.

"So, what's this going to cost us, Admiral Cole?" Gunny froze, I looked over the Admiral. He chuckled.

"How long did it take your system to recognize me?"

"10 seconds after you enter the hangar."

He nodded, "excellent work Captain. Is there somewhere we can talk in private?"

"May I include the rest of my board?"

"Certainly."

"Let's go to our conference room."

Jazz, Jade, and Aunt J were waiting when we arrived. We entered the conference room, I motioned to the sideboard, "coffee?" Everyone filled their cups and took seats. I made introductions, waiting to see how the Admiral would proceed.

"To answer the question on everyone's mind, why the cloak and dagger. The simple answer is, politics, and money," He said. "How much do you know about the ESFL?"

"The normal things I guess, loyal to no nation, only earth. Keeps peace throughout Sol space, earth finances it."

The General nodded, "there are politics in everything, and

where there is politics there's money involved, and where those two things meet, there is always a power struggle. It's no longer about global expansion, its space and solar system expansion, and mithrilium is financing it.

Like any other governmental organization, we have to submit budgets and requests. Not every country supports the ESFL equally, especially monetarily. Politicians put pressure on us using appropriation money to make us move in the directions favorable to those in power. We've held the line, resisting them mostly, which means we sometimes have to be creative to support ourselves and the mission."

"That's where Gunny Smalls comes in." I said.

"Him and those like him. Once Legion, always Legion. Unofficially, we keep our fingers in as many pies as we can. There is no official chain of command. But there is a network to keep us informed, and when needed, coordinated. We find people and companies sympathetic to the policies and the charter of the ESFL and work with and through them. That's the usual way, You and HMS are a special case."

"How so?" I ask.

"First, we have a common foe, you have become a thorn in the Corporation's side. Their owners are the powerbrokers and politicians who are attempting to manipulate the ESFL. The shipyards and refineries are where they get the money and control local economies and local politics. You have inadvertently disrupted some of their power plays. They are just getting set up here on Conclave, so they don't have all the pieces in place yet. That will not last forever. When they get more pieces in play, they'll be coming for HMS."

"So, if we are a special case, and you're not recruiting us, what specifically do you want from us?" He got up and refilled his coffee cup.

"That's where our creativity comes in, and the costs you ask me about earlier." He returned to his seat. "We want your ACE programs for our ships, if we buy, it politics will demand we give or at the least share it with earth. ESFL is not against sharing, but they won't approve the purchase unless they decide who gets the program.

They already had a few ships equipped with the ACE program through the Van Dam shipyards and have attempted to reverse engineer it." He smiled at Mal, "my compliments on your antitheft program. When they try to open the main processing unit all that was left was a box of black sand. So far, we've got no authorizations to buy the ACE programs, and I'm betting there won't be."

"So, you're here to broker a deal? What kind of deal are you offering? Equipment, services, information?" I asked.

"All the above, let me cut to the chase. We want the ACE programs on roughly 100 ships of assorted sizes, including support for the program. We want access to any other 'toys' you two come up with. We want re-fits and upgrades to our ships and equipment when needed, and when we are away from home port." My Eyebrows kept climbing as his wish list grew longer.

"And in return for us giving you the keys to the kingdom, what do we get?"

"A full mil-spec Med-bay, and when I say full, I mean full. Auto-Docs, cyber-limb capabilities, Nanite and Regen capabilities."

"As nice as all that sounds, we can buy all that, maybe not mil-spec but close. As you have noted we do a lot of upgrades in house."

"We'll give you a complete mil-spec loadout for a counter Intel and strike platoon of 30 men including all electronics."

"Again Admiral, nice and I'm sure Jim Jones would appreciate it, but how does it help us?" I saw it coming. The Admiral got that Cheshire Cat smile. Whatever he was about to offer was the juicy bait I would want so bad I'd take the deal.

"The ESFL will grant you all license approvals and charters for exploration and security company. Including authorization to own and operate a corporate security company. Mister Jones will fold up under your security company and work for you." He reached into his chest pocket and pulled out two data cards and pushed them to the center of the table. I knew what they look like, but I asked.

"And those are?"

"The keys to your Vigilance class exploration and security ship, Captain. And because you are a licensed security company, it is armored and armed." There it was, the eye candy to keep you from looking for the hook.

"I will need to confer with my board. How about a break for lunch?"

"Excellent idea." The Admiral said, rising. "I've heard wonderful things about your chef, you'll forgive me if I don't sit with you, we need to keep up appearances."

The Admiral sat with Gunny and his men, enjoying his lunch. We fix our trays and went into a separate private dining room. We talked as we ate.

"What happens to us when there is a change of command? Do we lose all benefits agreed upon?" Aunt J asked.

"We need to address that," I said.

Mal was nodding, "I don't like the part about the access to all our 'toys' as he put it. What about the things we haven't developed yet, do they get all those to?"

I nodded, "I don't like that part either. Anything new we develop needs to be covered under a specific agreement."

"What do we know about the Vigilance class ship?" Jazz asked.

"Major, display data on the ESFL Vigilance class ship," Mal said. Ship plans appeared on the wall. We walked along the wall, looking at the plans and reading the data.

"Impressive, I bet she's a dream to fly." Jade said. "Judging by her engines and gravitonics, she can dance the dance."

Mal was reading, "weapons, missiles, rail guns, ECM pods, shields."

"Crew berthing for 50, a big galley, and the cargo hold." Aunt J was saying.

"What's this?" Jade asked. We all looked.

"Major, identify this area," I said.

"Secured armory, and arms Bay."

"How many guns will she carry?" Jazz asked.

"Enough for a crew of 20 and a 30-man CIS platoon, I'm guessing," I said.

"She's four times the size of the beast." Mal said.

"Where do you plan on putting her?"

"A12 hanger along with the CIS platoon." I answered.

"We also need resupply of munitions and ECM pods if something goes bad." Mal added. I grunted and nodded my head.

"Anything else?" Everyone shook their head. "If they agree to our changes, are we all in agreement to accept their offer?" Everyone nodded yes.

We reconvened our meeting in the conference room. After an hour of back-and-forth the Admiral agreed to our changes, we agreed to house some ESFL personnel when they needed to keep a low profile and offer aid and assistance in emergencies. Which we would've done, anyway.

"I believe we have a deal, Admiral," I said.

We shook hands, "unofficially of course" he answered.

"Of course, you were never here."

"I'm guessing you'll want your ship and security equipment in A12."

"It's here now?" I asked.

"I never offer deals I can't pay with creds on the table." The Admiral said.

I nodded, "A12."

"Gunny," the Admiral said, "get us unloaded so we can be on our way. Thank you, ladies and gentlemen, stay safe and watch your six."

"You too, Admiral."

"Major, prep A12 to receive a ship, crew, and cargo."

"Yes, Captain."

"I wonder why he didn't ask for the Majordomo program?" Mal said.

"Oh, he will. You can bet on it." Aunt J said.

Gunny's cargo was unloaded, and their ship departed. We

watched by remote as our new ship was parked in A12, and the crew departed.

"Major, put A12 in security lockdown." I said.

"Understood Captain, we also have received all Documentation and authorizations for the new ship and our security firm. They have filed everything with the appropriate agencies." Major said in my ear.

We went to the med-bay, Doc was like a kid at Christmas. The three corpsmen from Jim Jones were there helping Doc uncrate and set up equipment.

"Do you need anything.?"

"Maybe a few more bodies to unpack. Also, the hand you ordered came in." He went over to an exam table and brought a cyber-hand over.

"let me see your arm." In no time he had changed my whole hand for the new one. "Once we get everything set up, we'll bring you in and see what the mil-spec cyber-limbs can do for you." Doc said.

"Before we do that, I want to see what I can do with the new programming." Mal said.

"Let us know if you need anything Doc, I'll get more help over to you." After leaving Med-bay we found Bob and told him to send Doc more bodies. "You know Mal, I think we need a tunnel through to A12, so we can come and go without prying eyes seeing what's going on."

Mal nodded, "Major pull up the blueprints of A12 and A14, plot the best placement for a tunnel between them."

"A tunnel already exists between A11, A12, and A14." Major said.

"That can't be right, I would've known about them if there were." I said.

"The tunnels run under all three hangers at the bottom of the heavy service lift. They seal each tunnel with a cargo hatch under security lockdown protocols. You need a special clearance to access that floor using the service lift." Major said.

"Who has access that floor?"

"Only You, and Mal Captain."

"Uh-oh, authorize new users, add Jazz, Jade, and Aunt J to the authorize users list."

"Done Captain."

I looked at Mal, "you want to take a walk?" I asked.

"Let's go by the shop first, I need some things."

"Should we ask the girls?"

Mal shook his head, "no, Jade went back to our apartment to rest, and Jazz went with her." We went down to the EL shop and got Mal's computer bag of tricks case. We return to the lift. There was no designation on the lift for any lower floors.

"Major, what is the designation for the tunnel floor?"

"Sub-basement echo, Captain."

"Take us down." The lift went down, and the doors open facing the cargo hatch. I walked over and palmed the pad on the hatch. It opened into a lighted tunnel. At the far end was another hatch.

We walked through the tunnel to the next hatch it opened to a lift door. We call the lift and went up to A12 hanger level. There sat our new Vigilance class E&S ship. She was something to see. She had nonreflective black skin shaped like an angel shark, but thicker with a shorter tail. We went around to the entry ramp I slotted the key card that the Admiral has given me into the entry panel and palmed the pad. The pad turned green, granting us access to the ship.

"Let's go to the bridge, I need to check things." Mal said. I nodded and followed him. I gave Mal the master key, and he slotted into the master control panel. He worked his magic, talking to himself, "standard control system, standard security systems, lots of storage space, decent processing speed. Need to fix that. There you are, backdoor closed. Authentication fully accepted. Ok, let's get ACE started."

Mal ran the ACE program. I did a walk-through of the ship. It was all still intact. This was not a stripped-down, De-Mil'ed Hulk. She was fully stocked and operational ready. Galley was online, I smiled. The cargo hold was full of cases and crates, probably the platoon's equipment. All systems seem to be over-engineered for her size. As Jazz would say, they dressed this girl to dance.

I went back up to the bridge, "she got a name?"

"Nope, just the designation number. You got something in mind?"

"*Vanguard.*"

Mal nodded, "I like it, want me to log it?"

"Yeah, *Vanguard* she is," I said.

"It will take a while before ACE is fully integrated," Mal said.

"Let's get back, it's almost dinnertime, anyway." I said.

"It should be done in the morning, we can come back then." Mal said, heading for the hatch. We stopped at the ship's hatch and Mal put in security lockdown.

"Major, put this bay in security lockdown."

"Yes, Captain."

On the way back to A14 I sent a message to Jim Jones, saying we needed to meet. He suggested 0900; I accepted.

Over dinner, "what have you two been up to?" Jazz asked.

"We looked in on Doc in the Med-bay, and went down to the shops, worked on some stuff getting ready to pay our trade deals," I said.

I messaged Bob, told them to proceed with the beast and put her back like Travis had her. We would put an ACE in her once the refurb was complete. He asked about Jade's tug; he said it would cost more to repair it than it would cost to buy a new one.

"Strip it out and take the hull to OEM refinery. Major, message *Humpty* to run out to the mining colonies and bring their loads back to OEM."

"Done Captain."

Jade was looking better, and the family was eating together and enjoying the company. "I'm sending *Humpty* out to the miners to make ore runs, we will suspend our tug operations for a few days. *Jingles* was a total loss; I'm having Bob strip it out and send the hull over to OEM." I said.

"If we stop tug operations won't that show them they scared us away, and they won?" Jazz asked.

"We aren't stopping, we are suspending ops until we can put *Vanguard* on overwatch. Then we'll get back out there."

"Who's *Vanguard*?" Jade asked.

"The new ship." Aunt J said, smiling.

"That'll put a kink in their chain."

"We have a meeting in the morning with Jim Jones to hammer out the changes and see if he knows of a captain with experience on that kind of ship and operations."

CHAPTER 14

We met with Jim the next morning. He seemed tense. We gathered in the conference room. Everyone got their cuppa, and we got down to business.

"I've got the file on the individual you requested." He flipped it to my P-comm.

"You seem tense this morning, Jim."

He took a swallow of his coffee, "it seems we work for you now, or more specifically my company is being absorbed by yours. I really don't have a choice in the matter, or not much of one."

"What did our 'friend' do?"

"My company's charter, which is issued by the ESFL, is being rolled up under HMS. We will no longer receive 'supplies' from him, it will all come through you. To be honest, and no offense to HMS, I'm not happy. I started my company because I wanted to make my own choices on assignments to take and what to walk away from."

"I don't blame you; I think we are both chess pieces in his game. He wanted things, I wanted things we traded. Then he threw the bait out on the table. I think his overall plan is to have assets in a place he could draw on when he needs to. He'll do what he has to do to win 'his' chess game. I'm sure he's thinking 10 moves ahead."

Jim nodded, "don't play poker with him either."

"You and he have a history?"

"Once Legion, always Legion. Don't get me wrong, business is good, and he's made us a lot of money. But like you said, he is a chess player, he may not use us as pawns, but we're still pieces on the board. You need to watch the moves being made."

"That's my impression as well. Jim, I don't want to take your company, I wouldn't know how to run if I did. I propose we run this like a sub Corp. You fold up under our new charter, but you run everything as before. You decide what jobs you take or not. You keep us safe and informed; I will provide supplies and facilities to be based out of. As icing on the cake, I think our friend left you a peace offering." I said.

"And what would that be?"

"It will be easier to show you; it's wrapped in our bait."

"He got you to, huh?"

"It's looking more like it all the time."

We all got on the service lift.

"Major, take us to echo deck." The lift descended to the tunnel level, the lift doors opened, and the cargo hatch opened as we approached. To their credit, Jazz, Jade and Aunt J acted as if they took this walk every day. We arrived at A12 hanger deck.

Jim whistled, "is that a Vigilance class E&S ship?"

"That's our bait." We walked around to the entry ramp, and up to the hatch. I palmed the pad. It showed green.

"Access granted, welcome aboard Captain." We went aboard, heading for the bridge. I felt like a tour guide, engineering, galley, crew berthing etc. we arrived on the Bridge, Jazz and Jade sat down at the helm and navigation stations, running their hands over the controls.

"Sweet." Jazz said.

"The ship is FMC, not stripped out needing a rebuild." Jim said.

"No, as far as we can tell she's fully mission capable, with a full load out," I said.

"If this is the bait, what's the hook?"

"Don't know yet, but I'm sure it's out there."

He nodded, "where's this peace offering you think he sent me?"

We went down to the armory; I palmed the pad, and the hatch opened. I motioned Jim to go first; he stepped in and froze. He looked back at me, and I stuck my head in. The place was packed, there was just enough room to walk down the aisle.

"All of this is mine?"

"Not all, but most. Some of it is for the ship's crew."

"That still leaves a lot of equipment, and some of this equipment is only one gen behind front-line troop equipment. This is bad."

"Why bad?"

"He gave you this ship, and me all this equipment, he wants something big. I hate not knowing when the other shoe will drop."

"You can always turn it down."

He smiled, "not likely."

We walked back out into the hanger.

"We're giving you and your company access to A12 to use as your business headquarters. Well, the first two levels anyway. You probably want to convert one shop to an armory and arms room for storage. Drop a requisition for it, and HMS will pay for it."

"When can we move in?"

"Right away."

"We'll move today."

"Also, we will give you a business office in A14 as the 'face' of the security side of our business," I said.

"I want all traffic to enter through A14, then move over here using the tunnels. I don't want to show all our cards. The team will still live and work over here, they'll just come and go through A14. Everything in A12 stays a secret for as long as possible."

Jim nodded, "make sense."

We look back at the ship.

I glanced at Jim, "you wouldn't know anyone who has captained a Vigilance class ship do you?"

He nodded his head, "I might, I just might. Yep, this is bad, but it should be exciting."

I looked at him, "you know that's a curse, right?"

He smiled, "oh yeah, I think the Legion thought it up. Captain, if there is nothing else, I got calls to make and orders to issue."

"Let's get to it commander."

Commander Jones left, and we went back inside *Vanguard*. On the Bridge, Mal checked the ACE program and crosschecking systems and electronics.

He looked up at me nodding, "looks good, we still have some tweaking to do, but we're good."

I nodded, "*Vanguard*, ship's status?"

"We are operating on shore power, and shore plumbing. All tankage is at 100%. Engineering boards are green and in safety standby. Weapons boards are green and in safety lockdown.

Armory is in safety lockdown. Shield boards are green. Scanner boards are green. Helm and navigation boards are green and in safety standby. Bridge and operation boards are green. Galley boards are green inventory at 100%.

ACE program 100% integrated. Integration with HMS headquarters complete. Safety and security protocols complete and online. Vanguard 100% operational and ready for deployment."

"Status of the ship's munitions load out?"

"Ship's munitions are at 100%."

"Contents of hold?"

"Hold contents are 2, riot suppression, armored grav-car's, and the rest of the CIS platoon combat loadout that would not fit in the armory and arms room."

"Bad indeed, Commander Jones, bad indeed." I mused. "*Vanguard*, do you have a flight Sim program for familiarization?"

"Yes, Captain."

"Jazz would you and Jade like to run through it?"

Both the girls yelled, "yes!"

I sent all our new paperwork, licenses, authorizations, and charters to Aaron, so he could do his lawyer thing. He messaged back he would take care of everything. Commander Jones moved his operations to A12 and A14. They did it at night, after the day crews had gone home. Doc and Mal had had their heads together making upgrades to the med-bay equipment.

***

It took 10 days for Commander Jones to move and set up his operation. They had moved all the CIS team's equipment from *Vanguard* and into their new armory in A12. There was apparently a lot of new equipment, all need to be integrated and teams trained on.

It would be another week before they were fully operational. However, HMS was fully covered and secured. A11 was now empty. After we found the tunnels, we thought it best to get A11 back under our direct control. Travis said they weren't really using it anymore, so he was glad to end the lease, move his materials, and save the money.

It took Commander Jones a week to contact the ship captain we had talked about, and another week for him to arrive. Jazz and Jade were occupying themselves on Vanguard's flight and operation sims. I was looking over engineering systems and shields.

The shield generators were over-engineered, and the emitters were twice the size of the ones on our tug's capture field. These were potentially shielding against missiles and rail guns.

"Are you about ready to break for lunch?" Jazz asked.

"Yeah, I was just looking at the shield generators and emitters."

"Something wrong with them?"

"No, the ship just uses them in a different way, and I was just looking at how it was integrated. I was thinking Mal can do his magic and step up their effectiveness."

After lunch, I went to the engineering shop. I had the cracked force emitters from Taurus on my test bench, with test leads attached to each section of a crack. I was applying power and watching the readings. Nothing unusual was happening. I tossed the socket wrench over the emitter, and it held it in place. I blinked my eyes through all the spectrums my eye was capable of and saw nothing unusual. This was becoming frustrating.

I shut the power off and caught the socket when it fell. I stood there, tossing the socket up and catching. It was like two magnets fighting to hold... It in place... I reapplied power, and tossed the socket back over the FE, it held it.

I got out an old test set with the old-style ring probes. Set the rings up on opposite sides and turned on the screen. There it was. The cracked FE had set up a magnetic fluctuating resonance. No wonder the emitter was holding it, the even cracked numbers kept the balance, odd number cracks held, but repelled when enough power was applied.

I needed to make an FE with insulated separations of odd numbers. I don't know how long I was in the zone, but when I stepped back from the odd-numbered FE's test, Jazz was standing there drinking coffee and eating pastry.

"Pastries for dinner?" I asked.

She smiled, "no baby, you missed dinner its breakfast, I brought you some." My stomach growled. I took a big bite of the pastry she handed me, and a swallow of coffee.

"I had a theory I need to see if I was right." She nodded in her pastry. She pointed with her chin to what I was calling an odd-numbered force, emitter or OFE.

"Where you right?"

"Yeah, tested good, now I have to apply power, and test the mag-flux-resonance."

"Pilot language baby," she smiled, I laughed.

"I'm testing to see if it will push back."

"If you wait a minute, Mal will be back he went to get breakfast."

"He was there before?"

She nodded, "all night, said you are on a roll, and he didn't want to stop you."

I was finished with my pastry and coffee when Mal got

back. He and Jade had brought a tray of pastries and coffee refills. I grabbed another pastry and refilled my cup.

"What you think?" Mal asked, looking at the OFE.

"We need to do a power test, but I think I'm on to something." He nodded and hooked up the low voltage leads of the test generator to the OFE leads.

"Do the odd leads go to ground or neutral?"

"Neutral, I think."

I turned the OFE on its side.

"Ok Mal, apply power." When power was applied, I tossed the socket toward the OFE. It caught and held socket. "Ok, the first test is good. Slowly increased power." As I increased voltage, the socket moved away from the OFE, suddenly the socket shot across the room bouncing around the shop.

"Ok, one last test. Turn the voltage up more, and everyone step behind the armor glass." I found the socket and moved over behind the armor glass. "Now I will throw the socket at the OFE and see if it holds it or throws it back." When we were all ready, I threw the socket, just as I ducked behind the armor glass the socket bounced off of. "Yes!" I yelled.

"Major replay video last test." The images appeared on the wall. The socket almost reached the OFE and at the same speed shot away.

"Amazing", Jade said.

"How much power did you apply to the emitter?" I asked.

Mal looked, "five VAC."

"Are you sure?" Mal nodded.

"Is that a good thing or a bad thing?" Jade asked.

"I've never seen a force emitter operate at such low voltage and not do what we saw. Major, all notes and recordings on these tests are now under the HMS company top-secret classification."

"Understood Captain." I need to get some sleep, you're all welcome to stay, lock up when you're done," I said.

A good night's sleep and a big breakfast did wonders. Standing at the galley's window looking out over the hanger, they were getting Jade's tug ready to go to OEM. Enough time had passed. Time to sew discord among the ranks of the enemy. I needed to talk to Mal; I knew he would want in on the operation. I found him in the EL shop; I made sure we were alone.

"Gilbert Planter," I said.

Mal didn't even look up from his work, "what about him?"

"It's time."

"You got a plan?"

"The beginnings of one."

"What can I do?"

I close the door and took a seat at the workbench.

"I'm sure you and Major have been gathering your own Intel on 'Gil', what I think we should do, is let our enemies take care of this little problem. They've been expecting us to confront Gil, go after him head on, I think we should make him a liability to his employers. Let them take care of him."

Mal was nodding thoughtfully, "what do you have in mind?"

"We need video of what he was doing before the attack. We've already got a video of him returning to port after the attack, we need icing on the cake."

"Major, display Planter's financials, displaying all video, display restaurant video, display bar video." Mal said. "You mean something like that?" Mal said, I chuckled.

"Remind me not to make you mad. Let's put together a montage of the time sequence, money trail, then leak it anonymously to the web, and anyone else you might think would be interested."

I was looking at the video of Gil and the bar, "please tell me he's dumb enough to brag about what he did."

Mal smiled, "Major, play bar audio."

"I had caught me a nice size rock, and was staying in the shadows, waiting for the right moment to strike. When the two of them were close together working on the same rock, I swung around the outside picking up speed. I held on to my rock until just before hitting them. I almost got both of them, but one got lucky and moved at the last second. I almost pushed that rock right through that tug." He laughed. "That'll teach those scabs to go against the union. I'll tell you this to, the bosses have got the same plan for those other scabs."

"Never underestimate the stupidity of your enemy." Mal said.

"When you're ready, make sure it plays in that bar last, everyone loves a surprise." I said.

Over lunch Aunt J asked, "have you seen the news about Jade's wreck?" Seems someone leaked video of Mr. Planter making the hit and run and bragging about it. They even had bank records showing credit transfers.

Strangest thing though, they can't seem to take the video off the net, one place will take it down, and it starts again somewhere else. It seemed to start at the union hall, they're thinking it must've been a whistleblower." Aunt J was watching our faces and the rest of the table while she was talking.

"Good for that whistleblower, I guess someone finally got tired of what was going on," I said, Mal nodded and kept eating. Jazz and Jade smiled at each other and went back to eating.

By dinner time Gilbert Planter was taken into custody, proclaiming his innocence to anyone who would listen. The Planter video mysteriously stopped running at 2100. I guess a whistleblower was content for the moment.

Commander Jones messaged us that the Captain he had recommended was on station. He requested a meeting in the morning at 0900. We confirmed the meeting and requested the file, so we could vet him, and be ready for the meeting.

Captain Welsbey's, late of the ESFL, the file was sparse. This file gave him high praise while on missions but was less than stellar on routine operations. Some highlights were; argumentative, reads into orders to suit his agendas, does not get along well with his fellow Captains, overbearing, etc.

"I hope he does better in person than on paper," I said.

Commander Jones introduced us to Captain Welsbey and left us. We all got coffees and took our seats.

"Good flight in Captain?" I asked.

"They rarely are," He said looking at each of us. "You're the HMS board?"

"We are." I answered.

"Did your rich parents buy it for you?" The tension in the room rose, I was wondering if he was testing me.

"No, actually it's been in the family for almost 100 years, I did however inherit when my parents were killed."

"Ahh." He said, as if that answered everything. "And the E&S ship I'm to command, how did you acquire that?"

"That's a classified corporate secret."

"It's legal I assume?"

"It is." He nodded, "I'll bring my crew."

"I'm sorry Captain Welsbey, I'm confused, I thought you were the one being interviewed, not us."

"Oh, you will hire me, I'm just deciding if I want to take the berth, I'm not a pleasure yacht Captain. I have some other requirements." I held my finger to stop him for he got on a roll. He stopped, looking angry that I'd interrupted him.

"Major."

"Yes, Captain."

"Pull up Captain Welsbey's ticket invoice for his entire trip to Conclave, double it, add 3000 creds to that number and credit his account please."

"Done Captain." Captain Welsbey's P-comm blipped receiving confirmation of payment.

"Thank you for your time Captain Welsbey we'll not be requiring your services, good day. The conference room door opened, and two security guards were waiting to escort him out. His face was bright red with anger. He left without a word.

Commander Jones stepped in, "I take it that the interview did not go well."

"That's one way of putting it," I answered.

"I'm sorry Captain, I thought he had learned after the last mission, but I guess not."

"I'm not even going to ask," I said. He nodded and left the

room.

"Why did you grab my arm?" Jazz asked Jade.

"Because you were about to go across the table and scratch his eyes out." Jade laughed, we all joined in.

"Major, pull Captain Williams' file, and message *Dumpty* to return to HMS for a maintenance inspection, once he has delivered his load to OEM."

"Done Captain." We reviewed Captain Williams's file; he had served as Second Mate on an E&S ship. He had excellent reviews and recommendations. We'll talk to him when he gets in from this run. We could find a hauler Captain easier than we could find an E&S Captain.

***

We had our three tugs in the hanger, having the graveler upgrade installed. *Beast* was coming along nicely with the refurb. I worked out with security teams on my hand-to-hand in the mornings. I was a little rusty, and had catching up to do, but I didn't embarrass myself. Training with the batons was great, I got to practice integrating offensive and defensive moves, and the "slap" let you know when you were too slow or out of position.

I asked Cmdr. Jones about setting up separate classes for anyone who wanted to train. To my surprise, Pam jumped at the chance. She said she knew I had trained in MMA to help my coordination and balance. She thought it would help her too.

CHAPTER 15

The *Humpty* was due in the next day, and I messaged Captain Williams to meet with us in the conference room at 1500, he confirmed. I was still working on the OFE's trying to figure out how we could implement and integrate what we had learned. This could mean a big jump in our shield technology, if I can get everything worked out. I needed a break, so I stepped down the hall to see what Mal was up to.

I stuck my head in the door, "hey, I need a break, want to go up for a coffee?"

He got up from the stool stretching his back, "yeah, I need a break too." We started up the stairs for the galley.

"What are you been working on?" I asked.

"I've done some tweaking on *Vanguard.* Streamlined her systems, and systems integration, also been helping Doc upgrade the med-bay equipment. You?"

"Not much, keeping HMS heading in the right direction, upgrading tugs, keeping *Beast* on track, working on the OFE's. If I can get the integration problem figured out, this could be big. I mean orders of magnitude big."

"What you mean integration problem?" He asked, filling his coffee cup. I filled mine and went over to the table.

"A normal FE is wired individually and then computer-controlled on how much force to emit. I'm thinking, since the OFE is already acting like more than one emitter, it needs to be connected and controlled differently."

Mal got "that look." "Have you thought about series parallel wiring and then the controller?" He asked.

I thought a minute, "wouldn't that require a controller at

the emitter?"

"Maybe not, let's try this, you build six or eight of the emitters and wire them in series parallel then I'll take them and see what I can do about controlling them."

"Sounds good." I said.

Captain Williams met with us at 1500. He gave us a full report on the runs and a few minor maintenance issues he had had. Overall, he had been making good runs and was turning a good profit, which made the crew happy because they made more money on their shares.

"We have another opportunity we'd like to discuss with you. We have gained an E&S ship, and we need a Captain for her. You'll be working with the security teams and as overwatch for HMS ships."

We laid out the whole picture for him on what had happened since he had been out on his runs. He listened, asking a few questions to clarify. He sat and thought, nodding with pursed lips.

Deciding, "I think what would be best for HMS and the security teams would be to have Captain Smythe move over to the E&S ship and slide me over to take the cargo ship. He's captained an E&S ship; I've only served on one. I'll even take First Mate on her under him, if you can get another cargo Captain."

I nodded, "Reggie's due back in a few weeks, we'll let things stand as is until he is back. Then we'll all get together and talk this out. You and your crew take three days off, then make another run out to the miners."

"Yes sir, the crew will be glad for the shore leave."

I was working down in my shop, making OFE's, just out of curiosity I made one that had seven sections instead of five sections. I tested the input and output and was shocked. The input was less, and the output was substantially more.

I realize that five and seven were prime numbers; I don't know if they had anything to do with it, but what the heck. I tried 11 and 13 as the readings kept changing, lower input, hirer output. There was no appreciable change after 13. Just off the cuff I made nine OFE's with 13 segments.

I wired eight of them series parallel and tested the input and output. Everything was holding steady. I wired in the ninth OFE, making the total an odd number. I tested again, the input remained the same, but the output increased by 25%. I wondered what would happen if I stayed with the prime number of emitters. I made more OFE's with the 13 segments and wire them into my test board. The input remained the same, but the output jumped up 75%. I couldn't begin to do the math to explain what I was seeing.

I ran down to the EL shop, "Mal, you gotta come see this!" He sat on the stool looking at the test board and listening as I explained what I found.

When I finished, he asked "why did you use prime numbers?"

"No reason, it struck me to try primes, we were already using odds."

He was deep in thought, "did you do a mag-flux-resonance reading?"

I face palmed, "I did not." We got out the magnetic field test set and set it up. The test screen lit up. There was a perfectly formed mag-flux-resonance shell covering the front side of the test board.

"It only covers the way the emitters are facing." I said. We shut down the power supply and disconnected six of the emitters. We reinstall them on the back of the test board. We kept the input power low and turned them on. We turned the mag field test set back on; the two sides had formed a perfect interlocking sphere. We looked at each other, "I'm not throwing anything at it." I said. Mal laughed.

"Major?"

"Yes Mal?"

"This is another corporate secret, lock it up."

"Yes sir, locked."

We worked on the C23 project as we called it. C23 was the position of the original cracked emitter that started all this.

After 10 days straight, we finally had a working prototype. Now we need to install it on the ship, and *Taurus* seemed the most logical candidate. She had plenty of power to drive the extra emitters, and Misty could control integration.

It took 23 OFE's to get complete coverage on *Taurus*. Weird. 23. Was the universe trying to tell me something, or just laughing at me. We placed a cover over the emitters so no one could see the emitter segments. They looked like any other emitter, only a little larger. Took us three more days to get everything tied into all of *Taurus'* systems.

"Feedback," Mal said.

"What?" I asked.

"Feedback," he said, "the OFE's will not work at the same time as the other FEs, they won't overlap they will fight each other."

"Okay, no problem, for now we'll just have to use one at a time."

"I think we're ready, we need to do a test flight," Mal said.

"I'll call the girls," I said.

***

They were ready for something new to do, the flight Sim had gotten old. Jazz filed a test flight, flight plan, and took us out into the rock field. Mal started his calibrations, and crosscheck tests.

"We're all green on the boards," Mal said, "I think we're ready for the next phase of our test."

"We all need to get into our vac suits just in case something goes wrong," I said. They all nodded and moved to get suited up. Putting on a Vac suit in *Taurus* gave me a déjà vu feeling.

We all took our places, "Misty, status of shield generators?"

"Shield generators online, green across the board, Captain."

"Ok, Mal, bring the shields online."

"Shields online, bringing power up slowly. Standby, we

have a little fluctuation. We're okay, just a minor adjustment. We are at 100% coverage on shields and holding. Shield generators holding a 20% output."

"Now the fun begins, find us some sand to fly through." I said.

"I know just the place." Jazz said. She flew us to a different area, and we scanned. "There's what we want." She said.

"Take us through slowly." I said. We moved through the sand and waited. Nothing happened, no sound, no nothing. "Any fluctuations on your readings?" I asked Mal.

"Nothing."

"I put us right in the middle." Jazz said.

"Take us back through. Mal, increase sensitivity readings." Jazz took us back through.

"Nothing, I have it at max sensitivity, and I barely read a blip." Mal said.

"Thicker sand maybe?" I asked.

"We came out here to test, so let's test." Jazz said, Jade nodded.

"Misty, scan for a denser sand field, and plot a course."

"Course on screen, Captain."

"Take us through Jazz." She nodded. As we passed through, there was no sound, but Mal got more of a reading.

I shook my head, "I'm so slow sometimes. Misty, show the view from dorsal camera."

"On screen, Captain." Everyone groaned.

"Misty, replay us passing through the sand field." We all watched, "Replay at 10 X magnification." We watched, "replay at 100 X magnification. Would you look at that."

"It's like the sand is flying right around us." Jade said.

"Around the shield actually." Mal said.

"Jazz increase speed and take us back through." We watch the same results.

"Mal, think she's ready for a small rock, a glancing blow maybe?" I asked.

"We can't find out any sooner." He said.

"Misty, scan for small rock about a pound in size and plot a course."

"Course plotted."

"Jazz, match speed and course, then slow down and turn in front. Everyone seal your Vac suit. Misty track the rock's impact on cameras."

"Yes, Captain."

Jazz got us in the position, slowed and put us in the path of that rock. We heard nothing, just saw a line across the screen, Mal registered a small blip.

"Misty, zoom in on the impact point and give us a slow-motion view." The view showed the rock impacting on the force shield, shattering then sliding around the shield. We kept trying bigger and bigger rocks, with the same results, no increase in power drain.

"Misty, percentage charge on force shield batteries?" I asked.

"Force shield batteries at 100%."

"The force shield generators are recharging the batteries?"

"No, recharge is coming from the energy of the impacts on the force shield."

"Incredible, the shield drains the inertial energy, and recharges the batteries." Mal said.

"We need a bigger impact."

"How big are you thinking?" I asked.

"One big enough and going fast enough to go through the ship."

"Oh, is that all, I thought you wanted to do something dangerous." I said.

"Ok, I know it sounds crazy, but according these readings the shield, for lack of a better word, steals energy from whatever hits it, and uses that energy against the strike."

"You're right, it sounds crazy."

"I can't believe I'm about to say this. Jazz, let Misty have the helm."

"Misty has the helm."

"Misty, find us a 100-pound rock, put us on an intercept course. Calculate speed of impact, that without shields, the rock would pass through the ship. Point of impact is to be where the rock would pass through cabin 2. Seal cabin 2 and evac O2."

"I have complied with all parameters set, standing by to execute orders."

"Strap in everyone. Dear God, don't let me screw this up. Misty, execute."

"Executing in, three–two–one–now."

The star field through the armor glass skewed, and we accelerated.

"All boards are green." Mal said.

"Force shield generators online, force shield batteries at 100% charge. Target acquired, Vector calculated and acquired, calculated velocity reached, impact in five–four." I close my eyes, gritted my teeth and gripped my seatbelt. "Three–two–one–now." There was no noise, no shuttering, no klaxon.

"Target destroyed, all systems and boards are green, force shield generator online, force shield batteries at 100%," Misty reported.

"Misty, all stop."

"All stop, Captain."

"Show rock impact area, slow-motion, 10 X magnification." The rock entered the frame and shattered, but this time it didn't go around us, it was just gone. "Speed of rock on impact?" I asked.

"250 KPH."

"Misty, did you detect anything breaching the force shield?"

"No Captain, it destroyed the target upon impacting. Force shield increased in power and 1% in size, it bled excess energy off, force shield has returned to original size." I shook my head and looked at Mal.

"Any ideas?"

"That's so deep into quantum physics and quantum mechanics, let's just say, it's beyond me." He said.

"I have a question." Jade said.

"You said we could only use the force shield or the FE capture field but not both at one time, right?"

Mal nodded, "right."

"Then how are we able to use our gravitonics and our force shield at the same time? Isn't grav and mag basically the same thing?" She asked.

"That's because they operate on different grav harmonics." I stopped and looked at Mal, "it couldn't be that simple." He shrugged his shoulders and started typing code.

"Give me a minute. Changing shield harmonic frequency. Would you look at that, out of the mouths of babes. Jade, you're a genius. Everything works together with no problems."

"Captain, Conclave Control is hailing us."

"Put them on."

"On Captain."

"*Taurus*, this is Conclave Control acknowledge."

"Conclave Control, this is *Taurus*."

"*Taurus*, this is Conclave is everything all right, you dropped off our screens like you blew up or something." I looked at Mal, he typed.

"No, control we're all good here."

"There you are, we have you back on screens. It must've been a glitch, will log it for maintenance, Conclave out."

"Roger, *Taurus* out. What just happened?" I asked.

"When I change the shield harmonic frequency, I inadvertently changed it to the same harmonic frequency as space. Our shields made us look like 'empty' space. I shifted our harmonics up a few octaves of frequency, so they could see us again," Mal said.

"So, we were invisible to their scans?"

"Yeah, for all intents and purposes."

"That could be useful, keep that setting handy. As of now, standard operation procedures are shields up all the time."

"Misty, test flight and results are corporate secret encrypted."

"Yes, Captain."

"Take us home Jazz, we have a lot of data to analyze."

***

Captain Smythe was inbound toward Conclave. I messaged him to bring the ship in for maintenance, give his crew a week of shore leave, and come in for a debrief.

Aunt J came into my office and sat down, "good morning."

"Good morning, long time no see, it's been what, 30 minutes sense we had breakfast together?"

She smiled, "I got some interesting news. Mr. Planter's wife went to visit him at detention yesterday." I waited for the other shoe to drop. "After the meeting, she went to the Port and boarded a ship headed for Titan."

"I guess she'd had enough."

"That's what I thought until they found Gilbert dead in his cell this morning. Poison, they say."

"It's not healthy to be a loose end with these people," I said, "If I had to guess, his wife took him a message. Something like, you die, or your wife and family does, you make the choice. She may have even given him the poison to do the job."

"On a brighter note, I heard I missed an interesting test flight yesterday."

"It was, this will be as big as ACE, when we announce it."

She nodded, "if the government doesn't seize it. We may want to talk to our friend and get covering before the vultures hear about it."

"You think it'll get that bad?"

"Something this big, it's not if, it's when. Tell him to bring one of his ships in for upgrades and tests." She said.

I sent an encrypted message to Admiral Cole that we had made a significant breakthrough in shield technology and suggested he bring a ship in for upgrades. The reply came back within the hour.

"30 days" was all it said. I went to find Mal, we had 30 days to come up with a plan. I found Mal in the EL shop.

"We have a problem."

"Anyone hurt?" He said, standing up.

"Not that kind of problem. When I said our shield tech would be huge, I was thinking too small." I relayed the conversation I'd had with Aunt J, and what she advised, and the message I'd sent to the Admiral. Mal paced the shop. I waited for him to process it all.

He turned, "I agree, we aren't thinking big enough. With our shield tech, we have just become the apex predator. The world powers and corporate powers will lose their minds. You have a plan?" He asked.

"We need to figure a way to make different levels of the shielding. Something like mil-spec, corporate level, and a civilian level. I don't like the idea of someone confiscating our ideas and we have no say so in the matter," I said.

"I would flush it before I let them take it." Mal said.

"I agree, I would burn it to the ground before I let them take it."

"As another precaution, I think we need to upgrade A11 through A14 shields, if push comes to shove, we can push back. Also, we will hold back the vanishing act from everyone, we'll keep that as our ace in the hole."

"My first thought of how to level the shield is to step down the primes. We'll start at five segments for the small civilian ships like tugs, seven segments for corporate and larger ships like haulers and cargoes, and 11 segments for mil-spec. We keep the rest for ourselves." I said.

"We need to come up with a way to tamper-proof the OFE's. The controllers are in the ACE, so they're safe." I said.

"I'll start on the tamper-proof OFE's if you'll make leveled OFE's," Mal said looking at his computer.

"Good, I'll make fives and have them installed on one of our tugs. Then some sevens for our haulers and cargoes, and 11 for *Vanguard* for now. We may upgrade her later. I don't completely trust our friend just yet, if ever."

"Yeah, if ever." Mal said.

***

The board met with Captain Smythe, and he gave us his briefing on the trip. It had been profitable overall. After he completed his briefing, we told him what he had missed, well most of it.

"We have a new E&S ship in our fleet, and we want you to Captain her. We'll shift Captain Williams over to take the cargo ship. You'll also be working with Commander Jones and the security teams on some of their missions and flying overwatch for HMS ships." He nodded.

Aunt J went back to her office. She was running the business more and more these days. The rest of us went to A12 to see the *Vanguard*. Tunnel traffic was more than when we first used it. The whole security company was now living in A12. We exited the lift into A12's hanger, and our first site was *Vanguard*. We walked over to her.

"I never tire of seeing these ships, a true thing of beauty," Reggie said.

"She is that." I answered.

"You know Nic, the legion is a small community, a kind of family. A dysfunctional one, I'll admit, but a family. I'm sure you've heard the phrase, once Legion, always Legion."

I nodded, "I have."

"When I was still active, there would be low visibility missions, we would visit different places to see different people. I will not ask where the ship came from, just know that strings will be attached."

I nodded, "want the ship?"

He nodded, "I do, Sir."

"Good, how many crew members are you bringing over from the cargo ship?"

He thought a moment, "maybe 10."

"Let's let Captain Williams know he'll need 10 new crewmen."

We pulled Earl and his group of engineers off of making Grav-bars and started them making OFE's. We made 11's for Vanguard; we figured we'd need 43 for full coverage. Once those were finished we start making fives for tugs and the Hab upgrades.

I messaged Reggie to meet us at *Vanguard*. We would move her over to A14. I had to call Jazz and Jade to move *Vanguard* because if I didn't, they would never find my body. We were on the Bridge of *Vanguard* with Jazz and Jade at the helm.

"*Vanguard*?"

"Yes, Captain?"

"Bring all systems online, make ready for departure."

"Bringing all systems to safety standby in preparation for departure."

"*Vanguard* notify A12 hanger control we will do a remote departure, but standby as a safety protocol."

"Remote departure acknowledged, Captain."

"*Vanguard,* open hanger doors for departure."

"Hanger doors opening."

"Bring gravitonics online, exited the hanger, dead slow."

"Exiting the hanger dead slow."

"Jazz, get us clearance from Conclave Control for a local test flight."

"Yes Captain, clearance granted."

"Bring engines online."

"Engines online, Captain."

"*Vanguard,* Jazz and Jade have the helm."

"Aye Captain, Jazz and Jade have the helm."

"Okay ladies take us out, so we can get a straight run it A14, and don't scratch the paint."

"If their grins get any bigger, their heads will split open," Reggie said chuckling.

"They've been dying to do this since we got her."

"This baby handles like a dream." Jazz said.

I let them enjoy themselves, "sorry ladies time to go back

to work. Jazz, all stop."

"All stop, Captain."

"*Vanguard*, do you recognize Captain Reggie Smythe?"

"I do Captain, Captain Smythe is Senior Captain of the HMS, assigned to the cargo ship *Star Duster*."

"Captain Smythe is being transferred from *Star Duster* and will assume command of *Vanguard* as of now. I relinquish captaincy of *Vanguard*, acknowledge transfer of command."

"Transfer of command from Commodore Haydock to Captain Smythe acknowledged."

I turned to Reggie, "you have the con, Captain."

"Thank you, Commodore. Jazz take us to A14 please. I think we have work to do."

"Aye Captain, returning to A14."

CHAPTER 16

We took 15 days to finish *Vanguard's* shield upgrade and integrating all her systems into the weapons grid. Mal was able to integrate the laser capacitors, rail guns and battery recharging into the shield recharge system. Once upgrades were complete, we were sending Captain Smythe and his hand-picked crew out for a shakedown cruise on *Vanguard*.

"Reggie, I want to make this clear, these systems, especially the shields, are top-secret. No one has anything like this. If the secret gets out before we are ready, well, catastrophic will be an understatement.

We called "our friend" and told him to bring his first ship in for upgrades. We need his covering to keep the wolves at bay, without us getting involved. We have enough trouble as it is," I said.

"I see. So, 'our friend' is pulling on the string for upgrades," Reggie said.

"Yes, but the shields weren't part of the deal, we had not invented them. To pay for getting the shields, he will have to cover us."

"If the systems test and perform like you said, he'll do whatever it takes to seal the deal, and he needs the deal. He has his own wolves to deal with. We'll give her a good shakedown test, Sir."

"You may depart when ready, Captain."

***

Aunt J had filled in for me as CEO, while Mal and I were upgrading ship shields and Hab shields in preparation for the

Admiral's visit. She hired another hauler Captain to fill Captain Williams vacancy. She also filled all other crew vacancies. We had not installed the new shields on the haulers or the cargo ship; we were waiting to see what kind of covering the Admiral could give us.

A11, A12, and A14 we upgraded shields to OEF 5's, except for the main Hanger doors. Those got OEF 11's. Call me paranoid, but the more I thought about the shields going public, the more concerned I became.

I received a message from Reggie, "astounding, returning to base." We had the haulers and *Taurus* out working the fields again. Jazz and Jade were going stir crazy, so we put them to work. So far, no other incidents occurred. We felt better knowing *Taurus* had her shields, and they were always online.

Vanguard returned to A12; we went over to meet them. Reggie had held the crew on board awaiting our arrival. We boarded for the shakedown cruise debrief.

We arrived on the Bridge, "gentlemen, we, the crew and I don't have enough words to explain how we feel about the *Vanguard*. We would put her up against any four of the legions' 'ships of the line' and win the engagement. The system integrations you have done, and what *Vanguard*'s ACE does is beyond compare. You'll get your covering, no doubt about it. He will do nothing to interfere with him getting these upgrades."

"Outstanding Captain, this is great news. We expect our friend to arrive sometimes within the next week. I'm sure they'll want a demonstration of our assessments. Do you have any recommendations on what we could do to show *Vanguard*'s capabilities?" I asked.

"Wargames." Reggie said. The whole crew was nodding their heads and grinning.

"Wargames? I have a general idea of what that is, but will that show them what *Vanguard* is capable of?" I asked.

"Well, we'll leave the final decision up to our friend, but I think they'll want it at some point. Either way, *Vanguard* will be ready."

Three days later the ESFL light cruiser *Invincible* arrived. They sent a coded message with coordinates for what I assumed was our meeting place. Within the hour Mal and I departed on *Vanguard*. Our rendezvous point was well away from traffic with plenty of room to maneuver. The Admiral arrived on *Invincible*'s skiff and joined us in the galley.

"Admiral, it's good of you to come. May I introduce Captain Smythe, Captain of the *Vanguard*."

"It's good to see you again, Reggie," The Admiral said. "I guess civilian life isn't too boring for you."

"No sir, these two keep things interesting."

"So it would seem. This new shielding tech, its operational on this ship?" He asked Reggie.

"It is Sir."

"Your assessment?"

"Easily twice as good as anything the Legion has, Sir." The Admiral look at Reggie for a moment, then looked at us.

"Captain Smythe is *Vanguard* prepared for level II battle Sim?" The Admiral asked.

"She is, Sir."

"Very well, shall we go to the bridge and tell *Invincible* the good news?"

The two ships separated, then faced off.

"Ok Captain, show me what you got." After the third pass, the Admiral stopped us. *Vanguard* was taking as many hits as she was giving, but the hits were barely registering.

The Admiral look to the readings, "*Vanguard* will stay at level II, *Invincible* will go to level III." We started again, same results.

"*Invincible* go to level IV," The Admiral said, his eyes glued to the readouts. We made another pass with the same results.

The two ships separated, "Admiral," I said, "you came a long way to see what we had, so allow us to show you what *Vanguard* can really do." The Admiral look at Reggie, he nodded.

"*Invincible*, take the gloves off."

"*Vanguard* confirm last transmission."

"Confirmed *Invincible*, take the gloves off, don't nuke us, but you have permission to rough the paint up."

"Roger *Vanguard*, roughing the paint."

I looked at Reggie, "give the Admiral the full show, give *Vanguard* the helm."

Reggie smiled, "Vanguard."

"Yes, Captain."

"*Vanguard* has the helm prepare for Sim engagement at level II."

"*Vanguard* has the helm, Sim engagement level II, acknowledged." The Admiral's eyebrows rose to his hairline.

"*Vanguard*, attack plan Victor one, engage," Reggie said.

"Engaging Victor one."

The star field out of the armor glass skewed. *Vanguard* went in hard and fast. We engaged a full spread of laser fire as we passed and were away. *Invincible* gave a good account of herself. She tried to rough up our paint. The readings on our shields got up to 18%, the batteries were still at full charge.

"*Vanguard* engage target 'to the knife' battle Sim level II." Reggie said.

"Engaging 'to the knife' battle Sim level II."

"This will show you what I think you came to see Admiral." Reggie said. There is no fancy flying this time, *Vanguard* went in toe-to-toe with *Invincible*. *Invincible* fired as soon as *Vanguard* was in range. *Vanguard* matched *Invincible* speed and vector and fired her lasers continuously, rotating to allow them to cool but maintain intensity.

Invincible was firing everything she had, lasers, missiles, and finally she fired one round from her railgun at our stern. The Admiral called a cease-fire.

"Standby *Invincible*," The Admiral said. "Replay your shield, laser, and battery readings during the last engagement." *Vanguard* did so. The Admiral watched the reading shaking his head, "she was never registering over 27% even with all the drain on shields and laser, capacitors batteries never drop below 96%. You didn't have this when last met." It was a statement, not a question.

"No Admiral, we did not."

"*Invincible*?"

"On speaker, Admiral," *Vanguard* said.

"*Invincible*," they answered.

"What did your battle Sim computer judge in the last engagement?"

"We died halfway through it, we kept firing trying to bring down those shields. How did we fare *Vanguard*, how close were you to shield failure?"

The Admiral laughed, "how close you came is classified, let's just say I have to buy a new set of dishes for their galley."

We heard laughter from *Invincible's* bridge, "you said rough of the paint, Sir."

The Admiral laughed, "that I did *Invincible*, that I did. *Vanguard* out. Let's get coffee." He said, heading for the galley.

Sitting around the galley table, "your assessment Captain Smythe?"

"Admiral, with this new shield tech, ESFL will have total space superiority, no one could even come close to this." The Admiral and looked at Mal and I.

"That's my assessment as well." The Admiral said, taking a swallow of his coffee. "Do you realize how big this is, how much you changed the status quo? Don't get me wrong, I'm not complaining, I just want you to realize that everyone will beat a path to your door."

"We're realizing it, hence our call to you as soon as we ensured they worked. We didn't want government agency showing up claiming national security and stealing our work."

"It wouldn't be governments. Conclave is an independent state so there is no 'national security' involved. I'm sure corporations will try to steal it as soon as the info is out, if it's not already. What's this going to cost me?"

"What are you offering?" I asked.

"Have you applied for a patent?" We shook our heads.

"Apply for your patent to the ESFL, that will keep the details as secret as possible, for a time anyway. I presume you have the equipment sealed against tampering and reverse engineering."

We nodded. The Admiral was deep in thought, probably looking at the chessboard in his head. Reviewing all the pieces and moves we changed on his board.

"How about lunch while you consider your options, Admiral." Reggie said.

"A fine idea, Captain." The Admiral answered.

We were enjoying a light lunch of soup and sandwiches. Chef sent out plenty of food he didn't scrimp on the galley supplies, and our messman knew his business.

"How long would it take you to upgrade *Invincible*?" The Admiral asked.

"Without looking at her equipment and engineering, I'm guessing a month, a little more maybe." I said,

The Admiral nodded, "you know I don't like coming to the bargaining table without my chips, so here's what will do. Reggie will give me a ride home; you take *Invincible* in for upgrades. I'll be back in three weeks with my chips. We'll go from there. I'll give *Invincible* her orders. No liberty, this will stay as low-keyed as possible. The crew will assist with the work."

The Admiral was more used to issuing orders than making requests. In this instance I didn't mind. Within the hour *Vanguard* departed with the Admiral, and we were on the *Invincible* on our way to A14. Upon boarding Mal and I gave Captain Parker, the commander of the *Invincible*, a gift. After introductions, I handed him a coffee mug from *Vanguard*.

"The only dish *Invincible* didn't break, the Admiral happen to be holding it, his uniform will need cleaning."

Captain Parker accepted the mug, laughing as he shook our hands. "No hard feelings I hope."

"Not at all Captain, glad were on the same side."

I messaged A14 to expect us with guests. We parked outside A14 hanger, *Invincible* was too big to fit completely inside our hanger. We told Captain Parker we would start upgrades in the morning. On the way in Mal and I had surveyed everything we need to see to do the upgrades.

***

We met with Bob and laid out the work we would do, and he put his crews together.

As a family we sat at dinner together, Jazz asked, "did you trade *Vanguard*, or is that one a loaner?" She smiled.

We chuckled, "it's a loaner, but needs work. The owner needed a ride home to get his checkbook. Reggie's given him a lift."

"I'm guessing he's interested in the product?" Aunt J asked.

"Very, he agreed with your assessment on the competition. That's why he needed his checkbook." I replied.

"We have to watch for wooden creds." She said.

"And hooks in the checkbook," I said. Lifting my cup, "confusion to the enemy" I toasted. Everyone raised their cups.

"Confusing to the enemy!" They replied.

We started work on the *Invincible* as planned the next morning. Mal was installing the ACE program and computer upgrades. Bob and his crews were starting work in engineering. I had Earl's group making OFE 11's. It would take a good bit of additional wire to install the new OFE's. We had to wire them in series parallel, it almost doubled our wiring requirements. *Invincible* had a good crew, and an excellent engineering department. Things were running smoother than expected. We cut no corners, but we didn't dawdle either. We all wanted to finish before the Admiral returned.

We completed *Invincible's* refit in 19 days. All test pad tests were successful, and Captain Parker took *Invincible* out for her shakedown cruise. Mal went with them, to make sure his baby was correctly and completely integrated. Jazz was miffed that she didn't get to man the helm. Everything checked out and *Invincible* had Mal back by midafternoon.

"Satisfied customer?" I asked as Mal came in.

"You could say so, if they smiled any bigger their faces would break."

***

The *Vanguard* arrived the next morning, Reggie came over for breakfast.

He came up to the family table, "have room for a party of one?" He asked.

"Always," I said, "Welcome home, have a good trip?"

"Interesting, we stopped by Titan and picked up another passenger. An engineer," We all continued eating, allowing Reggie to catch up with his meal.

Over coffee I ask, "an engineer, huh?"

Reggie nodded smiling, "Yep, our friend had him look over our equipment. He seemed frustrated. Said he understood what it did, and why. But did not understand how," Reggie said, chuckling.

"You saw our friend safely home I take it?"

"Yes Sir, he said he'd see us in a week or two. I also brought orders for *Invincible*, since their upgrades were complete. They are on their way home as we speak."

"You and your crew take a week off, and unwind, we'll call you if we need you."

We pulled the haulers in one at a time and installed OFE 5s on them and put them back to work. We'd upgrade the cargo ship the next time she was in port between runs. All our other ships, tugs, and Habs now had the new shields. We also upgraded the Hab's old asteroid defense grid rail guns, with heavier modified rail guns. Now we'd wait for the Admiral to return and see what kind of deal he would offer us.

***

Commander Jones stuck his head in my office, "got a minute?"

"Sure, come on in, grab a cuppa." He got a cup of coffee and took a seat while I refilled my cup. "What's on your mind, Jim?"

"I've been noticing all the upgrades to the ships and equipment."

I took a sip of my coffee, looking at him, "and?"

"And," he took a swallow his coffee, "I was wondering if you'd considered adding shields to the grav-cars."

I stared at him for a minute, considering, "no, actually, the thought never crossed my mind."

"Is it possible?"

"Hold that thought. Major ask Mal to come to my office, please."

Moments later Mal came in, nodded at Jim, "what's up?"

"Jim has an interesting idea; I wanted your take on."

"Ok, what's the idea?"

I nodded at Jim.

"Putting shields on the armored grav-cars," Jim said.

"How are they powered?" Mal asked.

"A small generator charges the batteries that runs everything." Jim answered.

"ACE control?" Mal asked, looking at me.

"Why not, that may be another market?"

Mal nodded, "I don't see why not. Sounds like fun. Let's do it."

I knew what Jazz would say, "boys and their toys..."

It turned out to be a little more challenging than we expected. In space we didn't have to allow for the deck, walls, or people. It took more flux manipulation control than we were used to. We thought we could use a small ACE machine to run it, but it turned out we needed a full-sized one.

We had to put low-power fives on them to handle the additional flux manipulation. Having a separate section that could be turned off to open the rear door while keeping the rest of the car covered was difficult.

"Captain, Mister Gunny is requesting docking instruction for his cargo ship," Major said.

"Have them dock at A14 and let them know we have company."

"Yes, Captain."

We all greeted Gunny, he had another shipment for Doc and other miscellaneous equipment. The Admiral was there as before blending in with the workers. We moved the meeting to the conference room. We had chef bring in coffee and snacks. After we all served ourselves, we sat down.

"Captain Parker reports all went well with his refit. He is extremely pleased with your work and the new equipment," the Admiral said.

"Glad to hear it, he's got a good crew, and they helped expedite the work," I replied.

"Any changes here, anyone come knocking on your door?" He asked.

"Not yet, we've kept everything in-house. We're only installing shields on our own ships. We've not offered them to anyone else yet."

The Admiral nodded, "I saw that you applied for your patent on the ESFL, so we're good there. Here's what I can offer you as far as covering you from governments and corporations who come at you legally. You are now contracted by the ESFL for R&D, this does not prevent you from selling or trading your tech. It will keep anyone from taking it from you legally. The illegal you'll have to deal with on your own.

What we want is the shield tech, but we'll not always be able to come here for the installation of the upgrades and repairs. What we'll offer for the shields, upgrades, and refits is a Space Dock and Repair Vessel (SDRV). That way we can meet you at different times and locations to have work done.

I will sign the SDRV over to you as payment. She's not as new as the *Vanguard*, and not in the same shape as the *Vanguard* was. She's being replaced and was being retried. She has some new tech, but she can't keep up with the fleet, she's just not fast enough. We loaded her with new parts that you'll need to make her FMC, and to help with upgrading her.

As part of the deal and turning the SDRV over to you, we

will need two of your 50 KLT tugs, with the new shields and crusher programs. They will be assigned to our new SDRV to feed her smelter. The SDRV you're getting also has a new full-sized Magna flux 3-D printer, and two smaller ones.

You, as a contracted R&D provider for the ESFL are authorized to have and use them. Gunny has all the authorization forms, and certificates for all the equipment on the ship. He also has other goodies being unloaded now.

The SDRV *Brokkr* should arrive in 2 days. We'll stay until then to take her crew back with us. Do you think you could install an ACE program on our cargo ship before the *Brokkr* arrives?"

I looked at Mal, "we can do in 2 days, unless something crazy happens," Mal said.

We signed over two of our upgraded 50 KLT tugs to the Admiral and had them loaded into the cargo ship. Mal started right away installing the ACE program on their cargo ship. We had gotten so good at installing the ACE programs that Van Dam had sold, Mal was done in less than a day.

CHAPTER 17

"Captain?" Major woke me.

"What is a Major?"

"Our security team guarding Mister Jocko is under attack and requesting backup and extraction."

"Take us to red alert, open channels to the Security Command Team."

"Channel open."

"Commander Jones, if you have not already, send a grav-car and back up to support Jocko's team."

"Backup will be in route in one minute," Commander Jones said.

"Send the second car and team to support Van Dam's team just in case."

"Roger, on it."

"Captain, there have been explosions at the Van Dam HQ."

"Let them know backup is on the way. Jim?"

"I heard we're on it."

"Captain, I'm tracking a tug pushing a rock vectoring toward us, there is an 87% probability the tug is lining up to releases payload targeting A14. Bringing shields from safety standby to online, bringing all defense rail guns online and targeting the rock when it's in range."

"Tell Gunny to keep his cargo ship where it is, it's safe behind our shields. And give Gunny updates on what is happening. Reggie, get *Vanguard* out on overwatch."

"Roger Sir, *Vanguard* will launch in two minutes."

"Captain we have incoming; the tug has released its payload targeting A14."

"*Vanguard* don't worry about the rock, Major has it covered, destroy that tug."

"Roger Commodore, *Vanguard* away."

"Time to railgun engagement Major?"

"30 seconds to the railgun engagement." The channels were quiet. "Rail guns engaging..., Main rock shattered..., Debris will still impact A14 shields..., Impacting now."

We felt vibrations through the ground, nothing got through our shields, but the landscape outside of our shields took a hammering.

"HMS base, this is *Vanguard*, target destroyed."

"Roger *Vanguard* assume overwatch."

"Roger HMS, *Vanguard* assuming overwatch."

"Jim, any update from our teams?"

"It was a double ambush. They attacked Jocko and Van Dam and were waiting for us to send backup. They ambush both backup teams, but they didn't know that our grav-cars had shields. They didn't fare so well. Some fool fired a rocket launcher, the impact blast killed most of the ambushers.

We've got casualties, including Jocko and Van Dam. They've blocked the way to Conclave Med, they're in route back to A14."

Doc cut in, "Med-bay standing by to receive casualties."

"Roger Doc."

"Team lead one to base."

"Go lead one." Jim answered.

"We are in-bound with casualties. We are being pursued by two grav-cars, team one and two will come together."

"Roger team leads, we are ready to receive you." Jim answered.

"Commander, have teams one and two drive all the way to med-bay and leave room for pursuing vehicles to enter behind them. We'll have a surprise waiting for them."

"Team leads, did you copy last?" Jim asked.

"Team lead, roger, ETA one minute."

"Copy, one minute." Jim said.

"Major, lower shields on Hab cargo door, allow our grav-cars to enter, then raise shields behind them."

"Yes Commodore, surprise ready."

I chuckled, *"learning program indeed."*

We were waiting outside med-bay when our teams arrived; they drove straight over to med-bay. I turned to watch the surprise. Both pursuing grav-cars impacted our shields, going full speed. Our shields didn't even flicker, taking the impact. It completely crushed the grav-car's front ends, and parts ricocheted all over the corridor. There was no movement from the passengers.

"Major, close doors. Notify authorities of some kind of traffic accident."

"Notified, Commodore."

Commander Jones was receiving the debrief from the team leads, I waited.

"Major, stand down to yellow alert."

"Yellow alert," Major said.

Commander Jones came walking toward us, "how bad?" I ask.

"Not as bad as it could have been, the grav-car shields saved a lot of lives. We've got 16 team members and 2 of Jocko's men with varying degrees of wounds. They're all in Auto-docs. Jocko lost his legs again, and is a bit singed. He's as mad as a bag full of cats. Van Dam is the worst, Doc is working on him now."

I nodded, "you said it was a double ambush?"

"Oh yeah, no doubt. They hit our principles to hold them in place, forcing the call for backup. Backup arrived right in the middle of their kill zone. The only reason they aren't all dead is the opposition didn't know about the grav-car shields. Backup was able to break through and evac everyone, no one was left behind," Jim said.

We walked into med-bay, everyone was being seen to, Chef had sent over coffee and sandwiches. Doc was still working on Travis, so I didn't interrupt. Jocko on the other hand was in rare form. He was sitting on the exam table yelling, promising to rain down damnation and revenge. His clothes and hair were scorched. His exposed skin looked like he had a bad sunburn. The whole thing struck me as funny, I couldn't help but grin.

He saw me, "and what are you looking at grinning!" He yelled.

"The only words that come to mind are, 'demon fart'. You are scorched from, well, everywhere. Singed hair, clothes still smoking. So yeah, Demon Fart," I said, smiling.

The whole place went silent. Everyone was looking back and forth between us, waiting for the explosion. Jocko looked down at himself for the first time since he'd arrived. He looked up at me, chuckling, then laughed.

"I guess demon fart about covers it," he said. Everyone laughed.

He shook my hand, "how's my boys?"

"Auto-doc."

"And your boys?"

"Same. Auto-doc. We lost no one, Doc's still working on Travis. He's in the worst condition."

"Someone will pay for this." Jocko said.

"Oh, you can count on it. They went after family, that's not business. They made this personal. Look on the bright side, you get a new pair of legs."

"I was just getting used to these." He said pointing at what they left of his cyber legs.

"Commodore, there's a news broadcast you should see."

"On screen, Major." The monitor in the med-bay came on.

"Repeating our breaking news, the enviro-terrorist 'Sol First', have taken credit for the attacks on Conclave Station. Citing the stealing of resources that belong to the peoples of the Sol system."

"What a load of crap, the Corporations funds those guys. They use them when they need to cover up the mess they've made." Jocko said.

"No Jocko, those terrorists are bad people, it wouldn't

surprise me if they weren't through destroying Conclave businesses," I said smiling. "Come on Mal, we need to go check on everyone else. We'll be back Jocko."

Mal and I went to my office, "what are you gonna do?" Mal asked.

"WE aren't going to do anything; those bad terrorists are."

"Ok, what are those bad terrorists going to do?"

"I'm thinking they will probably target the Corporation's shipyard, smelter, and the reactors that power them. I bet some kind of emergency would clear the facilities, so it hurts no one. Then all the power supplies would overload, causing all kinds of localized damage. Of course, that's just a guess I'm not the computer genius, mad scientist type."

"Now that you mention it, that sounds like exactly what would happen if terrorists attacked those places. Maximum damage, no casualties, and all that news coverage. That's just what they'd want," Mal said. I smiled, nodding.

I checked back on our people in Med-bay. Travis was now in the Auto-doc, as was Jocko. Doc had started Travis on nanite therapy, he would be in the Auto-doc for at least a few days. Bob was there checking on his old boss, asked if there was anything he could do.

"I think there is, as a matter of fact. Travis will be out of it for a while. I want you to put your assistants in charge here and go over to the Van Dam ship yard. Take charge and keep everything going over there. Tell everyone that Travis is doing ok and will be back soon. If you need anything to make things happen, money, resources, whatever, let me know."

He nodded, "that I can do, I'll keep you updated."

"Major, contact Aaron Stein, and ask him to come over. I'm sure the authorities will be here sooner rather than later."

"Done sir." Aaron arrived within the hour and met with everyone who is involved in the rescue.

"I think we have all we need, I'll take care of the authorities, I'll let you know if we need anything else."

All security team members were out of the Auto-docs that

afternoon except Cpl. Adams. Doc was holding him in Med-bay. Jocko's two men were still in the Auto-docs, their injuries being worse. Jocko was supposed to be out in the morning. I had Doc schedule him for new mil-spec cyber limbs.

The news is reporting that another terrorist attack had happened. There had been major damage and meltdowns at the Corporate shipyard, smelter and refinery, and their fusion plants. They estimated damage to be in the hundreds of millions of creds. Miraculously, no one was killed in the attack. We stood down from yellow alert to normal operations but stayed vigilant.

Mal and I were there the next morning when Jocko came out of the Auto-doc. We had breakfast ready for him, everyone was always hungry when they came out of an Auto-Doc. Jocko had finished his breakfast and was drinking his coffee, when Doc rolled the cart in with Jocko's new mil-spec legs on it.

Jocko looked at the cyber legs, and then at me and Mal.

"Mil-spec?" He asked Mal, and I nodded.

"Expensive, hard to get." He said.

We shrugged our shoulders, "found them in the back corner down at the secondhand shop, traded for them," I said.

"Uh-huh, then I need to start checking that place better," Jocko said.

"Let's get you back on your feet, shall we," Doc said. Mal and I chuckled.

Jocko smiled, "stick to medicine Doc, we already have enough comedians around here."

It took Mal and Doc a few hours to get Jocko up and going.

"Take it slow for a while Jocko, I got them dialed back until you get used to them." Mal said.

"If this is dialed back, I can't wait to see what these babies can do." Jocko said, grinning. "How's my boys doing Doc?"

"They should be out of the Auto-docs in about an hour."

"Thanks Doc, if there's ever anything you need, let me know." Doc nodded and left us alone with Jocko.

Jocko turned to us, "Nic, me and my boys appreciate all

you've done for us, but this goes beyond friends helping each other, and these." He knocked on his new legs, "these, when you can get them, ain't cheap. I pay my debts, what's it going to cost me, or what you need?"

I purse my lips looking at him, "my Dad used to say you can't put a price on friendship, and I can't wear but one set of legs at a time. You had a need. There may come a time when me or mine will have a need, you may be able to help us. May God grant that day never comes."

"Amen, but if it does, I'll be there." Jocko said, nodding.

Jocko looked up at the monitor frowning, picking up the remote he turned up the sound. They were interviewing people from the corporate shipyard and smelter.

"Authorities are still amazed that there was no loss of life in the terrorist attack on the corporate facilities. We are being told that the reactor is a total loss and the other facilities are just wrecked and ruined husks," The anchorman said.

"I guess we got off light, those terrorists really made a mess." Jocko said, looking around us.

"Yep, apparently the Corporation really made those terrorists mad," I said.

He looked back at the monitor, "remind me not to make them mad at me," He said smiling.

"Let's get your boys out and get lunch." I said.

***

The *Brokkr* arrives the next day. She was not a small ship; she was way too big to fit our hanger. She would have swallowed *Invincible*. They parked her on our yard, to the side of the hanger doors. She was close enough that our shield could cover her if needed. Her crew disembarked to Gunny's cargo ship.

We met Gunny and the Admiral on *Brokkr*. "It seems you have had excitement here on Conclave, someone should do something about those terrorists." The Admiral said, shaking his head.

I nodded my head, "bad business that."

"Let's take a walk through your ship," The Admiral said. She would definitely take more work than *Vanguard* did. The more we toured, the more work we saw that needed doing.

"What's her normal crew size?" I asked.

"A total of 100. 50 to crew the ship, 50 to work on refit teams, some doing double duty. With your ACE program, you could probably do it all with 60. Her materials holds are empty, but we've plused up on some equipment. The agreed-on magna-flux 3-D printers are on board. We've also left all the weapon systems active, with a full load out. Gunny has all the Documentation you need. If there is nothing else, I've got places to be." I looked at our group, they all shook their heads.

"You wouldn't know of a retired SDRV Captain looking for a berth, would you?"

"Nope, but Reggie might ask him," The Admiral replied.

"Then I think that covers it." I said.

"We'll be in touch," He said handing me the owners key cards.

"Give us some time to refit and upgrade her before calling us out. Until then, we can still do upgrades out of A14," I said, taking the key cards. He waved over his shoulder as he and Gunny left.

"We jump on this with both feet." Jazz said.

"Yep, lots of work." Mal added.

"Do we do the work here, or moved her over to the Van Dam shipyards?" I asked. "They have a better set up to work on a ship this size. We could augment them as needed."

Mal nodded, "let me survey the computers and upgrade them, and install an ACE on her. Then we can move her over to the Van Dam yards."

"I think that will be the smarter move. Let's beef up security while she's over there." Aunt J said.

"Definitely increase security. We need to talk to their structural engineers and designers about those engines, and what they can do. Besides, Bob is over there running things until Travis is healed and ready to go back to work." Everyone nodded, "let's get to work."

***

We had John Foster, Bob's assistant, get the work crews started on the initial inspections, and prioritized the work. The minor work they started right away. The big stuff was on hold until we moved her over to the Van Dam yards.

Doc messaged me that Travis would come out of the Autodoc in a few hours. Jocko was staying with us until his hab and HQ was repaired. We'd given him an office to run his operations from until then.

When Doc let us in to see Travis, he was sitting up eating.

"No wonder all my guys want to come over here and work, this food is great."

I laughed, "he looks like he's doing okay, Doc."

"He's doing good, it will still be a few days before he's 100%, if he doesn't push it." I nodded.

"Anyone catch you up on the happenings?"

"Some of it, one of my security detail told me about you sending in calvary and getting us here." We brought him up to speed on all the events and that we had sent Bob over to make sure they kept the yards on track.

"So, what had happened was," Jocko started.

"Don't you start that Jocko!" Aunt J said, laughing.

"What?" Jocko asked innocently. "I was going to tell Travis about the terrorists."

"What terrorist?" Travis asked.

"See." Jocko said, looking at Aunt J.

"I'll tell him," Aunt J said. "If you start one of your stories, we'll never get out of here." Aunt J turned back to Travis, "a terrorist group claimed responsibility for the attacks."

"That's a load of bull." Travis said, looking around us.

"Nope," Jocko said. "It was the terrorist. They hit us, but they really hit the Corporate facilities. Almost melted them to the ground. It will be months before they are operational again. According to the news, it did hundreds of millions of creds in damage," He said, grinning.

Travis looked at us for a moment, "well," he said, "it isn't smart to piss some people off."

"That's a fact," Jocko said, chuckling.

***

It took Mal a week to get *Brokkr* where we ready to move her over to Van Dam yards.

"I'm trying something different this time," Mal said. *Brokkr* is a more complicated ship, so I'm adding more processing power and more memory. She's not fully integrated yet, but we can get her over to Van Dam's."

"Good, let's get Jazz and Jade down here. They can move her over," I said.

I called Bob; they had yard space ready for us. We had gone through all the safety protocols and backdoor searches; all weapon systems were in safety lockdown. Jazz and Jade arrived and took the helm.

"*Brokkr*."

"Yes, Commodore."

"Bring all systems online in preparation for departure."

"Yes Commodore, all systems online for departure."

"Okay, Jazz take us around to the Van Dam yards."

It was an uneventful flight; it gave Jazz and Jade some stick time on *Brokkr*. She was the largest ship they'd ever piloted. We were the only ship in the yard, so we had plenty of room to maneuver. Jazz set us down as light as a feather.

They had us hooked up to shore power and plumbed almost as soon as we shut the engines down. Bob had crews ready to go to work as soon as we opened her.

Bob greeted us, "Mister Van Dam sent word that *Brokkr* had priority. Everyone was to work on her until she was finished. The structural engineers are waiting to meet with you to discuss engines and superstructures."

I went to meet with the engineers. Mal, Jazz, and Jade went back to A14 in one of our armored and shielded grav-cars.

We pulled up the ship's plans for the *Brokkr*. "They said she was being retired because she wasn't fast enough to keep up with the fleet anymore," I said. "What I want to look at is the possibility of adding two more engines or pulling out the two she has and replacing them with six smaller, more powerful and efficient ones.

We will also upgrade all generators. Refitting and upgrading, well, pretty much everything. We'll be bringing you lots of parts and equipment. Anything you need, let Bob know."

"Well, just from looking at these plans, and the placement of existing equipment, I can tell you it will be a lot easier, cheaper, and faster to remove the two engines and replace them with six. That will save room for us to put in other things," The head engineer said.

"Ok, let's go with that plan. Let me know if anything raises its ugly head."

***

I was in my office the next morning look at the ship's plans I have projected on the walls when Mal came in.

"Looking for anything in particular?" He asked.

"Not really, just looking things over, letting my subconscious work on it. There is one thing I was thinking," I said, pointing at the smelter refiner.

"What would that be?" Mal asked.

"We could increase efficiency if we added the crusher program and emitters in the smelter-refiner." I said.

"Makes sense." He said.

"I wonder if BB would let us look at his set up." I said, thinking out loud.

"I bet he would." Mal said.

I nodded, "let's call and ask." We called BB, and he said to come on over. We asked the girls if they wanted to go, but they said they'd rather be flying. They took Taurus and went out to wrangle rocks. Commander Jones sent a security detail with us in a grav-car.

CHAPTER 18

We arrived at OEM refining; BB met us in the lobby.

"We are so glad you could come and see our operation. It also gives us a chance to thank you in person. We appreciate all you've done and are doing for us. I must admit it was getting tight for us."

"We're glad to help. Everyone goes through tough times, someday we may be the ones that need the help." We walked as we talked.

"Is there any area you specifically wanted to see?" BB asked.

"The preheat and crushing processing area. We have an SDRV in the Van Dam yards for refit. We have some ideas that will make the smelter-refiner more efficient, but we'd like to see a working refinery to judge if our idea is workable."

"You boys have been good to us, so look at anything you want. I will tell you, I've noticed that your loads are crushed far finer than anyone else's. We can process your load in half the time it normally takes us. I have said nothing to anyone. That's proprietary tech, and no one's business. We're just folks talking shop."

I nodded, "Yep, just kicking around some ideas, I think they might be mutually beneficial."

"We got a load on the way in now, let's go see the operation in progress." BB said, taking us to the operations center.

We watched as a rock was taken in, broken up, and fed into the next process. We saw right away we could drastically improve his crusher program and equipment.

"This will show you the difference, *Taurus* is on the way in with a load. You'll see the difference between yours and everyone else's." *Taurus* fed her load in. It barely slowed at the crushing operation before it was on to the next.

I looked at Mal, raising my eyebrows, tilting my head slightly toward BB. Mal nodded yes.

"BB, when is your next maintenance shutdown scheduled?" BB glanced over at the schedule calendar.

"Three days, what are you thinking?"

"You're right, we have something that crushes rock, makes it easier for our tugs to move and load. We think we can save you time, money, and effort using our system."

"How much will it save me, and how much will it cost me?"

"It will, and I'm just guessing here without running the numbers, probably close to 50%." Mal was nodding. "The cost, we want 10% of OEM, we'll bring in all the special parts, equipment, and new computer controlling systems. You pay your normal shutdown cost; we'll pay the rest. Once you're back up and running, if we don't save you at least 40% you owe us nothing."

BB thought for a moment, "how long will it shut us down to make all the changes?"

"How long is your normal maintenance shutdown?"

"4 to 5 days."

I looked at Mal, he nodded, "we can do that, so it won't cost you any more time than your normal shutdown."

"Over 40%, or nothing." He asked.

"Over 40% increase in productivity or no cost to you above your normal shutdown cost."

BB nodded, "let's call the lawyers and get it in writing." We nodded and shook on it.

Three days later we were at OEM refining with four engineering crews ready to start work. BB's engineers met us and laid out what we needed so we didn't duplicate work, or work on top of each other. They did all our installs in three days, testing and ACE integration took another day. BB's engineering teams were finished about the same time.

We all gathered in the refinery operation control room for

startup.

"O'em, bring refining systems to safety standby in preparation for refinery startup," Mal said.

"Acknowledged, bringing all refinery systems to safety standby for refinery startup. All systems online in safety standby, all boards are green," O'em said. BBs eyebrows were at his hairline.

"Manual crosscheck, does everyone have green boards?" Mal asked.

BB looked around the control rooms at all the boards, "all boards cross checked, and are showing green," BB said.

"O'em, initiate refinery startup sequence," Mal said.

"Acknowledged, initiating refinery startup sequence," O'em answered. "Refinery systems online, all boards are green, refinery ready for normal operations," O'em said.

I looked at BB, "there's a lot of tugs out there, want to signal one in, and see how she does?"

BB smiled, "I guess we better."

O'em caught the first rock in her capture field and started the process. Our crusher program worked perfectly, the rock never slowed down, gravel moved on into the smelter. O'em processed three other tugs in the same amount of time the old system would have taken to do one. BB watched and shook his head.

"We'll have to hire more workers to keep up with O'em," He said smiling. "Boys, I don't need to see the numbers, that's easily over 50% faster. Welcome to the company," He said, shaking our hands.

***

We took a few days off after the refinery project. I slept late, but my idea of relaxing was tinkering in my shop. Jazz and Jade had other ideas. Apparently, we were going shopping. Of course, the "we" turned out to be eight of us with our security team. Better safe than sorry.

"We need to go in here." Jazz said. "That's a men's store." Mal said, I was nodding.

"They can read!" Jade squealed, and both girls clapped for us, laughing.

"Y'all should take that show on the road," Mal said, I laughed. They drug us in the store.

"Why is every time we come shopping, it cost the guy's money?" I asked.

"Yeah." Mal chimed in.

The girls laughed, "silly boys, girls don't spend their money on clothes, that's what guys are for." The girls laughed at us.

I looked at Mal, "we never had a chance."

"Never did dear, never did," Jazz answered, kissing me on the cheek. We bought what the girls told us to buy. Turns out it's easier that way. The security team members were all grinning when we came out. I looked at the one closest one, "not a word."

He smiled, "NDA, Sir." For some reason, and I'm sure it's a rule in the female handbook. Women have to visit twice as many stores to find what they need. Apparently, it was also true that guys are there to pay the tickets and carry stuff.

We stopped at a café for coffee and a snack; the girls talked about their purchases. I notice our security team listening to their earpieces and taking up tighter positions. I tapped Mal's foot with mine and nodded towards team. He nodded, we kept sipping our coffee while remaining alert.

We paid the tab and got ready to leave, "we good sergeant?" I asked the team leader.

"Just being cautious sir, we've picked up a couple of watchers, so far no threat."

I nodded, "recommendations?"

"Error on the side of safety Sir, grav-car is waiting outside."

"I agree, we moved to the grav-car."

We moved to the grav-car and headed back to A14. They made no moves against us.

"I'm glad to be in the grav-car, so I don't have to carry more bags." I said.

"At least you have a cyber arm." Mal said, rubbing his.

"Suck it up, Buttercup." Jade said. Everyone was laughing.

We saw Jocko and his boys at breakfast the next morning. Jocko joined us at our table.

"We'll be heading home this morning," He said.

"They got your place finished already?" Aunt J asked.

"Most, there are a few more security measures I'd like in place but we're working on."

"You can stay as long as you need," I said.

"I appreciate that, but I need to get back out there and be seen. We've already had a few hyenas sniffing around."

I nodded, "we'll send a maintenance team over with you, they can help on your security shielding."

He looked around the table, "thank you, thank you all."

After breakfast we went over to visit Travis. He had had his last checkup and was ready to go home.

Doc came over and asked Mal, "you talk to him yet?" Chin pointing at me.

"No, but there's no time like the present, you ready?" Mal asked.

"Yep." Doc nodded. They all looked at me.

"I've been working with Doc on upgrades to Med-bay, that includes the cyber tech equipment. I've tweaked the cyber limbs you're getting. So, while we talk to Travis, Doc will change out your cyber limbs," Mal said.

"Uh, okay, I guess."

"Right this way, we have a table ready for you," Doc said. "You'll also be getting nanite treatments." I put on a pair of shorts and took my shirt off, Doc got to work.

"So, what have you got on the burner?" Travis asked.

"*Brokkr*, our SDRV, is in your yard being refitted and up-graded. Thanks for the extra help by way.

Travis waved off with his hand, "no problem."

"I suppose you've heard about our new shield technology." I said. Travis nodded. Doc turned off my arm and leg.

"Yeah, I heard rumors about it while Doc had me chained to the bed." Travis said, Doc smiled as he worked on me.

"Well, the rumors are true; Mal and I came up with a new shield tech. We are ready to start selling. We want you, or rather Van Dam shipyards, to do the work. Same conditions as with the ACE programs. We'll still be selling and trading on the side, but you'll be the primary vendor." I said.

"How good are they?"

"That's classified, as we are under contract to the ESFL as their R&D provider. But we can still sell civilian models. I'll tell you this though, if *Taurus* had been equipped with them, Mom and Dad would still be here."

"That's tough, inventing something that would have saved your parents, I don't know how I'd feel." He said.

"Well, I'm looking at all the people we'll save in the future."

"Price range?" He asked.

"I don't know. Get your market research department to look at it, and we'll talk. We all want to make money, but I want everyone to be able to afford it, it's literally a lifesaver."

Doc removed my leg and replaced it with the new mil-spec one.

"I like the nonreflective black look." Travis said.

"Graphite-metallic-armor (GMA). Best mil-spec made." I said.

"Bet that was expensive."

"I could tell you, but..."

"Yeah, yeah, whatever. So, you're doing R&D for the ESFL, and I take it you'll do their upgrades and refits."

I nodded, "hence the SDRV in your yard."

Doc removed and replace my arm. Mal got busy doing his tweaks, as he liked to call them.

"The first shield install I want you to do is on the Beast. We'll have a media event to showcase it, like what we'll do for the ACE. This will be better."

Travis nodded, "ok, I'll get marketing on it. We'll be rich again." He laughed.

"I'd love to stay and watch the show, but I'm ready to go home, and I understand I have a ride waiting. I'll call you in a few days." Travis was gone, I looked over at Mal and Doc. They had their heads together at the test screen and computer monitor. You guys are making me nervous, you're too quiet.

"Uh-huh." Mal said, not even looking up.

"Can it do that?" Doc asked.

"Easily." Mal answered.

"Do what?" I asked.

"We'll have to do a shutdown to integrate it though."

"Do what?" I asked again.

"Is he always this nosy?" Doc asked.

"Oh yeah, he always wants to know everything," Mal answered.

"I hope you two are enjoying yourselves." They both laughed.

"Here's what we're doing, since these limbs are made differently, and have smaller but stronger parts and mechanisms, we could add stuff." Mal said, Doc nodded.

"Stuff? What kind of stuff?"

"ACE," Mal said. "We added a computer system, power supplies, and an ACE program. Because you have other cyber equipment, we can integrate them all through the ACE. I also wrote a program that will use your eye and ears as an early warning system by collecting data, correlating that data, give you a 360° situational awareness.

ACE can also tap other security feeds and boost signals to remain in contact with Major or other ACEs in our system within range."

"Are you yanking my chain?"

"No, but we need to shut down your CCU to integrate them. Then we'll bring everything back up slowly, you shouldn't feel a thing."

"Shouldn't?"

My cyber eye went dark, and the sounds dropped out. I waited. I was watching them out of my good eye, Mal was typing away. They were nodding their heads, talking, more typing. If I'd had known it would take this long, I'd have taken a nap. I close my eyes and tried to relax.

Someone tapped me on the arm. Opening my eyes, Mal was giving me the thumbs up. I nodded; sound came back to preset levels. "Can you hear me ok?" Mal asked.

"Yeah, that's good." The light in my cyber eye came up to preset levels.

"See that?"

"That's good there."

"We got your limb settings low; we will bring ACE online now."

"*Vigilance* program online." Everything became sharper, vision, hearing, tactile feedback, reaction feedback, strength, everything.

"Did you hear anything?" Mal asked. "Yeah, *Vigilance* program came online." I answered. Mal reached over and turned the volume up on his computer speakers.

"*Vigilance*, run a system check."

"Systems check complete, all boards are green."

"*Vigilance*, run ACE integration and all vigilance safety protocols."

"Acknowledged, ACE integration and vigilance safety protocols." The sharpness I experience seemed to double. Sounds are located, correlated, and identified. Sites were catalogued, facial recognition run and ID'ed. It was almost information overload. *Vigilance* seemed to realize he was giving me too much information and reduced data input.

I could tell they were 4 people in med-bay, voice analysis named the individuals. I could access their files if needed.

"This is incredible," I said, "but it will take time to get used to the interface."

"True, but *Vigilance* will start slow then increase the info as you can assimilate it. Anything you can't handle, he will filter the info for you, then pass the relevant info as required." Mal said. "*Vigilance* will also set and reset all of your settings based on your needs. You no longer have to do it manually, she will do it automatically. The more you interact with her, the more intuitive she'll become."

"Tomorrow morning's workout should be interesting." I said.

***

Painful was a better description. I got pummeled. Instead of flowing in the moment, I kept trying to read and interpret what *Vigilance* was showing me. This will take time and patience. Mal, Doc, and I kept this secret, another 'ACE' up my sleeve. Pun intended, I smiled.

Doc said the nanites would make their presence known in a few days. Nothing too drastic, small things to start, but no headaches, no muscle soreness, or anything like that. I was still getting pummeled in my workouts.

I noticed that *Vigilance*, or *Vee* as I now called her, had taken over passing messages and answering my questions unless I specifically ask for someone other than her to answer. It really didn't matter; *Vee* and Major were completely integrated.

I wanted to check on *Brokkr's* progress and asked if Mal wanted to go. He declined. He was locked in his mad scientist lab, working on something new. The girls were out chasing rocks, so they were happy. I wanted to walk the promenade in route to the shipyards, so I took two security guys with me. This would also give *Vee* and I some practice out in public.

I quit trying to keep track of all *Vee* was doing, and I only looked at things she would highlight, or transmissions and scans she would warn me about. She highlighted someone taking pictures of us, and she took some of her own. Facial-rec said green, but she logged it and sent it to Major.

Van Dam's yard had been busy. The whole aft engineering and engine section was open. They had removed the two big engines. They were adding superstructure supports for the new engines. Most everyone had been working at A14 was now working on *Brokkr*. We'd also brought *Beast* over to the yard, and they were installing shields on her.

Travis saw me, and came over, "what you think?" He asked.

"She's looking good, coming along faster than I would have thought."

He nodded, "they are moving right along on her. What you gonna do with the old engines?"

"I hadn't really thought about it, you got something in mind?"

"Maybe, some mining vessels like those big mil-spec engines, we could sell them to one of those outfits."

"If you get a chance to sell them, sell them. It will help offset some of *Brokkr's* refit costs." I said. "How is your marketing department doing on the shields?"

"I got an idea I want to bounce off of you." He said.

"Ok shoot."

"There's a small shield company, Aegis. They hold a few patents on different small shields. Mostly things like enviro-shields. They have a good product, and good service reputation. They already have a sales and marketing department; all they do is sell and service shields. They are well-managed and have little debt. But they don't have the backing to compete with the big corporations.

Once we sell our shields, they'll probably go bankrupt. I'd like to propose we buy the company and keep their management in place. We concentrate on our specialty and let them concentrate on their specialty. They sell and service, we install and refit."

"What will it cost us?" I asked.

"The rumors about our new shield tech are already circulating. Their share prices are suffering. Let's let the accountants dig in and see what the numbers say. Once we see that, we'll make them an offer, unless something comes up when the accountants start digging." Travis said.

"Sounds like a good idea, let's get the accountants and lawyers started. We'll split the cost of research and see where we land." I said.

Travis left to make calls, I continued touring the work on *Brokkr*. They were changing the engineering layout to account for the big magna-flux 3-D printer. We had also given the engineers the new specs on the smelter-refiner upgrades. *Brokkr's* crew berthing was for 100, we would only use 60, so we changed the berthing layout to make living aboard a little nicer. Some fine tuning would have to wait until we got her back to A14. We didn't want to show all our cards.

On a whim, "*Vee*, call Jocko."

"Online."

"Nic, what can I do for you?"

"Quick question, I know you're probably busy, what do you know about a company called Aegis?"

"I know the name, a small company, sells and installs shields I think."

"That's the one we're looking into buying the company, anything I should know?"

"I'll do some checking and get back to you."

"Thanks."

"Line clear."

"*Vee* call for the grav-car, we'll ride home."

"Yes, sir."

CHAPTER 19

I was still taking a beating at my workouts, but I was getting better, and my muscles didn't hurt afterwards. The bruises were gone in a few hours. I wasn't sure yet, but my natural reflexes seemed to get faster. "*Vee* keep a record of my natural reflex speed to see if they are increasing."

"Yes sir, but they probably are, that is a side benefit to the nanites."

"Sir, you have encrypted call from Jocko."

"Put him through."

"Online."

"Jocko, how's life treating you?"

"Better with my new legs. I got that information you wanted."

"What's the highlights?"

"The highlights are, Aegis is a front for the corporation, they use Aegis to bid small jobs to drive out other small business competitors, and cause riffs with the local workers. If I'm not crossing any lines, why are you interested in buying them?"

"Travis and I are about to market our ship shields. We were considering buying a small shield company to handle marketing and sales. Once the word is out about our shields, those type of companies will take a big hit in their stock value and sales." I answered.

"Ok, I see where you're going. Check out TranStar shielding. They are smaller than Aegis but have a better reputation and they are Aegis' biggest competitor. I know nothing about their financial situation though."

"Can I share this info with Travis?"

"Sure, no problem. He would've probably found it in his checking, anyway."

"Okay, thanks, see you."

"Later."

"Line clear." *Vee* said.

"*Vee* send a message to Travis, to cease-fire on Aegis, they are a front for the corporation, per Jocko, look into Tran-Star shielding instead."

"Sent."

"Message Reggie, we need a Captain with SDRV experience. Do you know of any who might be looking for a berth?"

"Sent."

"Locate Mal."

"EL shop." She answered.

"Message from Reggie: I'll make some calls."

Mal was intent on his workbench. He was studying something and had his test probe's out.

"Don't just stand there, come on in." Mal said.

"I didn't want to jog your elbow," I said, stepping up to the workbench.

"I finished the final adjustments." He stepped back. There lay a mil-spec cyber hand. "I'm finally done with it." He said.

"What did you do to it?" I asked.

"Come sit here, I'll explain while I work." I took a seat. "Rest your arm on the bench." I did, Mal detached my hand from my arm. "I ran across something interesting while researching and adapting our batons. Did you know a small grav-pulse near the skull, behind the ear, will cause unconsciousness?" He took off my hand.

"I didn't know that." He took the end half of my lower arm and pulled the tube out about half the size of the baton.

"So I had an idea to augment your hand with that capability, and the punch only capability of the baton, that's why this one is so small," he inserted a half-size baton back into my lower arm. "This will give you two more functions for self-defense."

He attached the new hand, "tell *Vee* to run diagnostics and if she gets a green board to run the 'finger tap' program and integrate."

"*Vee* says we're good."

"Feel any different?"

"Nope."

"Good, the way it works is, when you want to knock someone unconscious, you point with your index and middle finger curling the other two fingers in, this activates the 'pulse mode', When those two extended fingers are tapped behind the ear, it's lights out.

To use a 'punch mode' flex your hand like you will deliver a palm strike, when your hand is flexed up out of the way, its armed. Ask *Vee* if the new programs are active and ready to use."

"*Vee* says the program is online."

"Have you tried it?" I asked Mal.

"Well, no, but records show they have tested it, and it works."

"Well, let's hope if I have to use it, it works correctly."

"It will work fine, trust me."

"Uh-huh."

***

My morning practices were getting better, I could hold my own again. I had to turn off the tap and palm punch during my practices, but I practiced with them in private.

Business was good, the haulers and the cargo ship were making good creds. Jazz and Jade had been choosier with the rocks they grabbed, seeking the higher value ones. BB would not advertise the fact, so we were okay so far. That was bringing in the creds nicely.

Travis wanted to meet to talk about the TranStar acquisition. I walked to the Van Dam yards; it was an opportunity to train with *Vee*. My two security guards and I walked along the Promenade, heading toward the yards. *Vee* ID'ed two people with encrypted comms, but no one made any overt moves against us.

We got to the yards, Travis had all the information and financials on TranStar shielding. The company didn't look bad. Good reputation, good customer base, had some debt but not too much. Their stock prices were dropping on news of a new type of shield coming out. They were mostly a service and repair company. They were doing better than other shielding companies. We gave the lawyers the go-ahead to start negotiations to buy the company.

I took the opportunity to tour *Brokkr* while I was there. They had all six engines mounted and were replacing the hull. The upgrades to the smelter-refiner were complete, as were the placement of the new generation of generators. Everything was coming along nicely, but it wasn't cheap.

I varied my routine. Instead of taking the grav-car back we walked to an alternate route through the Promenade. *Vee* didn't ID any followers this time, and the walk home was uneventful.

The next morning over breakfast I caught everyone up on *Brokkr*'s progress, and where we were on buying TranStar shielding. After breakfast, Jazz and Jade were off in search of the next big strike, Mal went back to his dungeon, Aunt J was doing whatever Aunt J did. I was doing some additional one-on-one, hand-to-hand training. Those two hours flew by. Afterward, *Vee* confirmed that my natural reflex speed was increasing, my eyesight, and coordination were also improving.

Jim caught me leaving the practice mats, "you're doing a lot better, I'm impressed."

"Thanks, good instructors and lots of practice."

"Yep, that's the way to improve at everything. On another subject, we need to consider changing your attire." He said.

"Oh?"

"If you're going to continue to take walks, we need to upgrade your clothes and accessories. Not only yours, but all the boards clothes, or at least some of their clothes."

"Why the change?"

"We've noticed an uptick in sophisticated surveillance on

us, they're getting better or have hired better. So, we need to up our game."

"You got my attention."

"I'm bringing in a specialist, all this company does is provide protective clothing, and offensive and defensive accoutrements."

"Ok, set it up will be there."

Over lunch I told everyone what Jim had said, and he had someone coming in to show us what was available.

"He wants us to wear body armor?" Jazz asked.

"He would probably like that, but these clothes don't look like body armor, they look like regular clothes that protect like, light body armor. To the casual observer we look like were dressed in everyday clothes."

"As long as they don't want us to wear ugly clothes, I'd rather be shot than have to wear ugly clothes." Jade said.

"I'm sure we all feel the same way; I know I do." Mal said, with a hint of sarcasm in his voice, but he kept a straight face.

Jade looked around at him and smiled, "keep it up, I see a sofa in your future." We all chuckled, except Mal.

"On another subject," Jazz said, "we had hyenas following us and grabbing rocks from where we get ours."

"Any hostile moves or aggression toward you?" I asked.

"No, they think we know something, and they want to get in on whatever it is." Jazz answered.

I nodded, "I think it's time for another upgrade. Mal, let's look at replacing those small rock defense rail guns with something with a little more teeth."

"Yeah, I don't like them being out there alone was just those little pop guns. I know we have the shields, but I feel better with adding more teeth." Mal said.

***

I looked down from my work platform and saw Jazz and Jade standing there, "what's up?"

"When are you guys going to be finished? It's been four days. I didn't think replacing a couple rail guns would take this long."

"This is Mal's fault, I install what I'm told," I said.

"And there he goes, right under the bus, I thought he was your friend." Jade asked smiling.

"He is, until his girlfriend asks questions with my girlfriend standing there as a witness," I said laughing.

Mal came walking up, and looked at me, I shrug my shoulders.

"So, this is your idea?" Jade asked.

"What was my idea?" Mal asked.

"That's what I thought," Jazz said looking at me.

"Ok, we took a little longer than we first thought. Once we checked our inventory for replacements, we found mil-spec rail guns, lasers, and stuff. So, we decided to use them, rather than let them gather dust on the shelf." I said.

"So, you two have made our tug a gunboat?"

"It was his idea!" Mal said, pointing. We all burst out laughing.

"Boys and their toys." Jazz said.

"How much longer?" Jade asked.

"After lunch we can take her out to calibrate all the weapon systems and let Misty integrate everything." Mal said. An hour after lunch we were pulling out of the hanger.

"Okay take us away from traffic and find us a rock we can use for target practice, to calibrate the rail guns and lasers, and get them zeroed in." I said. Jazz took us out on the fringe of the rock field we fired and calibrated the weapons and weapon systems until Misty had full integration. Mal added combat programming to Misty like *Vanguard* uses, just to be on the safe side.

We moved back into the rock field. Sure enough, a few hyenas followed us.

"Misty, find the most useless rock in this area, and highlight it." Misty scanned the area and highlighted one that was just a rock, no minerals. "Jazz, vector toward that one but move in slowly, let's see what the hyenas do." Jazz moved us toward the rock, taking her time to line up on it. As soon as they were sure which rock we were after, they swooped in and grabbed it.

"Open a channel to them Misty."

"Open."

"Hey, back off belters, that's our rock, don't be claim jumping."

"Ain't no claim jumping, you didn't mark it, you're just too slow today! Better luck next time."

"Close channel." It was a good size rock, and they were only 50 KLT tugs, so it took both to get it to the refinery. "Serves them right, they'll lose creds on that run."

"We have an encrypted call coming in from Jocko." Misty said.

"Putt it through."

"Good afternoon *Taurus,* are you out in the fields?"

"Good afternoon Jocko, we are. We're trying to make a living. What can we do for you?"

"God bless you good hard-working people," He said, laughing.

"I want to ask a favor, there's a family of rock hounds that are having a bad run of luck. They could use some of your luck picking rocks. The thing is, they won't take charity, they are hard workers, but prideful. So, you need to be your usual sneaky self and help them out if you would."

"Us sneaky?" I said.

He laughed, "that's the rumor, anyway."

"Are they out on the fields?"

"Yeah, I'm sending you their transponder data, any help you could give them would be appreciated."

"Data received." Misty said.

"Glad to help Jocko, just paying it forward."

"Thanks *Taurus*, next round is on me."

"Channel clear."

"Misty, find the tug from the data Jocko sent us."

"Located, they are about 15 minutes away."

"Plot a course to that area."

"Jazz take us over. I think I'm gonna make coffee, anyone else want a cup?" Three hands raised.

We moved into the area, but not too close to make it obvious we were looking for them.

"Misty scan for the biggest richest rock you can find in this area."

"Scanning." I brought everyone a coffee, and we were relaxing, watching the readouts, making small talk.

"That one looks promising." Mal said. The closer we got, the higher the readings went.

"Whoa baby, would you look at that, 32% and she's a big one. It would take us 4 trips at max load capacity to get all of it."

"Tag it Misty."

"Tagged."

"That was perfect for what we need." I said.

"Misty contact our target tug, what was her name?"

"*Night Wanderer*."

"Open a channel to them."

"Open."

"*Night Wanderer*, this is the *Taurus*, are you busy?"

"Hi ya *Taurus*, not busy yet, just scouting."

"Interested in a shared run? We hooked a big one and we will need help. We can't leave this one unguarded. We got it tagged, but you know hyenas, they'll move in on anything they can, tagged or no."

"We see you're close *Taurus*, sure, we'll share a run with you."

"Great, come on over and look. We'll see the best way to skin this cat."

The *Wanderer* arrived. She was an older 200 KLT tug, and she looked a little worse for wear.

"That looks like a good catch *Taurus*, how do you want to do this? To be honest with you, they rate us as a 200 KLT but her condition she can only handle about half of that."

"No problem *Wanderer*, we've had a run of good luck lately, and have had refits done. We got a new crusher program that will let us pulverize rock, so we can handle it easier.

Here's what I'm thinking, *Taurus* chews this rock down to size and makes the runs in, once we get her down to the right size, we'll make the last run in together."

"How do you want to split? It seems you should get a bigger share."

"No, I'm thinking equal split after expenses, if you are out here guarding our rock you could be working your own find. I think that's only fair."

"Okay *Taurus*, 50-50, but only after expenses, you're the one burning fuel."

"Deal *Wanderer*, after expenses, 50/50."

"Deal *Taurus*, let's get to work."

As we headed in with our first load, "Misty, tell me about the owners of the *Wanderer*."

"Family owned 200 KLT tug, family comprise husband, wife, two sons. They appear to be making a living, but only barely. They own their tug free and clear."

"Stop, that's all I need to know at the Moment."

"What are you thinking Nic?" Jazz asked.

"They remind me of our family, living on the tug, working the belt."

It took *Taurus* 4 single runs, and the last run *Taurus* and *Wanderer* made together. On our way in I messaged BB, and told him to do a 70/30 split, with the 70 going to *Wanderer* but to swear it was a 50/50 split.

BB sent back, "done." We unloaded at OEM, and BB settled with the *Wanderer* on the spot.

We called *Wanderer* before he called us.

"*Wanderer*, that was a sweet run! I love these kinds of pay-days!"

"*Taurus*, you sure about the creds split?"

We heard a woman in the background, "Tommy, don't be rude."

"Yeah, 50/50 after expenses like we agreed, right?"

"Yeah, just seems high for a 50/50 split even on a shiner like that."

I laughed, "my girl better never hear me complain about making too many credits, she'd choked me out."

Tommy laughed too, "yeah, Momma is giving me that look right now."

"Great run *Wanderer* we'll give you a shout if we hang into another one like that."

"Thanks *Taurus*, we may be down a while, were going in for maintenance."

"If you don't already have someone, check with Travis Van Dam, he's a friend of the family, tell him *Taurus* sent you he'll treat you right, not that he wouldn't, anyway."

"Will do *Taurus*, thanks again."

"Channel clear." Misty said.

***

The sale of TranStar shields looked like it would go through. We had a meeting schedule for 1500. Travis and I were there to hammer out the last few details. The overall price wasn't too bad, if the sale went through, we stood to make good creds.

We arrived in our two armored grav-cars, with our security teams. They showed us right into the owner's office. After introductions, we took our seats.

The owner didn't look thrilled, "Sir, if you don't mind me saying so, you don't look happy to be selling your company."

He looked at me with sadness in his eyes, my adrenaline spiked, "I'm sorry." He said.

His desk became red highlighted, "BOMB!" *Vee* shouted in my ear. Time slowed. I twisted from my seat, picking Travis up with my cyber arm, kicking off toward the door with my cyber leg. There was a white blinding flash as we crashed through the door. Then blackness...

"Get the bleeding stopped, put the tourniquet on," Someone was saying.

"Med-bay, this is team one, were coming in hot, no pursuit, one critical."

Blackness...

"No pain, I'm okay, just get me up."

Mal was shouting, "*Vee*, command override, shut down cyber limbs."

Blackness... Bright lights, white ceiling.

Blackness... Beeping machines.

Blackness...

"MOM!" Blackness...

CHAPTER 20

"Nic... Nic... Nic..!" Someone had my hand, "you're safe Nic! It's me, Jasmine!"

"Jasmine?"

"Yes baby, I'm here, you're safe."

"Safe?"

"Let me get Doc, lay still."

"Doc?" The fog was lifting, I was in Med-bay strapped to a bed. I focused on Doc coming toward me. "Doc?"

"Hello Nic, how are you feeling?"

"No pain."

"We got you nerve blocked while you heal."

"Why am I in Med-bay?"

"What was the last thing you remember?"

"I was going somewhere."

"Do you remember where?" Jazz is holding my hand. She looked like she hadn't slept in forever.

"Nic, do you remember where you were going?"

I looked at Doc focusing on him, "To. A... Meeting?"

"Good, what kind of meeting?" I blinked my eyes, trying to concentrate.

"We went to meet to buy TranStar... Travis! The bomb! Travis, where is Travis?" I looked around for him, "I tried to throw him away from the blast."

I looked at Jazz, tears were running down her face. She shook her head. I felt the ice-cold fury rising in me.

"Nic!" I look back at Doc. "Travis died in the blast, along with all the owners of TranStar. There was nothing you could have done to save them. It's a miracle you survived." I was finding it hard to focus.

"Nic, listen, you are badly hurt. You lost your other leg, a broken pelvis and fractured your spine in several places. God only knows how you survived without being blown in half. We had to do a lot of work on you. We've added mithrilium graphite composite for bracing, to support your bones, and we hit you with another nanite treatment."

"How long have I been out?"

"You've been in a Med-comma for a month, while we worked on you."

"Why did you remove my cyber limbs?"

"Safety, we didn't want your limbs coming online at an inopportune moment."

"Prudent," I said, "I guess I must learn to walk again."

Doc was nodding, "yes, but it will go much faster this time."

"Ok, where are my limbs?" They both smiled. "Don't tell me you let that mad scientist have my limbs to tweak." They both nodded. "So, I've been out for a month, what did I miss? What's happening at Travis' shipyard? Do they know who bombed us?"

"Stop," Doc said. "Everything is being taken care of. You have good people around you. The only thing they can't do is get you better. Right now, that's your job. Concentrate on getting better. Everything else can wait."

"Can I have visitors?"

"Yes, unless I want to start a riot. But no business is to be conducted."

"Okay Doc, no business." I said.

"Yeah right, that and a cred will get me a cuppa coffee."

Mal, Jade, and Aunt J came in. They look like they hadn't slept in a month.

"Y'all look like hell, except for Aunt J she's as pretty as ever."

Aunt J smiled, "sell many used tugs?" I smiled.

"You don't look so good yourself, you know all the hair is

burnt off the back of your head, right? And when they sewed your right ear back on, it's a half inch lower than the other one," Mal said. I stared at him for a moment. The girls looked aghast that he would say something so heartless.

"How long have you been waiting to use that one?"

"Two long weeks!" We all laughed.

"You guys ok?" I asked.

"We are now," Jazz said. Everyone nodded.

"I told Doc I wouldn't talk about business."

"I heard that." Doc said from across the room.

"And I'm not going to!" I said back. "Because I know it's in good hands with you guys running it. I'm sure Bob is still over at the Van Dam shipyards, keeping it running until his next of kin can take over." They all looked at each other.

"What?" I ask.

"Travis didn't have any family, and after the last attack almost killed him and Jocko, he changed his will."

"Changed his will to what?"

"If you survived him, everything went to you. Lock, stock, and barrel as they say," Aunt J answered. "You're right, Bob is over there running it."

"No family?"

"No, none," Aunt J said, shaking her head.

"Except us." I said. They nodded.

"So, they went after family, again." The cold rage was upon me, again...

"Their biggest mistake was not going after my family. Their biggest mistake was leaving me alive."

Mal moved up to my side, putting his hand on my shoulder and whispered into my ear. "Patience brother, I have lots of info, and Commander Jones has someone you'll want to talk to. That will keep for now. First you get better. Business is war."

I nodded, "business is war."

Because of my nanites, I was out of Med-bay in a week. Mal had been busy working on my cyber limbs for the past month, while I was in the coma. He had been busy; he'd use the magna-flux 3-D printer to miniaturize everything to get them to fit inside my limbs. I now had an extra cyber leg, and that gave him more room to work with.

Jazz said he had been driving himself, feeling guilty, wondering if there was more he could've done. The final stages of my cyber upgrades were done and were down his shop behind locked doors. He and miniaturize a short-range tri-dar scanner and had fitted it into one of my legs, with a mini power supply. To the other leg he put a mini shield generator and batteries.

The mini OFE 5s were in the front, back, and both sides of my cyber limbs. They were mag plates on the soles of my cyber feet so that when the shield was active, it completely enclosed me inside the shield. The shield wasn't as strong as the full-sized 5s, but it would stop a railgun round, or a rocket launcher round. My shield was a prototype. He was working on one he and the girls could wear. *Vee* also got an upgrade to handle all the new equipment.

"Are you making me a superhero?" I asked. "Can I fly?"

"Not in my shop."

"Oh well, one can always hope."

"Maybe out in space using the Mag-fields in your shields, but that's just a guess."

"Have you tested the mini shields yet?"

"Kinda."

"kinda?"

"Well, the first one cut the dummy's legs off, but don't worry you don't have legs, anyway."

"Ha-ha-ha that was a joke, right? You are too funny. You know Jazz will kill you, right?"

"There is that." He said.

I was still walking with a cane to help my balance, practicing my katas in private, working on my coordination and balance. I felt it was time to go pay Commander Jones a visit, so Mal and I walked over to A12.

The walk was good practice, and it was good to be out and about. When I came out of the lift at the A12 hanger Reggie was there.

"Good to see you up and about, Commodore."

I smiled, "good to be seen Reggie. Were you able to find us a SDRV Captain for the *Brokkr*?"

"I have someone I think you should meet; he was the captain of the *Brokkr* before they promoted him and moved him to the ESFL home port shipyard."

"Sounds interesting, how long will it take for him to get here?"

"He's actually already here, he's been staying with us here in A12 for a couple weeks awaiting your recovery."

I know my eyebrows were at my hairline, "okay, that's unexpected."

"I'm sorry sir, if I overstepped."

"No, no, that's fine you did the right thing. We've all been flying by the seat of our pants. I'll meet with him in the morning."

"Yes sir, he'll be ready I'm sure."

Commander Jones was waiting for us in the team's ready room.

"Commodore, it's good to see you."

"Thank you, Jim, what have you got for us."

"How much do you know?"

"Nothing."

"Take a seat and we'll get started."

"Thanks, but I'd rather stand, I'm retraining my balance. The two of you feel free to sit."

Pictures appeared on the wall as he began his briefing. "There were three of them, a contracted hit team. One did the job, the other two were for support and to cover his escape. We cornered them at their ship. The two support guys didn't make it. The triggerman was severely wounded but survived."

"He give us any usable Intel?" I asked.

"Not directly, we used facial rec, and their ship info to track them from one of the Mars orbitals to here."

"Did you get anything?"

"His real name is Samuel James; he's married and has two daughters. He works mainly freelance. But has been called on from time to time by the Baxter Consortium when they want a problem to go away permanently."

"The owner of TranStar told me he was sorry just before the explosion. I'm guessing they were using his family to apply pressure." I said.

"They may have been, but all of his family is ok." Mal said.

"Cred trails?"

"Layered, but we could follow it."

"So, there's a good chance Mister James doesn't know or care who paid for the contract."

"That'd be my guess."

"Can we say for sure who ordered the hit?"

"There is a 90% probability it was the CEO of Baxter consortium, Donald Baker, and his fixer Ray Hardisty." Jim said.

"Who paid Samuel James?"

"Fred Durant, they have apparently worked together for years. Durant used to do jobs, but a car bomb put him behind a desk."

"The only pressure point I see his family. I wonder how he would react to seeing pictures of his family. Be ready to flash them on his wall." I took a contact case out of my pocket, "I had Doc make me a black see-through contact to hide my eye movement and pupil dilation. I thought it might be useful for this interview."

I put the contact in, "*Vee*, match cyber eye color to contact." both eyes were completely blacked out, my vision was unaffected.

"That looks creepy." Mal said smiling.

"Let's see how Mister James likes them." I left my cane with Mal.

I entered Samuel James' holding cell; he was seated and handcuffed to the table.

"You people can't hold me here like this, it's against the law. This is kidnapping. I want a lawyer. I'm just a ship's pilot, flying for other people. I know nothing about what they were doing, I'm just a pilot."

I sat and watched him for a moment. waited; he didn't get fidgety or nervous.

"I'd like to keep this professional. Mister Durant liked it better that way, too." His eyes flickered for a millisecond, and then it was gone.

"That name supposed to mean something?"

"Fred Durant, the man who pays you, Samuel James from Mars orbital. Married, two daughters." Their pictures flashed on the wall behind me. He looked at them and then at me.

"Okay, we'll go the professional way." He said.

"Who paid for the hit?"

"Don't know, I get money and target information."

"Have you ever missed your target before?"

"I didn't miss Mister Haydock, you were not the target, Travis Van Dam was."

"And everyone else?"

"Collateral damage, nothing personal."

"Nic, I have more info, Samuel James is another false ID, including his wife and daughters. His true name is Jon Vector, divorced wife Linda, son Jon Jr." Mal said in my ear.

"So, you used the owner's families as pressure points to get them to detonate a bomb, to kill Van Dam."

"Essentially, yes."

"And if they had not, more collateral damage?"

"Sometimes but, usually I have an alternate detonation device."

"You said it wasn't personal," he shrugged his shoulders. "Maybe not for you, but you killed a member of my family, that makes it personal."

"So, what you gonna do, kill my wife and daughters."

"Oh no, I would never kill that lovely woman and those two young girls, after all they are only actors playing a part you paid them to. Now Linda and Jon Jr, well as you said, collateral damage. That seems to happen a lot of your line of work."

He went still, "what do you want?"

"I thought it would be obvious, I want the man who ordered my brother's death."

"Van Dam was not your brother."

"Not the same mother." I answered.

"Baxter consortium, I get my orders from Ray Hardisty, he's their fixer. He takes his orders from whoever is a top guy at the time."

"Donald Baker," I said.

He nodded, "I guess now you want me to kill him? I could kill you instead."

"People keep thinking that."

His image turned highlighted red, "he's augmented, his adrenaline is spiking, he's about to attack!" *Vee* said. My adrenaline spiked.

He snapped his handcuffs as he stood up. He lunged across the table feet first. I stood and shifted to the right, causing his attack to miss. His roundhouse kick came at my head. I ducked under it, blocking the follow-on back fist. I hit him in the back with my cyber palm strike, shattering his spine. Another palm strike to the back of his head, crushing his skull, launching his body over the table. He hit the floor and didn't move.

Security busted into the room. "We're good guys," I chin point at the body, "bag 'm, and tag 'm."

"Roger Sir, we'll take care of it." I nodded and left the cell.

I went back to the ready room. Mal handed me my cane and a cup of coffee.

"That solves that problem," Jim said.

"It's not what I planned, but he was of no further use to us. As far as the consortium knows his mission was a success. They were after Travis, everyone else was collateral damage."

"Which is what he turned out to be." Mal said sipping his coffee. I nodded, sipping mine.

"Now we know who our enemy is, but they don't know, we know." Jim said.

"We're safe for the moment, we'll be watching for their

next move. Have Doc do an autopsy on him, they augmented him." I said.

***

I was up at 0600 the next morning practicing my katas, my balance was improving and my movements becoming smoother. I had slept peacefully, the demise of one piece of human garbage hadn't bothered me at all. If anything, I felt I had collected a little toward the debt that was owed for Travis.

I knew Jazz had been standing there watching me. When I finished my last pass, I looked at her.

She reached for me, "got time for a shower?"

"Yeah but we'll be late for breakfast."

"That's okay, I know the chef, he'll save us something." She laughed. We were late for breakfast.

We met with Admiral Archibald "Archie" Gallant Ret. formally the commander of the ESFL's fleet shipyard.

"Admiral, Captain Smythe tells us you were the Captain of the *Brokkr* before they promoted you and you took over the ESFL shipyards."

"Call me Archie please, I'm retired, and the answer to both questions is yes."

"Okay, Archie, call me Nic. I find myself in need of a yard manager, if you'd rather talk about that, than captaining the *Brokkr*."

"No, thank you, worst job ever had, I hated that shipyard job. I wound up sitting at a desk looking out the window pushing papers and going to meetings about going to meetings. I should've turned down that promotion and stayed on the *Brokkr*, a good ship and crew.

Admiral Cole said he needed me, so I took it. If you'll have me, I'll take the *Brokkr* and be glad to have her back."

I nodded, "There is a chance we may take hostile fire. I don't want you going into this thinking we won't."

Archie took a swallow of his coffee looking at me.

"You know, all of us Legionaries talk to each other. These men respect you. You've had some dustups. But every time, you were in the middle of it with your men, or you sent enough backup to hold off a company of Marines.

You got all your people home and got them patched up. The only time you didn't, they pulled you out of the rubble where they found you trying to save a comrade. You stand by your friends and help others when you can. And God have mercy on anyone who harms your family, because you won't.

Reggie told me of the saying you like to use, so Commodore, if you'll have me, I'll proudly 'ride for your brand'."

I stood reaching my hand across the table, "welcome aboard Captain, we're proud to have you. Gather your crew."

"Aye-aye, Sir." He said as he shook my hand.

Doc messaged me, saying he needed to see me. I assumed it was about the autopsy. Mal and I went over to med-bay.

"What did you find Doc?" I asked.

"You were right, they augmented him. He had an implanted CCU pharmaceutical injection system. The system could administer pain meds, stems, and adrenaline. Pretty sophisticated stuff.

Also, his bones were covered with a mithrilium carbon fiber that made his bones three or four times harder than normal. It killed him when you hit him in the back of the head and cracked his vertebra but broke none clean through. You jellified his heart though, and you crushed his skull. His system was also flooded with nanites."

"Mil-spec?"

"None I know of; these are better the mil-spec."

"How could they cover his bones?" Mal asked.

"Nanites, some kind of building or enhancing ones, as close as I can tell."

"Mal, you and Doc have a look at that pharmaceutical CCU, see what you can learn. See if we can use the tech. Doc, were you able to isolate any still functioning nanites?"

"Some, but I don't how long they'll stay viable." He answered.

"Do we have some kind of nanite medium that can keep them suspended or something?" I asked.

"That's what I've got them in, but that's not my field, however I know someone who works with them."

"How well do you know him?"

"Pretty well, he's my brother. Last we spoke he had quit Titan Technical Institute, said they were too narrowminded."

"He was going to TTI?"

"No, he was teaching there."

"Contact him, we'll fly him here, first class, and pay him for his time. See what he can make of these nanites." I said.

CHAPTER 21

Aaron Stein came to see me to get Travis's will settled.

"I'm deeply sorry for your loss Nic, Travis was a good man, and a good friend."

"Yes, he was, I will miss him. I know he changed his will."

"He did that right after he, in his words, 'dodged a bullet' in the attack that almost killed him and Jocko."

"He had no living relatives?" I asked.

"None, like you, he had a kind of adopted family. He left 80% of his assets to you, and 20% Jocko. He named you as executor of the estate."

"Okay, let's keep this simple, your firm will keep handling all the legal affairs, I'll check with Jocko and see if he wants to cash out. Are there any changes that need to be made?"

"None, he was the sole owner of the company, and had little debt. The only outstanding contracts are with your company."

"Ok, keep everything running the same for now, let me know before you change anything. I plan on making Bob the yard manager, I'll let you know of anything other than that."

"Fine, we'll take care of all you need. They threw the other lawsuit brought by the Conclave Council out of court, so that's finished. They had to pay all costs, and we charged them to the max."

"What suit?"

"Sorry, I thought Julia told you. Conclave Council wanted to confiscate your shield tech, claiming national security issues. We pointed out they weren't a nation, and you are a chartered R&D for the ESFL. The judge sided with us."

"Jackasses, I was afraid someone would try something like that. Anything else?"

"That's it for now until you make any changes to the company. You signed everything; the Van Dam yards are now yours."

"Thank you, Aaron, I appreciate all you've done for us."

I didn't want to rename the shipyards; I didn't want the Van Dam name to die with Travis. "I need to go over to the yard; you want to come?" I asked Mal.

"No, you go, I'm looking at that Pharma-CCU and working with Doc."

***

I called my security team; I wanted to walk, so I could work on my balance and coordination. We took a slow and easy pace through the Promenade. The enhanced *Vee* gave me an even better 360° awareness than before, and my shield worked in perfect sync.

"*Vee* message Jocko and see if he is available for a drop by visit."

"He says he's in his office and you are welcome anytime." We strolled along toward Jocko's office. People seem to recognize me more than I remember. Shop owners, waived, and passersby greeted me. I'd rather have the anonymity, but at least they are friendly, for now.

Security took me straight in to see Jocko.

"Got any coffee in this place or should I have brought some?" I asked, smiling.

"I think we can scare up a cup or 2. Come on in and have a seat. I hope you didn't take it amiss that I didn't come and see you. I thought it would be better to wait until you are up at around. We found out we were being watched. They wanted to see what we did after the attack on you and Travis. I felt that it would be safer to stay away for a while." Jocko said.

"I understand Jocko, that was a wise precaution. No hard feelings, we're good. I just talked to Aaron Stein; Travis made me executor of his estate." Jocko was nodding. "Travis had changed his will and left the yard to us. 80% to me and 20% to you."

"What? He left me 20% of the yard?"

"Yep, one reason I stopped by is to let you know about the shipyard and see if you wanted a buyout, or if you want to retain the shares."

"You'd be willing to keep me on as a shareholder?"

"Of course, I didn't know which you'd rather do."

"Who are you going to get to manage the yard, or are you going to manage it?"

"No, I will offer Bob the job, he's been doing great at it so far."

Jocko nodded, "Bob is a solid hand, he'll do ya right. I think I'd like to keep the shares. That'll give me a solid, steady income."

"Any luck on finding out who was behind the attack?" He asked.

"Baxter Consortium."

Jocko gritted his teeth, "mafia in nicer suits."

"I guess we need to make some powerful friends who aren't crooked in their own right." I said.

"Good luck with that." Jocko answered.

"Do you know a politician we can help and who can help us in return?"

Jocko thought a moment, "there is a local Conclave rep, a straight shooter. He could use help to further his career and influences. I feed him info from time to time, he does the same for me. What you have in mind?"

"The Conclave Council tried to confiscate our shield tech; Aaron Stein shut them down. So, if our rep could talk HMS into giving shield tech to emergency vessels and emergency services, that should give them a big boost in public opinion."

"That's actually a good idea. Helps them, the Conclave, and your company. I'll set up a meeting for you and him to talk," He said.

"You're not coming?"

"Nope, you and his dealings don't need me associated with it. I work better behind the scenes."

"Okay, set it up and we'll see how we can help each other. Send Aunt J your account info where you want your shares paid out to. I need to get to the yard, if anything changes, I'll let you know."

"I'll get a meeting set up, be careful out there," He said.

When I got to the shipyard, I went into Travis's office.

Travis' admin assistant came in, "good morning Mister Haydock, do you need anything?"

"Mary Jean, isn't it?"

"Yes, sir."

"Just show me to the coffee."

"It's right in here, sir." We went into a butler's pantry, where all the coffee and fixings were. "Sir, if I may ask, what will happen to us?"

"The shipyard?" She nodded; I could tell she was very concerned. "The Van Dam shipyards will continue as it always has. The yard is not shutting down, no one is losing their job."

She let out a breath, "thank goodness, we were all worried that you would merge the yards or sell it off. This will be good news for everyone."

I nodded, "I guess we should let everyone know. Would you call Bob to the office, please? And email all employees that the Van Dam shipyards will remain in business, no one will lose their job."

"Yes sir, right away."

"Thank you, Mary Jean."

Bob came in the office, I was over by the display case reading the tickets Travis had gotten saving my life, wishing I could've returned the favor.

"You wanted to see me Mister Haydock?"

"I do, grab a cup coffee, and let's talk."

Bob got him a cuppa and came back into the office. "Bob, we're gonna make changes, and you will not like them." He was a little shocked but said nothing. "I'm promoting you to yard manager, so you'll be pushing papers rather than working crews."

"What about Mr. Beck, the old yard manager?"

"Retired, there will also be a substantial raise in pay with the position to help with all the headaches. After a year, if we are still making a profit, you'll get a bonus of 10% of the Van Dam shipyards."

He looked stunned. "All right sir, any changes you want made?"

"Only the ones you make for now, it's your yard, don't lose money. Where do we stand on finishing the *Brokkr*?"

"We will finish the yard work in two days. Then we can move her back over to A14 for final testing and shakedown cruise."

I nodded, "good, before we move her, we'll be changing her name to the *Travis Van Dam*."

Bob smiled, "I think he'd like that, sir."

***

We were all on hand for the launching of the *Travis Van Dam*. We kept the ceremony low keyed, close friends and employees only. Mal had changed the *Brokkr's* ACE designation to the *Travis*. Captain Gallant, Mal, Jazz, and Jade brought *Travis'* new engines online. I broke the champagne bottle on her bow, and she backed out of the yard.

Aunt J and I were there as VIPs and stayed to reassure the yard employees they all still had a job. We had called the *Wanderer* and made him a deal to get her into the yard to reassure everyone we were still a working shipyard.

"What do you want to do with the boneyard, sir?" Bob asked.

"What boneyard?" I said.

"The parking yard where we have several ships and pieces of ships, engines, some of it is just junk."

"How many ships, and what kind?"

"Off the top of my head, six or eight ships, two hulks, I'd have to pull up the list to be sure."

"Pull it and let's go look."

Aunt J went back to A14, saying she had no interest in scrap yards. Bob and I took the yard tug and flew out over the boneyard. There were two mid-sized ore haulers, too large ore haulers, four 200 KLT tugs, a good size cargo ship that needed engines, the rest hulks and pieces.

"What you think?" Bob asked.

"Where did these come from, and what was Travis planning on doing with them?"

"All the haulers were loan defaults, and they are or were for sale. The cargo ship was a trade in, he was going to put the engines out of *Brokkr* in her and put her up for sale. The tugs, he never was sure about what to do with them. They were trade-ins too." We hovered over the yard while I thought.

"Ok, takes notes. Inspect the two big haulers and make sure they are FMC. If they are not, fix them and move them over to A14. The mid-size haulers and the 200s were going to combine into a new hybrid hauler-tug combo. We'll need to talk to the engineers and draw up new ship plans for them. The hulks and scraps we'll feed into the *Travis'* smelter-refiner, to fill her holds of raw material."

"What about the ship commander Jones said to hold on to until you decided on her disposition? He said the owners might want a refit, but was not sure."

"Show me." Bob flew us over to the edge of the yard by the scrap heap. There's a small nondescript cargo ship that looked a little worse for wear.

"Does she look odd to you?" Bob asked.

"Yeah, odd shape for a cargo ship, the engines seem a little bigger than standard." I said.

"Not much room for cargo, she must make her creds on fast runs rather than bulk." Bob said.

"That must be it," I answered. "Have her moved over to A14

until they decide what to do with her. Let's get back and talk to the engineers about the new hybrids were going to build."

***

We met with the ship design engineers I told them what I had in mind. I wanted to separate the hauling part of the ship away from the crewed and power part of the ship, making it basically a barge with gravitonics to load and unload cargo. Take the leftover parts and combine them with the 200 KLT tugs. That way the tugs could separate from the barges and mine rocks to fill it, then reattached to the barge and "tug" it to the smelter-refinery. With all the ships and parts we had, we should be able to build two complete barges. The designers love the idea and got right to work.

I called Jazz to see if they had parked *Travis*.

"Yep, we parked her right where she was before." She answered.

"Good, bring *Taurus* back over and pick me up, I want to show you something we're going to do."

"Okay be there in 30."

Taurus docked at the yard and I joined Jazz on the Bridge.

"What's cooking?" She asked. We flew over the boneyard and I told her the plan and showed her the hulks and scraps we will feed into the *Travis*. We then moved to the mystery cargo ship.

"Capture that small cargo ship we're moving it around to A11 and don't scratch the paint or shake her up."

"Are you doing this or am I doing this?" She asked.

"I'm having it done." I said, grinning.

"Don't make me hurt you."

Taurus picked up the cargo ship, and we started toward A11. "*Vee*, have Major prep A11 for our arrival and be ready to Grav-sling the cargo ship inside the hanger. Once that's complete lockdown A11, no entry."

"Done sir, standing by."

Jazz set the cargo ship down on A11's grav-pad, and Major moved her inside A11's hanger and closed the hanger doors.

"Home." I said.

"Home it is." Jazz said.

We parked at A14s hanger and shut *Taurus* down. Jazz put her hand on my arm, "Nic can you tell me about that ship?"

"It belonged to the hit team that killed Travis. We'll see if it holds any more answers."

"And the hit team?" She asked.

"There were three, two died trying to get away, the last one was wounded, when our teams captured him. I went to talk to him to get answers, and he attacked me."

"And?"

"He seriously overestimated his abilities; he didn't survive the encounter."

"Are you okay?" She asked.

"Yeah, I hadn't planned on killing him, but we had gotten what information he was willing to give, when he attacked me, I didn't hold back. I don't feel good about it, but I don't feel bad either."

"If you ever need to talk, I'm here for you." She said.

"I appreciate that, and I'll come to you if I need to talk."

***

I found Mal in his shop, "you busy?"

"Not really, what's up?"

"We moved the hit team's ship over to A11. We're going to open her and see if there's any useful Intel we can gather. Bring your goodie bag and let's go see Commander Jones."

"We need to be careful opening and going into that ship." Jim said.

"Those guys are professional killers, they stayed alive by being paranoid in the extreme. There is no telling how many booby-traps, both electronic and mechanical, there will be."

"Before we go in Mal will hack the computer core and suck

all the info out of her. When he's done with that, we'll look at go inside. I totally agree with you, these guys will have set traps. We'll just go slow, and if we decide is too dangerous, we'll make scrap out of her."

We went over to A11 and took a tour around the outside of the cargo ship. We moved up to the personnel hatch, and Mal opened his bag of goodies. He plugged into the palm pad and unleashed his cracking program.

"That was too easy," He said. The door entry pad turned green. "A head fake, huh? Let's see what you got." He sat down with his keyboard and began coding and code breaking. "There you are, that was a nice touch."

"Is he always talked himself?" Jim asked.

"Yep, and if he wasn't, I be worried," I said. Jim just shook his head.

"Ok I'm past the ship's computer safeguards, I'm downloading the core now. This will take a while, you might want to go get dinner, and bring me something back."

After we finish eating, we went back to check on Mal's progress; we took him some soup and sandwiches.

"So far, the information is just about the ship, plot plans, maintenance schedules, and overalls. I suspect there's a secondary system. I haven't found where they are connected, but I will."

He finally found it the next morning. "They hid the connection in the ship's maintenance routines. They had installed multiple self-destruct programs and devices. I've downloaded the second computer core, but I need to dig into it deeper and make sure I missed nothing."

"Ok, I need to check on the *Travis*, and check in with Doc, I'll be back." I said.

Captain Gallant had assembled his crew and settling in on the *Travis*. "I'm impressed with the upgrades and the additions you made on the old girl. I'm looking forward to getting out there and seeing what she's got. The specs on the new shields are impressive, this is a whole new generation of technology. I can see why you could operate her with so few crew. The ACE system is outstanding. No wonder the ESFL contracted you to do R&D for them."

"How long before your crew will be here?"

"A week, 10 days at the most."

"Ok, I want to be ready to leave on a shakedown in say, 15 days. Fully supplied and mission ready."

"Can-do, sir."

"Thank you, Captain, carry on."

I found Doc in the galley where he was getting coffee. "Any word from your brother?" I asked.

"He'll be here in a week; I think the first-class tickets sold him." He laughed.

"If he can answer our questions it'll be worth the price. I've been thinking about the mithrilium carbon fiber covering for bones, would that help my pelvis and vertebra?"

"I was having the same thoughts. That would be a great tech to have."

"We'll pursue it." I said.

"You have a message from Commander Jones," *Vee* said, "He says the Tailor is here and ready to meet with you."

"What time would you like to meet?"

"1500."

"Ok, we'll see them at 1500, message the rest of the board about the meeting."

"Sent."

CHAPTER 22

"The Tailor" was an actual Tailor. All his clothes were custom-made using mithrilium carbon silk, backed with polarizing padding, that turned hard when anything impacted it. He had hats, gloves, glasses, secure P-comm's, secure wrist columns, scramblers, anything you wanted, or he could get it.

He gave an impressive ballistic demo and even demoed for our batons. We ended up each getting two casual sets of clothes, two business casual sets, two business sets, and one formal set. The contact lenses protected your eyes and were heads up display capable that interfaced with our secure P-comm's.

We all got new wrist comms, P-comm's, contact lenses with HUD capabilities. Earbuds with noise canceling capabilities. We also got concealable dart guns, powerful enough to go through thick layers of clothing or light armor. Commander Jones and the security teams needed resupplying of several items which the company paid for. All-in-all, it was a very profitable afternoon... For the Tailor.

First thing we did was give Mal all the electronics gear to let him check them and tweak everything. The first thing he did was to upgrade the encryption on everything.

I was in my office later looking over resumes of people from the yard to fill the crew of the *Travis*. *Vee* was helping me sift through the information. Mal came in and sat down.

"How's tricks?" I asked.

"I've been over the data from the cargo ship, and I think we're clear to enter, but carefully."

"Ok, you got a plan?"

"I've thought about introducing an ACE from the outside

terminal, but it would take a long time, and I really need to see the system to see how I need to handle it.

The next best solution is for you to go in by yourself with your shields up. *Vee* will be scanning everything, helping me watch for system spikes. Once you get to the bridge safely, then I'll come in and we'll program an ACE in her."

"Sounds reasonable, out of curiosity, does she have a name?"

"No, just a number."

"When do you want to do this?"

"Now, while no one is around to get in the way, and possibly get hurt."

"Okay, let's get this done."

***

We got to the ship, and all was quiet. I had Major open the hanger doors and put shields up between the ship and the rest of the hanger. If it went bad Major was to let the blast go out the enviro-force-field. Mal would stay on the safe side of the force shields.

Mal remotely opened the personnel hatch.

The hatch looked empty and innocent. "*Vee*, give me full-spectrum scans and analysis, interface with Mal and keep watch for anything out of the ordinary no matter how small."

"Understood, interfaced, ready to proceed."

On my HUD, I saw my shields were online and green. I stepped into the ship, stopped and waited.

"Nothing so far," Mal said, "ease on in."

"Roger, easing in." I took a step and paused... Step, pause.

"Hold," *Vee* said, "a sensor just went live on your right."

"I got it," Mal said, "quite the trickster aren't you. Okay, I took care of it. It was an ID sensor, we're good. You may continue."

"Roger, continuing."

At the T junction, left went left toward engineering, right

went toward operations and the bridge. I took a step paused, step paused, all the way to the bridge.

Vee scanned everywhere for things out of the ordinary, "Suspicious device under the captain's chair," and highlighted the area.

"Standby Mal, I'll take the side panel off of the captain's chair and look."

"Standing by."

The side panel opened slowly. The chair was booby-trapped to arm when you sat down in the chair, and it would explode when you got up. I deactivated the arming device and checked the other chairs; they were all clear. I went back to the personnel hatch and got Mal and brought them to the bridge.

Mal plugged into the bridge systems and checked for booby-traps.

"This looks like a standard cargo bridge, nothing special." I said.

"I think it's designed to look that way in case they get boarded and inspected." Mal said.

"Makes sense." I said. Mal started his systems checks, I waited.

"Yeah, this is a standard small ship CCU, we must replace it before I install the ACE. The other CCU seems big enough to run the ACE."

"And where is the other CCU?"

"According to what I could glean, it's behind the bulkhead at the back of the flight deck."

"And how do we open it?" I said, looking at the bulkhead.

"That, I haven't figured out yet."

"If it were me, I'd have an electronic and a manual release lever for emergencies."

We looked around, "and I believe easy to get to. *Vee*, scan the deck and bulkheads for a release latch to this area."

"Caution, there is a release lever behind the support beam on the right, there is also a tripwire connected to another explosive device like the one under the captain's chair. The explosive device located across the passageway aimed at the lever."

I looked behind the column and found the lever and trip-wire. I disarmed the tripwire, "are you ready for me to pull the release lever? You might want the plug-in for this. This is where I'd put my last ditch stop to protect my home."

"You're right, hold on." Mal said plugging in, getting ready to cover us.

"Okay, let's do it."

I pulled the lever; it was a loud click. I looked at Mal; he shook his head no and shrugged his shoulders. I ran my hand along the bulkhead, "*Vee* scanned the deck and bulkhead for switches and relays that move or slide this wall when acti-vated."

"There is a relay switch two meters to the left, but it can only be reached from the other side of the bulkhead."

"Okay," I said, "I'm going slide the wall one meter to the left and see what we have. Are you ready, Mal?" He nodded; I slowly slid the wall one meter open. Mal was watching the readouts.

"*Vee,* do another threat scan of this room."

"Scans read clear."

"I'm opening the access panel to the relay and removing its arm, so it can't activate. I'm leaving it wired in case it reads a fault and triggers something." I said. The room behind the bulkhead seemed to be a command bridge, battle bridge or ops command-and-control area. This was where all the high-tech equipment was located.

We looked in and scanned everywhere we could to find booby-traps. We finally decided it was clear and Mal plugged into the main systems computer.

"Oh yeah, now this is more like it. There's plenty of room and power for ACE to operate in." He started the ACE program upload and integration. "This will take a while, I wrote a special package for this upload. It will trace and track traps while it's taking over the systems."

"Turn it loose, the quicker it starts the quicker it's fin-ished." I said.

Mal hit the enter key, "let's go get breakfast, time flies when you're having fun."

Bob messaged that the two large haulers were FMC. He would have them fully tanked and ready to run in two days.

I went to Aunt J's office, "you got a minute?"

"Yeah, come on in."

"Those two large haulers from the boneyard I told you about, will be here and ready to work in two days. We need captains and crews for them. You seem to be in your element running the circus, do you want to fill them, or do you want me to?" I asked.

Aunt J smiled, "I am having fun, busy, but I'm enjoying it. Let's call Jocko and see if he has a line on anyone who needs a berth."

I nodded, "Major, call Jocko."

"Online."

"Jocko?"

"Nic, what's new?"

"I'm here in the office with Aunt J. We have two large haulers, that we need to put to work. We need captains and crews. We were calling to check and see if you might know people in need of work."

"I know folks who need to work, timeframe?"

"We can fill berths in two days but need captains first," I said.

"No one shady, Jocko," Aunt J said, laughing.

"Julie, you wound me. I would never send anyone shady… Ok, I might, but not to you," He said, laughing. "Let me make some calls, who should I send the info to?"

I looked at Aunt J, she nodded, "send it to Aunt J, she's running the store," I said smiling.

"Wise decision young man, with her running things you won't lose your shirt. I'll get the info to you shortly, Julie."

"Thanks Jocko," Aunt J said.

At lunch I noticed Bob and Pam eating together.

"Did Bob just start coming over for lunch with Pam or is

there a HR issue?"

"Boy, you don't miss a thing, do you," Mal said, smiling.

"Well, I was in a coma for a month. So I may have missed some things."

"Okay, I'll give you that one. They've been seeing each other for a few months. I guess they knew each other back when they both worked at the Van Dam's."

"Good for them, Pam is like a different woman since then." I said.

"Where's J&J?" Mal asked.

"Out on the rock field, doing what they love, just flying around." I answered.

Mal nodded, "I checked on the ACEs' progress, we're at about 70%, shouldn't be much longer."

I nodded over my soup and sandwich, "I think I'll go practice my hand-to-hand, I still have kinks to work through."

***

The ACE finally reached 100%, Mal was doing the last check and discussing integration with the ACE when I arrived.

"What do you want to call her?" Mal asked.

I smiled and said, "*Loki*."

Mal smiled, "the trickster, I love it! ACE, your new designation is *Loki*."

"Acknowledged, designation *Loki*."

"Did you find anything new?" I asked.

"Yep, two more traps, one engineering and one in the galley. I saved them for you." He said chuckling.

"Thanks, buddy."

"Hey, you're the one with the shields."

"There is that." I disarmed the explosive traps. Someone had designed them to kill people, but not disable the ship. I open one of the crew's cabin doors, it stopped halfway open, so I slid it the rest of the way open. There was a flash of light and a loud bang; I took a shotgun blast on my shielded chest.

"You okay?" Mal ask over comms.

"Yeah, thank you for my shields, otherwise your shares in the company would've got a lot bigger. Lessons learned, don't assume, take it slow," I said.

"Sounds like a smart thing to do, you get to open all the doors from now on," Mal said, chuckling.

It took the rest of the day to go through the quarters methodically. We finally felt like we had cleared the ship of all the traps. We took a real look at her; she was a trickster.

Loki had top-of-the-line, oversize engines, better than mil-spec. Everything we saw was mil-spec or better, except where they wanted a smoke and mirror show. She had a full sensor suite, ECM suite, weapons suite, full gravitonics, and oversize tankage for what she was.

They had converted one of the crew cabins to an arms room and armory.

"All this with three people?" Mal asked.

"I think most of this was for one person, the triggerman," I answered. There was a small med-bay that was fully automated, and fully equipped.

"We'll let Doc check this out, there's equipment here I don't recognize," Mal said. The cargo bay held 2 grav-cars, or one grav-car and a small delivery work grav-van.

Mal left the cargo bay for safety while I opened all the vehicle doors and access panels. After the all clear, Mal climbed in the grav-van.

"I'll say this about those guys, they didn't scrimp on equipment."

The grav-van was full of electronic surveillance equipment, and armored.

"I think I'm in love." Mal said.

"You better not let Jade hear you say that," I said, chuckling. The grav-van had plenty of power for speed and pushing. But from the outside you'd never know it. But I guess that was the point. The grav-car was an armored four passenger model, with plenty of power, and some surveillance gear. She looked to have been built to work together with the grav-van. We designated the grav-car L1, and the grav-van L2.

Mal went back up to the bridge, and I went to engineering. *Loki* was a trickster. When anyone scanned her, she would look like any of a 1000 other small cargo haulers but could outrun the best of them. Everything was over-engineered, I bet once Mal does his tweaking she'll do even better.

I went back up to the bridge, Mal was deep into his programming. I sat down and waited.

"I've been thinking," Mal said without looking up, "I'm stepping up my ACE game in *Loki*, there's more here to work with. I think we should keep *Loki* a close hold secret." He stopped and looked at me.

"Ok, who gets access?" I asked.

"The smoke and mirrors area, commander Jones, he already knows about her. Doc sees the med-bay. Jazz and Jade get full access."

"Yeah, we want to live," I said, chuckling.

"Everyone else will be on a case-by-case basis. I have a feeling we may need her in the future." He said.

"She's gonna need new papers and transponder codes." I said.

"I'm already working on it. We can change the transponder codes at will. They designed her that way." Mal answered.

"Okay, close-hold above company top-secret. Aunt J?" I asked.

"Only if she needs to know. I don't want to worry her, but I'm not against it." Mal answered.

"We've still got a lot of work to do on her, starting with shields. I'm thinking 11's." I said.

"Definitely 11's," Mal answered, "and 7s on the vehicles."

"Yeah, more is better." I answered.

***

Aunt J had our new haulers crewed and working by the end

of the week. Commander Jones asked about *Loki.* I told him it was top-secret, need to know.

He nodded, "you're the boss."

J&J brought over scrap from the boneyard and feeding the *Travis* to fill her raw materials holds. The *Travis* was working perfectly. She would crush the metal to gravel size pieces and feed them into the smelter-refiner. Once the boneyard was clear, they would find and bringing in rocks of specific content to finish topping off *Travis'* holds.

Mal and I took Doc over to *Loki*, "before we go inside, what you see in there is top-secret, close hold." I said.

"Okay, I appreciate your trust." He said.

We took him straight to med-bay. He said nothing as he looked around. The more he looked, the more contemplative he became. He crawled under the big Auto-doc and traced tubes over to the bulkhead and open the access panel.

He stepped back staring, "oh my God," He said.

Mal and I looked at each other and moved over to see what he had found. There were four tall cylinders containing fluid and other equipment keeping it all circulating. I looked at Mal, raising my eyebrows. He shrugged his shoulders.

"What is that Doc?" I asked.

"This is a nanite production generator, and stasis medium. I think this is the nanite's we're looking for. Was there another CCU here in the med-bay?" Doc asked.

"Not that we found. *Loki,* is there another CCU in med-bay?"

"Yes, Commodore." A panel slid open, revealing a CCU. "*Loki* are you fully integrated with a CCU?"

"Yes Mal."

"Ok Doc, you can look at it. *Loki* grant Doc access to the med-bay's CCU." I said.

"Access granted."

Doc looked through data screens, "this is amazing."

"Is it mil-spec Doc?" I asked.

"No, it's above mil-spec," He said, without looking up. "I

don't know of anyone who has this. They either stole it from somewhere, or someone highly classified, or killed for it."

"Based on where we're standing, I'd bet they killed for it, or it was a corporate payment." I said, looking at Mal.

"Well, either way, I'd bet my last cookie that the ESFL doesn't have it. And if they do, it's someone's super-secret spec ops group that has it. 'Eyes-only' secret." Doc said.

"When does your brother get here?" I asked.

"Due in tomorrow." Doc suddenly turned around, "can you make another one of these, I mean build it from scratch?"

"I don't see why not, the only parts we can't make would be the nanite suspension medium." I said.

"I have that and can get more of the suspension medium."

"Okay, so yeah, we could probably make another one," I said, Mal nodding.

"I really think we need to do it. If we lose this one, there is no getting it back." Doc said.

"Okay, will make another one. It will take time, and Doc, remember. No one must know about this."

"Are you kidding, this is the kind info that will get you killed," Doc said. Mal and I nodded. Doc took samples of the nanite's to compare to the one's he had in his lab.

***

Aunt J did interviews for the engineering crew we would place on *Travis*. We were looking for individuals who are single, and we were offering a 10% raise to sign on. We only looked at people who were already working for HMS or Van Dam. In the end we had 50 who signed on. Captain Gallant and his new crew took the *Travis* out on a shakedown cruise.

I was heading into the hangar, going to lunch, and glanced over at the last 50 KLT tug, and a thought struck me.

"*Vee,* call Bob."

"Online."

"Bob?"

"Yes, sir?"

"Are you at the yard, or here at A14?"

"Sorry sir, A14."

"No, that's perfectly all right, enjoy your lunch with Pam. I'll be up in a second."

"Line closed."

CHAPTER 23

I went over to Bob and Pam's table, "May I join you for a moment?"

"Please do," Pam said.

"I don't want to interrupt your lunch, so I'll be quick. The yard boat we used the other day on our tour, that was a tug, right?"

"Yeah, it was a cutdown 15 KLT tug. Sometime in the past they made the cabin bigger to seat 4 and replace the full-sized tanks with smaller ones." Bob said.

"What kind of shape is she in?"

"Not bad, she hasn't been put under any strain in years, she just looks rough."

"Okay have someone fly her over here and take back the 50 KLT to use in the yard."

"I'll make the call right now."

"Thanks, pardon the interruption, and both of you take an extra 30 minutes for me interrupting your lunch."

"Thank you, sir" Pam said. The 15 KLT tug had arrived by the time we finish lunch.

Mal and I walked over to look at the yard tug. It was an old 15 KLT tug, that had been made into a yard tug. She looked a little rough, but that's what I wanted.

"What are you up to now?" Mal asked.

I pointed at the tug with my chin, "for *Loki*." He looked back at the tug and tilted his head to the side, smiling.

"Oh yeah, that's perfect, it will add to the camouflage and give us transport, so we don't have to Dock if we don't want to."

"My thoughts exactly." I said.

We called Buck, one the foremen over, "Replace the small tanks with full-size ones from the 25 KLT tug. Then check her over and fix all the other systems for open space ops, not yard ops. Don't worry about the looks, or paint, we'll take care of that later. We'll bring you the shield emitters to install later, change the tanks first." They got to work.

Doc's brother arrived that afternoon.

After some quick introductions, "we got one of our larger rooms ready for you why don't you go up and relax and unwind from the trip. We'll talk tomorrow." I said. He thanked us, and Doc took him to get him settled in.

The foremen we had talked to about *Loki*'s tug came over to us.

"Got a minute, Sir."

"Yeah, Buck, whatcha got?"

"Well Sir, it's about your small tug."

"What about it?" I looked over to see what wrong.

"Well Sir, I can do what you want, or I can do what I think you're asking for."

Mal and I looked at each other, "go on."

"Sir, I'm former Legion and we had small, low-slung tugs that were armored and armed. You know, in case we had to operate under fire."

"And you think that's what I need?"

"Based on your recent history, yeah that's exactly what you need."

Mal and I both laughed, "okay, point taken."

"What do you need to make me one, and how long will it take?"

"We need to set that old 15'er over to the side and start with a 25. We'll take it from there and be finished in about the same amount of time as converting the 15'er."

"Ok, hold that thought. *Vee,* is Bob still in the galley?"

"Yes, sir."

"Call him."

"Online."

"Bob."

"Yes, sir?"

"I need you down on the hangar floor, we have a change of plans."

"On the way, Sir."

"Line closed."

Bob arrived, and we all talked over what we needed to make the tug I wanted.

"Is there a used ship lot or yard you can halfway trust to buy from? Not some snake oil salesman who'd cheat his own mother."

"There is a guy we've dealt with; he usually shoots straight with us." Bob said.

"Okay let's go ship shopping. We'll take the 15 KLT tug as a trade-in and see what we can find."

***

Bob, Buck, Mal, and I went to see "Red" at Johnson's used shipyard. Some things are a cliché for a reason. Red came out of his office as soon as we landed, and it was obvious why he was called red.

"God what a mop of hair." I said as he approached.

"Good afternoon, good people. Fred Johnson is my name and I'm," that's as far as I let him get.

"Whoa Red, hold on, you don't have to sell us, we're already sold." I said. "You know Bob from the Van Dams shipyards?"

He nodded, "yeah, how ya doing Bob?" They shook hands.

"The thing is Red, I'm the new owner of the Van Dam shipyards." Red looked at Bob, Bob nodded. "In the past you've done a lot of business with Van Dam, and if you want to continue, don't try to skin me and I'll do the same for you. We're both in business to make creds, just don't try to make this month's rent off one sale to me. You with me so far?" He nodded.

"I'm trading in that cut down 15 KLT tug for a 25 KLT tug that's in good condition. I'm not looking for new, just a good mechanically sound ship. You got something like that, or do I need to go somewhere else."

He looked at me closely, "okay Mr....?"

"Haydock, Nic Haydock."

"Okay Mister Haydock, if you'll do me right, I'll do you right. Sometimes I need some work done on some of my trades. You take care of me and I'll take care of you. Also, I'll sell you whatever you want at cost plus 2K credits."

"Sure, and I'll fix anything you want for cost plus 30%."

Red laughed, "okay, so this ain't your first rodeo. Cost plus 500 creds."

"We'll do your repair work for cost plus 7%." I replied.

He nodded smiling, "sounds like we have a deal. Let me show you what I've got that may work for ya."

We took his yard ship and went over to his tug line. He had a good selection, I'll give him that. What condition they were in was another matter. We hovered over the line of 15s, 25s, and a couple of 50s.

"Here's what I've got, do you think one of them will do?" I was looking them over when Buck touched me on the arm and pointed with his chin. Over in the corner, in line with a lot of donor tugs, sat a Legion armored tug. I nodded.

"Red, shoot me straight, which one of these 25s has the best engines?"

Red looked down at the line, "the second one from the end there, the black and yellow one."

"Okay, I'll take that one, and that 25-donor tug, and that other one over by the fence. No, never mind it doesn't look like it's got all its parts."

"No, it's all there, it's just no one wants an old Legion tug." Red said.

"If it's all there, I'll take it too."

We came to an agreement on price and exchanged creds and paperwork. We had all our new-old tugs back to A14 in two hours, and Buck went to work.

"Buck, I want you to leave the outside a little rough looking, not too bad, but not too good. Know what I'm looking for?"

"We got it covered, Sir."

We were looking over the Legion tug; she was a little beast. They had pulled all her weapons, but the cable runs are still there, for the rail guns and lasers, and she still had all of her armor. The cockpit cabin was a little rough, so we pulled the interior out of the best 25 along with the engines and generators. She still had her full-size tanks; Buck was like a kid in a candy store.

"Buck, use whatever you want to make me a beast with teeth."

"Can-do boss." And off he went.

We met with Doc's brother after breakfast the next morning. He signed the NDAs, and we went to med-bay to talk. We gave him a brief history of our run-ins with the corporation and the assassins that killed Travis and almost killed me. He was no fan of the corporations.

He worked for them briefly and they had confiscated some of his work, and he got nothing out of it. After I was satisfied, I told Doc to tell him what we found during the autopsy and show them the samples from the body. I wasn't ready to show him the new samples from *Loki* just yet.

He listened and looked at the samples. He had the same look that Mal gets when he looks at computer stuff.

"I will need equipment, and yes, I want in. Whatever the terms, just house me and feed me, and I'm in."

"I think we can do a little better than that. Give your brother a list of what you need, and we'll get it. I looked at Doc, "you may need to call Gunny." Doc nodded.

Captain Gallant and *Travis* were back the next day, reporting excellent run. They had a few minor calibration issues, but the shields and the ACE were 100%. They refilled all her holding tanks and supply holds in preparation for the next mission.

The cargo ship from the yard, designated *Cargo 2*, now had new engines and was ready to work. Aunt J had a captain, and crew ready, and the ship left a week later.

Admiral Cole messaged us with coordinates, date, and time to meet a ship for upgrades. We loaded *Loki*, the Legion tug designated *LT*, on to the *Travis* along with the *Taurus*. Jazz, Jade, Mal, and I were going on this trip. Aunt J was staying to run the business. Buck was coming too. We wanted him to finish the *LT*. We also took along a 10-man security detail. I figured some paranoia was a good thing.

The *Travis* departed the next morning in route to Admiral Cole's coordinates. While in route, the work crews worked on the *LT* and on installing OFE's on the outside of *Loki*. The four of us did all the work on the inside of *Loki*.

It took six days to receive the coordinates where we were to meet the Legion ship. There was no ship at the coordinates, so we waited. We were on the far side of Jupiter from Conclave Station, so we did some scanning to see what resources were in the area. Nothing special came up.

Buck finished *LT*, and Mal was programming an ACE into her. There was a deck hatch in the *LT* that matched a dorsal hatch on *Loki*, so we could enter and exit without EVA. Mal added the combat tactics portion of the ACE program to *LT*, because she was armed.

We had done all the testing to *LT* that we could do inside the *Travis*. The four of us loaded in *LT* for a test flight and weapons calibration. Jazz and Jade took us for a joy ride. *LT* was quick, I guess when you're not trying to tug 25 KLTs of rock those engines can do other things. Mal calibrated our rail guns and lasers, and we did some targeting runs on local rocks.

We took *LT* back to the *Travis* and parked her by *Loki* in preparation for locking her onto *Loki's* dorsal.

"Buck, lock *LT* to *Loki's* dorsal hatch and make sure everything works properly." I said.

"Roger Sir, on it."

I went to the bridge to see Captain Gallant. Something felt off by the other ship not being here.

I stuck my head in his ready room, "Captain, do you have a minute?"

"Of course, come on in. Coffee?"

"Yes, please."

"How's the test flight?" he asked.

"All green."

"So, what can I do for you Commodore?"

"I'm not sure, this just seems odd to me. I would've expected a Legion ship to be waiting here, or here by now. This is normal for the Legion?"

"It is not, and what makes it even more odd is they should have messaged us by now."

"Well, there's nothing we can do about it. We will take the *Taurus* out and see if we can find anything we need in these local rocks. We'll give them a bit longer before we message anyone." I said.

"Good, we're still a little low on some materials."

We took *Taurus* out and did some scouting; we found nothing special. There were a couple of small spikes, but nothing worth our time.

"Commodore, we have two ships approaching our coordinates." Misty announced.

"Two ships?"

"Both are cruiser sized."

"Jazz slide us down behind some rocks. Misty open a channel to the *Travis*."

"Channel open."

"Captain, I see we have company."

"Yes, two light cruiser class ships. But something's not right, they are not responding to our hails. I'd recommend yellow alert Commodore."

"I agree, yellow alert Misty."

"Yellow alert, all defenses systems online."

"Our shields are up, right?" Jade asked.

"Always," Mal answered, "that is now SOP on all of our ships. If we are flying, our shields are up."

"The *Travis* is being hailed." Misty said.

"On speaker." I said.

"*Travis Van Dam*, this is a corporate ships *Ajax* and *Sampson*, respond."

"Give me an encrypted channel to *Travis*."

"Channel open."

"Captain Gallant, mind if I take this?"

"By all means, please do."

"Okay, but if they open fire, light them up."

"With pleasure, Sir."

"*Travis Van Dam*, this is a corporate ships *Ajax* and *Sampson*, respond."

"*Ajax*, what can we do for you."

"Shut down your engines and prepare to be boarded."

"*Ajax* we are independent vessel under contract to the ESFL operating in free space. On what grounds are you going to board us?"

"Shut down your engines and prepare to be boarded."

"I don't think so, *Ajax*."

"If you don't, we'll start by destroying your tug you have out working the field."

"Go ahead, it's unmanned anyway, we'll sue for a replacement." I typed in "go dark" on the terminal. Mal nodded and gave me a thumbs up, and Taurus disappeared from their scans.

"There, we saved you a missile, she self-destructed. What's your next threat?"

Another voice came on, "Mister Haydock, this doesn't have to get messy. Just give us what we want, and you and your people can go about your business."

"Oh, it's already messy, you'd have to destroy us or capture and kill us. You can't afford to leave any witnesses. Baxter must be getting desperate."

I typed, "take us to their 6 o'clock high and be ready to fire weapons," Mal and Jazz nodded and started us moving.

"We don't get desperate; it's surrender or will take what we came for from your wreckage."

"And you are?"

"Ray Hardisty."

"The man himself, Baker sent his fixer to fix this. Well, since you represent the Baxter consortium, why don't you buy my tech, you can afford it. Or doesn't Donald Baker want to write a check?"

"Mister Baker has decided you are too much of a nuisance, this is your last chance to surrender."

"You know that if you fire on the civilian ship that's piracy which is an automatic death sentence, right?" Jazz had us in position to take out their engines.

"Not if there are no witnesses."

"There will be these recordings."

"They'll never find the wreckage, enough talk, you have three seconds to surrender." I close the channel to *Ajax*.

"Captain Gallant when they fire, we'll take out her engines, if they keep firing, rain hell down on them until they surrender."

"Roger Sir." The speakers are still open for us to listen to *Ajax*.

"So be it, you made your choice, *Ajax* and *Sampson* fire at will."

Both ships fired on *Travis*.

"Target both of their engines with the rail guns prepare to fire, then change positions and prepare to fire again."

"Engines targeted on both ships standing by." Misty said.

"Fire." I said. As soon as we fired Jazz moved us to their 6 o'clock low position. "Misty jam all signals coming from the enemy ships."

"Signal jammed."

"Destroy any buoy they launch."

"Targeting buoys standing by."

The missiles and rail guns they hit *Travis* with, barely charged her batteries. Misty had shredded their engines.

"Open a channel."

"Channel open."

"Had enough *Ajax*?" They kept firing. *Travis* opened fire putting two missiles in the ship. That decided the issue. Neither ship fired after that.

"*Ajax*, do you want talk terms?"

"As you pointed out Mister Haydock, piracy is an automatic death sentence, Mr. Baker underestimated you. Admiral Cole made a good choice in you." Both *Ajax* and *Sampson* self-destructed, leaving nothing but a debris field.

"Captain Gallant, do you have an alternate way of contacting Admiral Cole to get him an encrypted message?"

"I do, what's the message?"

"He has a mole."

"Roger, I'll send the code he'll understand." I also sent a company encrypted message home warning of probable hostile actions. I doubt there's anyone alive over there, but we might as well gather all this metal and fill Travis's holds."

We sanitize the area to leave Baker guessing. We took four days even with *LT's* help, but we got the debris field cleaned up, giving us literally a ship load of materials. There were no survivors.

We received a new encrypted message from the Admiral the next day. He sent new codes using Captain Gallant's old Admiral codes. I wasn't sure how secure they were, but we had to start somewhere.

The message was "go somewhere and wait, he needs to kill a rodent or nest."

"Let's move and go prospecting." I said.

"Dealer's choice," The Captain said, "we'll go where you think best, you showed good instincts in the battle, so what's your gut tell you."

"Not instincts, lots of video games during my hospital stays at rehab."

"Nice trick disappearing from tracking." He said, I smiled. "Anyway, pick a direction and we'll follow you."

"We'll want to stay in the thick of the belt, so we can prospect, let's try over there." I pointed to a random place on the belt map. It was the closest large bodies. It would take us a day or two to get there, but we were in no hurry.

We had made schematics and blueprints for the nanite machines and had Buck make parts. We would not assemble them, just box them until we got back home. Mal and I worked on *LT*, tweaking her a bit more, then moved on to working on L1 and L2. The girls were training under Captain Gallant and the flight Sims. They were training on navigation and piloting larger ships.

When we arrived in the area we had picked, we found a nice clearing in the field to park *Travis*. We'll just sit here quietly for a while and see what happens. We finished installing shields on L1 and L2, Mal was working on L2 install an ACE. He said he'd do L1 later, he wanted to see what L2's equipment could do and how he could improve them.

CHAPTER 24

We started the engineering crews making standard parts we would need for any upgrade we would do; Ajax and Sampson had given us plenty of raw materials. Buck had done a great job on *LT*. She looked like a cobbled together little beast, and a beast she was.

We were in *Loki's* galley talking over coffee, "I think it's time for us to take *Loki* out for a shakedown run." I said.

"Yes!" Jazz said, we all chuckled.

"We need to see what she's capable of, and we can look for shiners while we're out and about." I said.

"Sounds like fun." Jade said.

"I'll let the captain know we can be off whenever we're ready. With all that's been going on, I think we need to bring an engineer on for *Loki*. Mal and I are spread thin working on other projects, we need someone we can trust to keep Loki in top shape." I said.

"Do you have anyone in mind?" Mal asked.

"I was thinking Buck might be a good candidate, he's been with the Van Dam since he left the Legion, and then with HMS. Solid guy, knows his stuff, shows initiative, thinks outside the box." I said.

"*Vee,* pull up Buck's records. God, no wonder he wants everyone to call him Buck. His name is Willard Buckmire, with a name like that you have to be tough. Display Buck's full record." The data appeared on the wall screen.

We read through it. All his training came from the ESFL. There is a list of ships he had served on and positions held.

"It looks like he served a long tour with special ops support group. That's probably where that outside the box thinking came in."

"Let's bring him in and talk to him. We'll keep him in the common area here in the galley for now." Jazz said.

"Vee, message Buck and have him come to *Loki's* crew hatch, I'll meet him there."

"Message sent."

"Let's make soup and sandwiches and have lunch while we talk." Jade said. I met Buck at the hatch when he arrived.

"Let's go to the galley and get lunch."

We all sat down and ate, "thank you for the great work you've done on *LT*. You showed initiative and insight into solving problems, you'll be getting a bonus for this run." I said.

"Thank you, Sir. I really enjoyed the challenge, that was more fun than just changing parts and welding cracks." He said smiling. We continue with small talk as we finished our lunch.

Buck was looking around the galley area, taking it all in.

"What you think of our ship?" Jazz said.

"Kinda disappointed Ma'am, the betting pool has high odds it's a leisure yacht in disguise," He said. We all laughed.

"I see you served with spec-ops support for a time," I said, over my coffee cup.

He lifted his eyes to me then back to his soup, "yes sir, I was on a team that kept their equipment repaired and maintained for immediate deployment. I was strictly maintenance though."

"Supposedly, even maintenance crews had to be qualified in spec ops training to even work in the support side." I said.

"We trained with the team some but not much, mostly just emergency drills," He said, dodging the question.

I got up to refill my coffee and looked at Mal and the girls, lifting my eyebrows and chin pointing toward Buck. They all nodded yes.

I returned to my seat, "so you like the challenge of working on *LT*?"

"Oh yeah, I love stuff like that. That's what I enjoyed most about spec-ops. They were always customizing equipment to get the most out of it or use it in unusual ways."

"Would you like to keep doing that kind of work?"

He sat back looking around, "this is more than just a small cargo ship isn't it?" I shrug my shoulders. He nodded, "to be honest, I've been bored working in the yards, I can do that work blindfolded. So yeah, I'd like to keep doing the 'custom work' for you."

"Good, we are about to take *Loki* out for a shakedown run, you'll be coming with us." He nodded smiling.

***

Loki gave us green on all systems. We eased out of the *Travis* and started our shakedown run. Jazz ran *Loki's* engines up and put her through her paces.

We were still in the common area bridge, "so what do you plan on doing with her?" Buck asked.

"You understand this is top-secret, the people on the ship right now are the only ones who know her true nature. We discuss nothing about the ship, off this ship."

"Understood, Commodore."

I nodded to Mal, "Loki, open operations bridge." Mal said. The ops bulkhead slid out of the way.

"Sweet," Buck said.

"Loki bring up full sensors."

"Full sensors online."

"Jazz take us around and see if we can find something worth our time. Buck let's take a tour. Buck was all eyes.

When we got to the cargo bay, his grin almost split is his head in two, "oh yeah." He looked over the grav-vehicles, and around the bay."

"What do you think?"

"I can make one improvement right now."

"What's that?"

"We need to install a small magna-flux 3-D printer in here

ASAP."

Mal and I looked at each other shaking our heads, "why didn't we think of that."

"Fresh eyes," Buck said. "And we had one in spec-ops."

"If you need anything else let us know, the budget for the ship is kinda big." I said. Buck and Mal talked about L2. They were under the hood in no time. I headed back up to the ops bridge, stopped by the galley and got coffee.

"How's Buck doing?" Jazz asked.

"Kids and candy." I replied.

"More like boys and toys." Jade said.

We chuckled, "ok that too," I answered. "Anything on sensors other than rocks?"

"No, we can still see *Travis*, which is impressive given the distance we traveled." Jade said.

I went over and took the ops seat and looked at the readings. There was nothing special in this area, I change the settings to look for iron and mithrilium. After a while I went to the galley, and got coffee for the girls when I refilled mine.

I brought them their coffee, "does he clean house too?" Jade asked Jazz. Jazz gave her "the look". "hmmm, too bad, I thought he might could show Mal how," Jade said shaking her head.

My sensors terminal pinged, and I went over to see what had triggered the sensors.

The iron and mithrilium readings were climbing, "Jazz take us 20° to port please, let's see what we have."

"20° to port." She answered.

"The reading strengths is on the uptick, take us down 10°, we may have found a nice one," I said. Out of the armor glass we could see we were coming up on the huge rock, a couple of them.

"Readings are still rising, take us around to the other side of that one," I said, pointing. Jazz slid us around between the two big rocks, and the readings pegged.

"*Loki* localized readings." I said.

"The strongest readings are 2° to port, distance uncertain due to interference." *Loki* replied.

"Ease us forward, Jazz." We eased around the rock in the readings, kept rising.

"Commodore sensors show there is a ship on that asteroid dead ahead." *Loki* said.

"Go to yellow alert. What kind of ship?"

"The best answer I have is a large one." *Loki* answered.

Mal and Buck came on the Bridge, "we've apparently found a ship." I told them.

"*Loki,* go dark," I said.

"Dark."

Mal took his sensor station.

"Take us in Jazz, ahead slow," I said.

" Ahead Slow," Jazz said. We rounded the asteroid, and an open plain came into view.

"She's a big girl," Mal said. "No obvious energy readings, no comm emissions, she's dead quiet." We continued to glide closer in. "Mithrilium readings are high down there. Probably why they're here," Mal said.

"Try a direct laser calm to them we want no misunderstandings."

"No answer to laser comms." He said. We were a kilometer out from her when we saw debris.

"Circle us around Jazz." When the other side of the ship came into view, we saw the damage. Mal was right, she was a big girl, huge would be a better description. She was way bigger than *Travis*. She had taken some hard meteor hits; the whole area looked like it had taken a huge meteor storm. There were impact craters all over the place.

"All stop," I said.

"All stop," Jazz answered.

"Take us lower and tell me what that looks like to you."

"Mining equipment," Jazz said.

"And bodies," Buck said.

"Set us down Jazz, looks like will have to go knock on the door."

Jazz set us down beside the ship. She dwarfed us. "Jazz you

and Jade take *LT* and keep overwatch for us. We'll suit up and take L1 over to see if anyone is home."

LT lifted and did a circuit of the area, "no signs of life," Jade reported.

We lowered Loki's cargo bay ramp, and drove L1 through the enviro-field, and headed toward the bodies first.

"It looks like five or six people in the group, they got caught outside in the meteor storm. They never had a chance."

We turned back toward the big ship it was the oddest-looking ship I'd ever seen. It looked like a giant cylinder with flat sides and a cone on one end. We found a cargo ramp was down, where the unfortunate crew must have left their ship. We drove up the ramp hoping the hatch would auto open. No such luck. We sealed up our suits, evac'ed the air out of L1 and got out. We walked over to the personnel door to see if it worked.

"No palm pad, this is an old ship." Mal said. He plugged in and by-passed the lock and the outer airlock door opened. "What do you think?" Mal asked.

"From what I see 80 to 100 years old." I said.

"At least." Buck said.

"Try the comms, see if anyone answers." I said.

"Hello, anyone home?" Mal said.

I shook my head, "original."

"Whatever works," Mal answered. No one answered.

"Take us in," I said. Mal bypassed the lock and cycled the airlock open. "Let's stay sealed until we see what we're dealing with. *LT*, do you copy?"

"Copy Nic."

"We're inside, no life signs yet, will leave our mic's open for you."

"Roger, be careful."

We passed through the airlock and stood in a dark passage-way.

"Bridge or engineering?" Mal asked.

"If she's been sitting here for 80 to 100 years, she will be dead. We'll need a portable generator to get things up and running again." I said.

"There's a small one in L1, I'll go get it." Buck said.

While waiting for Buck to get back, "so which way engineering or bridge?" Mal asked.

"I've been thinking about that, this ship is not a normal design, I think engineering is in the ship's bow. Ops and the bridge are probably somewhere up there too. So, let's head for the front of the ship. Any change out there, Jazz?" I asked.

"No change, we were just listening to your stimulating conversation," she answered.

"Ha-ha you girls are so funny," Mal said. Buck got back with a portable generator and we headed toward the front of the ship to find engineering. We found signs that point the way to main engineering. We arrived in main engineering and plug the generator into the engineer's main console. The console powered up and showed engineering readouts.

"Will she still have fuel after all this time?" Mal asked.

"Yeah, but it's frozen. We'll have to thaw it out to get things started again. There should be a ready tank that is smaller that we can heat to get us started." I said. We found a ready tank and started the heaters. We look through the engineering logs while we waited. "She went in to safety shutdown when no one reset her maintenance safety protocols." I said.

"What's the name of the ship?" Mal asked.

"The *ESS Duty*." I answered.

"No way!" Buck said.

"You recognize a name?" I asked.

"Yeah, and the 80 to 100-year timeline fits. My Dad, who is an engineer and conspiracy theorists, used to talk about the *Duty* all the time. He said the government took her because she was too advanced, or she crashed somewhere out in the galaxy. Or the newly designed engines just blew up. No one knew for sure.

Some rich genius built the ship using supertankers. He invented a new type of drive engine that was to revolutionize space exploration. Dad's gonna be disappointed that there is no conspiracy here, just bad luck."

"*Vee,* cross-reference *ESS Duty* and see what you find."

"I found that basically, what Buck said is true. They built the ship as a proof-of-concept mining colony ship. Miners would live aboard until they hollowed an asteroid out enough to start Habs. The drive he developed was a theoretical concept called a grav-cone-drive."

"I remember studying about the GCD, it creates a tiny Blackhole in front of the ship and pulls the ship along. More power you applied, the bigger the Blackhole would become the faster the ship would be pulled along. No one could ever make it work, except, I guess, Mr. August. Too bad he didn't get to show the world he made it work."

"We have enough fuel to start one of the standby generators, diagnostics show a green board. But do a visual inspection just to be sure." I said.

"On it."

"Let's pull up ship plans while Buck checks the generator." I said.

"Geez, this thing is huge, it looks like he desired to house 1000 people. He was way ahead of his time. There's a bridge elevator down that way." I pointed.

"The generator is good Commodore," Buck reported.

"Ok, let's see what we got, prime; heat; start; and if all is well, running, and we have power." We brought engineering systems online and thawed out the main tankage. "We'll concentrate on engineering and then the bridge," I said. "Jazz, we still good out there?"

"Yep, all clear."

"Ok, return to *Loki* and Dock *LT*. Take *Loki* up and assume high cover position but stay dark. I'll feel better with you covering us out of sight."

"Roger, returning to *Loki*, then high cover, keep your comms open."

"Roger, comms open."

Engineering systems came online. We got Amber and red boards from the major damage. We made sure we had shut those areas down. We left Buck in engineering watching the generator and went up to the bridge.

We plugged the portable generator into the main bridge console but kept isolated from the ship in case some safety program tried to lock us out.

"Ok I'm in," Mal said, "just as we thought, safety protocols shut everything down. A distress signal was sent, but the satcom was damaged in the meteor shower. No one ever heard, not that it would've done them any good."

"True," I said, "at least we don't have to search every nook and cranny for bombs this time."

"What, this time?" Jazz said.

"I was hypothetically speaking," I said, crossing my fingers.

"Well, we are going to, hypothetically talk, when you get home Mister." Someone chuckled but said nothing.

"Anyway," Mal said, "Mostly, the ship is in good condition for a derelict. We can claim salvage rights on her, she's ours." Mal was looking through the computer systems while I was reading the logs. Mal got my attention and made the "cut the mic" sign. I nodded and close the open channel.

"You know this will be worse than the shields, right?" Mal asked.

"What is?"

"The GC Drive, we thought the shields would cause a ripple, this new drive will cause a tidal wave."

"Oh crap. I hadn't thought that far ahead. They will try to take *Duty* from us, and the only ones who have this tech will be the corporations." Mal nodded.

"You know how you feel about people taking our inventions, and in this case our property." I said.

"I agree, we have to be ready, because it's not if they come, it's when they come," Mal said. "We need to talk to the girls."

I nodded, reopening our channels. "Buck, how's it looking down there?"

"Everything's looking good, tankage is thawing. The only problem I see so far is environmental. All the O2-ponics in the matrix died when it froze. I'm looking for the stores and supplies now to see if they have replacement 'soup', hopefully they do."

"Keep everything moving slow and steady, we're going out to get the girls and bring them in. Jazz?"

"We heard, we'll land at the entry ramp."

"See you there but hold when you come inside." I said.

"Copy," she answered.

We headed down to the personnel hatch; the way was now lighted. We got to the airlock and Mal entered the code "123456" I looked at him and shook my head.

"What?" He said. "I'll install a palm pad later."

Loki landed, and we drove L1 back into the cargo bay. We went up to the galley, I looked at *Loki's* camera and made the "cut the channel sign".

"Channel muted." *Loki* said.

"*Loki* monitor Buck, if he calls, announce it and open a channel."

"Understood Commodore."

"What's wrong?" Jazz asked, concern on her face.

"We've been blessed and cursed." I said. "Everyone grab a cuppa and let's talk."

Everyone had their coffee and was seated at the galley table. "You heard what we found on the *Duty*, what you didn't hear because we cut the mics, was what we fear may happen," I said. Mal and I shared our concerns with them.

"Bottom line is, they'll want *Duty*," Jade said. Mal and I nodded.

"They want everything. They've already sent two ships out to kill us, to take our tech," Jazz said.

"I think this is the beginning of some major moves by the Corporation. They got a mole, and God only knows what or who else inside the ESFL close to Admiral Cole. They sent assassins to kill Travis and Jocko, I think it'll get worse before it gets better." I said.

"What do you think we should do?" Jazz asked.

"I think the first thing we should do is get *Duty* repaired and install shields and an ACE on her. Then no one can just take her from us. That will give us time to explore our options." They nodded.

"Are we calling in the *Travis*?" Jazz asked.

"We have to, if we want *Duty* FMC anytime this decade," Mal said.

I nodded, "that's my thinking too. We're already on standby until we hear from the Admiral, so we might as well make good use of our time." They all nodded. "*Loki* send an encrypted message to the *Travis* with our coordinates and asked her to join us." I said.

"Message sent."

Glossary

A.C.E. : Automated Control Engine. Computer program, like artificial intelligence

Aaron Stein: HMS Lawyer , from Randall Jones and Associates

Aunt J: Julie Moore, Chief of Supply and Acquisitions. She owned and ran a small breakfast bar called the "Breakfast Plus". All the kids just called her Aunt J.

CCU: Computer Control Unit

CIS: Counter Intel Security

Conclave Station: mined out asteroid where Haydock HQ is located.

E&S Ship: Exploration and Security Ship

EL shop: Electronics repair shop.

ESFL: Earth Space Foreign Legion

FE: Force emitter

FMC: Fully Mission Capable

GCD: Grav Cone Drive

GMA: Graphite Metallic Armor

Hab: Habitat

Jade: HMS second pilot, and Mal's girl friend. Spiked blond hair.

Janet "JJ" Jennings: HMS lawyer, from Randall Jones and Associates

Jasmine "Jazz" Duvall: Chief Pilot and Chief of Flight Operations.

Jocko: Boss of A, B, C rings

KLT: Kilo tons, Weight rating for rock tugs, and other ships.

M3D (Printer): Magna Flux 3D printer

Malcolm "Mal" Calhoun: Chief Information Officer.

Miss. T': it sounds like 'Misty', the 'T' stands for *Taurus'* AI.

MKT: Metric Kilo ton

Nicolas "Nic" Haydock: HMS CEO

O'em: the name of OEM's ACE Computer

O2Ponics: Oxygen Hydroponics

OFE: Odd-numbered Force Emitter

P-Comm: Personal comm unit

Randall Jones: HMS Lawyer. Owner of Randall Jones and Associates

SDRV: Space Dock and Repair Vessel

S-Tube: Subway tube

Taurus: Haydock's family 200klt rock tug.

Uncle J: Lou, Aunt J's husband (Deceased)

The End of book 1

Duty Calls, book 2 of the *Duty* trilogy coming soon.

OTHER BOOKS BY JAMES HADDOCK

Duty Calls

Duty Calls continues the story of Nic, Mal, Jazz and Jade as they fight to hold what belongs to them. The Corporations are becoming more aggressive in their effort to steal their inventions. Our four friends are matching the corporate's aggression blow for blow. The fight has already turned deadly, and the Corporation has shown they aren't afraid to spill blood. Nic has shown restraint, but the gloves are about to come off. They've gone after his family and that's the one thing he will not tolerate.

From Mist and Steam

Searching the battlefield after a major battle Sgt. Eli finds a dead Union Army messenger. In the messenger's bag is a message saying the South had surrendered, the war was over. Along with the Union Messenger was a dead Union Captain carrying his discharge papers, and eight thousand dollars.

Sgt. Eli decides now is a good time to seek other opportunities, away from the stink of war. While buying supplies from his friend the quartermaster, he is advised to go to St. Louis. Those opportunities may lie there and a crowd to get lost in. Sgt. Eli, becomes Capt. Myers, a discharged Union Cavalry Officer, and strikes out for St. Louis.

The war has caused hard times and there are those who will kill you for the shirt you are wearing. Capt. Myers plans on keeping his shirt, and four years of hard fighting has given him the tools to do so. Realizing he must look the part of a well-to-do gentleman, he buys gentleman clothes, and acts the part. People ask fewer questions of a gentleman.

What he isn't prepared for is meeting an intelligent Lady, Miss Abigale Campbell. Her Father has died, leaving the family owned shipping business, with generation steam-powered riverboats. They have dreams of building steam-powered airships, but because she is a woman, there are those who stand against them. Capt. Myers' fighting is not over, it seems business is war. They decide to become partners, and with his warfighting experience, and her brains the world is not as intimidating as it once seemed.

Hand Made Mage

Ghost, a young Criminal Guild thief, is ordered to rob an ancient crypt of a long dead Duke. He is caught grave robbing by an undead insane Mage with a twisted sense of humor. The Mage burns a set of rune engraved rings into Ghost's hand, and fingers. Unknown to Ghost these rings allow him to manipulate the four elements.

Returning to the Guild to report his failure, everyone thinks he has riches from the crypt, and they want it. While being held captive by the Criminal Guild, Ghost meets Prince Kade, the fourth son of the King, who has troubles of his own. Ghost uses his newfound powers to escape from the Guild saving the Prince in the process.

Spies from a foreign kingdom are trying to kill Prince Kade, and Ghost must keep them both alive, while helping Prince Kade raise an army to stop an invasion. Ghost finds out trust to soon given, is unwise and dangerous. He is learning people will do anything for gold and power. As Ghost's power grows, his enemies learn he is a far more deadly enemy than anything they have ever faced.

Mage Throne Prophecy

A routine physical shows Captain Ross Mitchell has a flesh-eating virus that specifically targets the brain. Prognosis says he'll be a vegetable by week's end. Having survived numerous incursions in combat around the world, he decides he's not going out like that. He drives a rented corvette into a cliff face at over 200 MPH. The fiery impact catapults him toward the afterlife. Instead of finding the afterlife, he finds himself in a different body with an old man stabbing him in his chest. He fights free, killing the old man before passing out. He wakes to find he's now in the body of Prince Aaron, the 15-year-old second son of the King. In this medieval world, the Royals are Mages. The old man who was trying to kill him was a Mage "Vampire". Instead of blood, the old Mage was trying to steal Ross/Aaron's power, knowledge, and in this case his body. When Ross/Aaron killed the old Mage, his vampire power was transferred to him. He now has the memories, knowledge, and powers of the old Mage. Ross/Aaron must navigate this new environment of court intrigue with care. His older brother, the Crown Prince, hates him. His older sister has no use for him. The King sees him as an asset to be used, agreeing to marry him to a neighboring Kingdom for an alliance. Before the marriage takes place, the castle is attacked. Someone is trying to kill him but is finding it most difficult. Where Mages fight with Magic, Ross/Aaron fights with magic and steel. It's hard to cast a spell with a knife through your skull, or your throat cut. As Ross/Aaron travels with his fiancée toward her home for the marriage to take place, they are attacked at every turn. Someone doesn't want this wedding to happen. Ross/Aaron has had enough of people trying to kill him. With Aaron's knowledge, and Ross' training, they take the offensive. The Kingdom will never be the same.

Made in the USA
Columbia, SC
15 June 2020